BARBELLS
AND
SAXOPHONES

ALSO BY DAVID RITZ

Novels
SEARCH FOR HAPPINESS
THE MAN WHO BROUGHT THE DODGERS BACK TO BROOKLYN
DREAMS
BLUE NOTES UNDER A GREEN FELT HAT

Biographies
BROTHER RAY (with Ray Charles)
DIVIDED SOUL: THE LIFE OF MARVIN GAYE
SMOKEY: INSIDE MY LIFE (with Smokey Robinson)

Lyrics
"SEXUAL HEALING" (recorded by Marvin Gaye)
"BROTHERS IN THE NIGHT"
(Theme Song to Film "Uncommon Valor")
"RELEASE YOUR LOVE" (Recorded by The Isley Brothers)
"LOVE IS THE LIGHT" (Recorded by Smokey Robinson)
"EYE ON YOU" (Recorded by Howard Hewett)
"GET IT WHILE IT'S HOT" (Recorded by Eddie Kendricks
and Dennis Edwards)
"POWER" (Recorded by Tramaine Hawkins)
"VELVET NIGHTS" (Recorded by Leon Ware)

BARBELLS

AND

SAXOPHONES

BY

DAVID RITZ

DONALD I. FINE, INC.
New York

Library of Congress Cataloging-in-Publication Data

Ritz, David.
Barbells and saxophones : a novel / by David Ritz.
p.   cm.
ISBN 1-55611-158-4
I. Title.
PS3568.I828B37   1989
813'.54—dc20   89-45333
                                                      CIP

Manufactured in the United States of America

10 9 8 7 6 5 4 3 2 1

DESIGNED BY IRVING PERKINS ASSOCIATES

FOR ROBERTA,
the love of my life

Thanks to Aaron (my main man) Priest, Don Fine, Alison Rebecca, Jessica Nemeroff, Esther (for many wonderful ideas), Elizabeth, Brad (fellow artist and workout partner), Marc (for Marvelous Medusa), Jenny, Julia, Gabriel, Sarah, Mom, Pop, Mom—Florence M. Plitt, Herb Boyd, Fernando Feldman, Flame (famous female wrestler), Hans (badass bodybuilder) Olin, Vince (iron guru) Gironda, Tommy Chong, and the many immortal saxists—Pres being the most prominent—who've brought me closer to God.

THE SHOWDOWN

"Can you describe the scene?" asked Klaus Mueller, my tall thirty-year-old dressed-to-the-teeth shrink.

"I don't think I want to," I answered, squirming on his butter-soft leather couch. I could never lay still. I never thought it was fair that he could look at me, but, flat on my back, I couldn't see him. Plus, I hated the way he put a sheet of designer paper towel on the pillow under my head—like I had cooties or something. I also hated the photo of Sigmund Freud hanging on the wall, looking so smug, like he was sure something was wrong with me.

"I wonder what's holding you back," Mueller wanted to know.

"I don't wanna think about it," I said, suddenly sitting up straight. I wondered whether I intimidated this guy. I might have been five years younger than him and a whole lot shorter, but I keep my body hammered in shape and that makes lots of guys jealous. See, I like wearing tight T-shirts. I like the way I look in snug jeans. Pumping iron is pure pain, which is why I feel like I've earned the right to show off. I like it when the girls notice. I like it when my biceps bulge and my triceps swell; hell, that's the whole point.

"You brought up the subject of fighting your father," said the shrink.

"Let's drop it."

"That's your option."

"Look, Doc, I know my options. You don't gotta remind me. And I don't gotta remind myself of bullshit I'd rather forget. See, that's what that fight was all about—bullshit. Just like the bullshit in here."

"Yet you return. You've been coming here for nearly two months."

"You egg me on—that's why I come back. You punch my buttons. You do it on purpose."

"I'm trying to be a good listener."

"Then listen to this. I think you always gotta have the upper hand. It's like you *make* me talk about certain things."

"Like what?"

"The fight I had with my father. The one in the gym."

"Do you think you might be fixated on that fight?"

"You're the one who's got a fix on me—just like Pop had a fix on me. Just 'cause he was a weightlifter, just 'cause he was Mr. Olympia of 1948, doesn't mean he's dumb. Fact is, Pop's a fuckin' genius. It's just that his head's screwed on wrong. He thinks he's God. He thinks you should worship him and not Jesus—that's what's wrong with Pop. And so when I came along, I was supposed to worship him. See, that was my job in life—to make my father look big. He's always had this thing about being so short. So he made me feel like a shrimp so he wouldn't feel like a shrimp. Yeah, that was his trick. I caught him at it early, but it didn't make a damn 'cause one thing about Pop, he'll never change."

"How did he make you feel small?"

"Posing. When I was eight, nine, ten years old, we'd stand in front of the mirror, and he'd start flexing his muscles, and I'd start flexing mine, and he'd say, 'Look at me, son. Watch how I do it. Imitate me.' With him looking down at me and me looking up at him, I felt puny."

"How old were you when you finally confronted him?"

"Sixteen. The old man had just left my mother for a bitch named Patty. I wanted to murder him for that. And I knew he'd wanna murder me when he found out I'd just quit high school."

"So you went to the gym to tell him."

"To get it over with. That's always been my policy with the old man."

"And what happened?"

"First, you gotta picture the gym. It's down there on Mulberry Street in Little Italy where I was raised, a few blocks from our apartment on Broome. It ain't even on the street. It's down in this cellar. Pop took over someone's basement in 1940, put up a sign that said Gino's Gym and he's been pumping iron ever since. Gino never makes it easy. Even to get in the gym you gotta pull on this forty-pound dumbbell that's supposed to be a door handle. Pop put that on there to scare off the wimps. So if you got the strength to open the door, you step into this dark torture chamber that smells of old wood and leather and iron and salty sweat. No windows, no fans, just a nasty old heater for the cold weather. See, the whole gym is just one room—maybe twenty-five feet wide by sixty feet long—crowded with equipment made by Pop himself— benches, pulleys, presses, squat stands, hack slides, racks of barbells, rows of dumbbells, piles of weights and the walls covered with dozens of photos of guess who? Gino—Gino when he was twenty, Gino at thirty, Gino at forty, Gino posing for this contest and that contest, Gino winning awards, Gino showing off his tree-trunk thighs, Gino sticking out his power pecs.

"Now on this particular day, Pop—he was about fifty then—Pop was sitting behind this long counter in the back of the gym. That's where he always sat so he could yell at everyone. He'd sit on this high stool that'd make him feel tall, even though he's shorter than me. I'm telling you, Doc, that's his problem, being short. But you know this shrink stuff, not me. All I know is that he was back there yelling at a couple of musclemen. Gino loves to tell the big boys they're doing everything wrong."

"You were angry to start with."

"Fuckin' furious. The day before he had moved out of the house, telling Mom how he didn't love her no more. He tried to explain to me about Patty, but I already knew about Patty. Everyone knew about Patty. She was this waitress down at Crestini's. She was a knockout, maybe the best body in the neighborhood, closer to my age than Gino's."

"Did she work out at Gino's Gym?"

"Are you kidding? No woman ever has or ever will work out at Gino's Gym. Gino runs the last all-men's gym in New York City. He's got this whole philosophy about it. Gino's got a philosophy about everything. He says women are distracting. 'Mind to muscle'—that's Gino's code. No dames, no music, no aerobics, just pumping."

"How'd you first learn about Patty?"

"I saw him down there having lunch one day, which was very unusual since Gino's lunches usually consist of a half-dozen raw eggs mixed with Tabasco sauce. The old man's a protein freak. He thinks vegetarians are worse than Nazis. Gino says, 'Let the cows eat the grass and I'll eat the cows.' He lives on raw meat. So when I saw him eating a plate of fettucine and noodling around with Patty, I knew what was happening. Things were especially rough back then with my folks. The gym was barely breaking even. How could the place ever make money when Gino's favorite pastime was kicking out customers who did his exercises wrong? Mom had also started talking about quitting her job at Stella's Hair Salon and borrowing money to buy a beauty parlor of her own. That drove Pop crazy. Deep down, he was scared she'd wind up making more money than him, which is just how things turned out."

"You found yourself in the middle of your parents' marriage."

"They drove me crazy. He'd talk about her, and she'd talk about him. They both told me I was their best friend in all the world. It's like they expected me to choose one over the other."

"And on this day, you were prepared to do just that—choose Mother over Father."

"That's you talking, Doc, not me. I didn't feel like I had any choice. The truth is that it was easier to tell Pop I was quitting school than to tell Mom. Mom would be more disappointed. She was more interested in my education than Gino. Neither of them had graduated high school, but Mom wanted me to be an accountant or a lawyer. Gino just wanted someone to take over the gym."

"Was that ever a real possibility?"

"Sure, I thought about it. I thought it'd be great. But that's when I was ten or eleven. That's when I started training seriously. If you can believe it, Gino had me bulking up that early. He couldn't wait to train me. Now I can see you're a skinny guy, Doc. You got no chest and you got no arms..."

"I'm a cyclist," Mueller told me, like I really gave a shit.

"That's cool," I told him, "but riding a bike and building bulk ain't the same. Building bulk means pain, like a blowtorch shooting through your muscles. That's a hell of a thing for a little kid to feel, especially when the kid just wants to be home feeding his birds and playing his flute."

"Birds?"

"I didn't tell you?"

"I don't think so," said the shrink, straightening his pink paisley silk tie.

"I don't think you've been paying attention, Doc. I know I mentioned the birds. See, birds are my best friends. That's where I get the music from. The way they sing. By the time I was thirteen, I had canaries and lovebirds all over my room. Plus homing pigeons up on the roof. The birds were beautiful. Their colors were gorgeous and they had these different personalities—some of 'em sweet, some of 'em shy, some of 'em perky, but all of 'em made me happy. Like I was protecting them. I gave them names, I took care of them, but Pop hated them. He said they gave him a headache. I didn't care what he said. I cleaned their cages and fed them vitamins with an eyedropper and Mom told Pop to leave me alone, she said there was nothing wrong with birds. Pop also hated when I started up with the flute and the sax, and Mom wasn't too crazy about it either 'cause she saw how I started running around with the blacks, but I did what I wanted. And what I wanted was to quit high school—I hated high school—and start making money playing music."

"How did he respond that day when you told him you were quitting school?"

"Like he didn't hear me. The gym was filled with big guys, serious muscleheads. As usual, he wanted me to show off, he wanted to show the guys how he had taught me, his prize student, perfect form. See, up until then, that was the story of my life. Pop showed me off like I was his own personal creation. That goes back to when I was ten and he started entering me in these kids' weightlifting contests. If you think Little League fathers are bad, you should have seen Gino at these junior bodybuilding meets. It should be against the law. I remember once I dropped a barbell on my chest—I wasn't any older than twelve—and he starts yelling at

14

me and I go into shock. Mom's watching all this and she nearly dies. She starts screaming—she never wanted me in these contests —and here she comes, running over to see if I'm okay, and Pop pushes her away and tells me to brush it off and start pumping again and I try, I give it all I got, but I can't, I'm too freaked, I'm too scared, and I start crying and he starts screaming louder and I want to die, I pray to God to let me drop through a hole in the floor. The amazing thing is that by the time the next contest comes around, Gino has me pumped up and psyched up all over again. And I win it. And I'm glad, 'cause he brags about me all over the neighborhood."

"In many ways, you became an extension of him."

"You got it, Sherlock. But by the time I was sixteen, I was fed up—fed up with training seven days a week, fed up with entering bodybuilding contests to make *him* happy, fed up with schoolwork I fuckin' hated. All I really cared about were my saxophones and my birds."

"Yet you also identified with him. The first time you mentioned him in here, you did so with great pride."

"Look, Doc, in my neighborhood Gino Viola commands respect. Fact is, for years Patty had been the girlfriend of one of the big wiseguys."

"Wiseguys?"

"Mafiosi. This big shot had broken up with her, but no one would have the nerve to touch her except Gino. That's 'cause the wiseguys loved Gino. They never asked him for protection money, they never fucked with him—not once. Not 'cause they were scared—those guys ain't scared of no one—but 'cause they were proud of him. They respected his muscle. They liked the way he got his picture in the magazines. Sure, they knew he was a lousy businessman, they knew he'd never make big money like the other guys who started out the same time as him, guys like Vic Tanney,

Jack LaLanne, Joe Weider and Joe Gold. Maybe that's why they left him alone. Maybe if they thought he could make big bucks, like a prizefighter, they would have gotten involved. But it wasn't like that. Back then, there was no money in bodybuilding. And Gino was such a lousy salesman he never even thought of franchising a chain of gyms. The wiseguys didn't see him as a money source. They saw him as a guy with balls, a *paisan* who was strong as a fuckin' bull, the only guy from the neighborhood ever to become Mr. Olympia. They'd come by just to watch him throw the weights around. Gino was a hero. In school—even when I was in the third and fourth grade—I was famous just for being Gino Viola's son."

"Which infuriated you, perhaps even causing you to quit school."

"What do you mean?"

"He robbed you of an identity, and you wanted to get back at him."

"I wanted to get away from him."

"And he didn't want to hear what you had to say."

"'Pick up those hundred-twenty-five pounders, kid, and show the guys the way to do dumbbell inclines,' he says. 'No, Pop,' I tell him, 'I ain't picking up nothing.' 'Pick 'em up,' he starts screaming. 'You better stop screaming,' I scream back, trying to build up my nerve, ''cause I'll walk outta here just like I walked outta school today.' 'You did what?' 'I quit school.' 'Over my dead body.' 'If that's what it takes.' See, I never talked back to Gino—no one did—and here I was, acting smart, acting up."

"You were itching for a fight."

"There you go again, telling me what I was doing."

"Surely you knew what you were doing."

"He had crushed Mom."

"And you wanted to crush him."

"No one can crush Gino. Gino's the one who does the crushing."

"Had he ever hit you before?"

"You kidding? When I was a kid, he'd lose his patience all the time and whack me on the ass. Once he hit me across the mouth 'cause I wasn't being respectful to Mom."

"Did he hit her?"

"Never. That's one thing about Gino. He ain't no woman-beater."

"But you knew you were going to get it."

"I don't know what I knew. I was just pissed about this Patty broad. And I also had a chance to play in a band with a steady gig in Jersey. That meant decent money—and I wasn't about to pass up on it."

"Did you explain all that to Father?"

"Look, Doc, I wish you wouldn't call him 'Father.' That's how people talk on 'Leave it to Beaver' or 'The Brady Bunch.' I don't talk that way."

"Sorry."

"I was sorry 'cause I didn't have time to explain shit to Gino. He went off on me. He shoved me so hard I fell against the squat rack and wrenched my back."

"So you didn't hit him back."

"Fuck yes, I hit him back. I hit him with a right to the jaw. I'd been waiting to throw that punch my whole life. The problem is, he was also waiting. He's got this steel jaw. It was like I'd hit him with a feather. I remember the look in his eyes—Gino's got these deep blue eyes—before he leveled me with a left uppercut. He's a lefty. And I was a goner. Next thing I remember, I'm stretched out in my parents' bed with Mom putting a cold compress over my forehead, saying 'Only a monster would do this to his son.'"

"I'm afraid that's all we have time for today," said the shrink, getting up from his fancy English armchair and buttoning his blue English blazer. He must have been six feet three, with wheat-thin light brown hair and pale skin. It didn't look like he ever needed to shave. He wore these old-fashioned eyeglasses that made him look like a well-to-do bookworm.

"You're cutting me off, just when it's getting good?" I asked.

"Our forty-five minutes are up," Klaus said calmly.

"But I got more to say."

"You'll say it on Friday."

"But maybe I don't wanna wait till Friday."

"Then write it down."

"Some racket you got here, Doc. A hundred bucks for a forty-five-minute hour."

"Another patient is waiting."

"I haven't even discussed my problem."

"We've discussed whatever was on your mind."

"I've got decisions to make."

"If you have an anxiety attack, feel free to call me."

"Life is one long anxiety attack. What am I supposed to do, call you every five minutes?"

"Then you see my problem."

"*My* problem is my girlfriend Kathy, not me. We haven't even talked about Kathy."

"Next time, Vince. Now if you'll excuse me . . ."

I walked out of Klaus Mueller's Madison Avenue office into the killer afternoon heat. July in New York. The garbage stunk and the city sweltered. The taxis were belching and the busses were farting; the pedestrians were sweating and the cops were running across Sixty-eighth Street, chasing down some nut who'd probably just ripped off one of those snooty high-priced boutiques that deserved to be ripped off.

Over on Lexington, I dropped in at Nick the Greek's coffee shop where big Nick makes a mean tuna melt. I needed some kind of quick satisfaction. I was pissed. Sitting at the counter, I remembered how, in this very spot, Kathy had talked me into seeing a shrink. How could I have been so stupid? Who needed Mueller, with his tasseled Bally loafers and his butter-leather couch? What a waste of money! It was all about money.

I passed by a record store and stopped to look in the window. Look at the shit that was selling—Guns 'n' Roses, Poison, Def Leppard, Cheap Trick, David Lee Roth. Heavy metal makes me sick. I don't even consider it music. Those creeps are more like wrestlers than musicians. Their shit is fake—fake feelings, fake songs, fake sex. Music is real. You can feel when it's true and you know when it's jive, and to me, arena rock is super-jive. Then why had I been playing it for the past six months?

Money.

Basically, I can play anything. A couple of sax solos behind a heavy metal band is easier than buttering toast. If you can play jazz—and believe me, jazz is my native tongue—everything else is kid's play. Playing teeny rock is like stealing candy from a baby. It's like stealing money, and money is something musicians are always looking for. Ever since I left home, I've had to make my own money. Pop wouldn't give me a dime and I wouldn't take a cent from Mom.

So there I was, standing out in front of this record store, looking over the piles of CDs and cassettes and wondering how come not one of them had my picture on it. Not one of them had my name. Ever since I was a teenager, ever since I started hanging out with the real musicians—the black jazz musicians—in the Village, all I'd heard was, "Vinnie, you got the sound. Vinnie, you got the feeling. Vinnie, you got what it takes." Then what was I doing here in 1987, twenty-five years old, and still without a band of my own? All I'd done was play behind other people, jumping from one gig to another, sometimes for the love of it, sometimes for the money.

I decided to walk in the store and look around. Don't ask me why. Maybe I was looking for aggravation, maybe for motivation. Who knows? Anyway, I'm in there, and I see this display, this life-size cardboard cutout figure of a saxophonist named Kenny G. Ever hear of him? You probably have, 'cause he's popular as all hell, and there he is, wearing a tank top with his skinny arms and his hair almost as curly and long as mine, hair to his shoulders, his sax hiked up towards the heavens and a big sign over his head that says, "Featuring the Instrumental Smash Hit, 'Songbird.'"

I can't help but feel a little sick inside 'cause the first song I ever wrote was called "Songbird," written for my white-throated finch named Gus. No one's ever heard my song and here everyone in America is listening to Kenny G's lame-ass ditty. Kenny G is to the saxophone what sugar is to soup. It ain't a taste I like—no bite, no balls. Okay, maybe he's got a sweet sound and maybe "Songbird" is a pretty melody, but mine was a burning jazz line with two modulations in the middle and one night at Draper's on Avenue D, the joint where we used to jam, the great saxist Sonny Stitt came by and heard it and said, "Man, that's a motherfucker."

"I'd like Kenny G on compact disc," said this hot-looking Japanese lady who was looking me over out of the side of her eyes. Her eyes were coal black and her broad-shouldered suit said she was an executive. Her clothes were too loose to tell much about her body except for her long luscious legs.

"You like Kenny G?" I had to ask her.

"I find his sound romantic," she answered in perfect English.

20

I knew she was into me by the friendliness of her voice, and I almost started to make a move. I wanted to tell her that I was a musician, that I could blow away Kenny G any day of the week, that, compared to my sax sound, he was nothing but a half-hard dick. But I hated it when I started acting like Gino—he was always showing strangers this postcard-size picture of himself as Mr. Olympia which he carried around like fathers carry around photos of their kids—and besides, it was already five o'clock and I'd told Kathy I'd be home by six. The last thing I needed was another distraction, even though this one was extremely classy with perfume that smelled like the first night I flew into Rome with that heavy metal band when the Italian stewardess wound up staying at our hotel and she and me wound up staying in the same bed and I got all wound up in the way she smelled, like this woman buying Kenny G, all fresh and exciting and new.

"How do *you* feel about Kenny G?" asked the gal with the burning black eyes.

"The way Mike Tyson feels about Bonecrusher Smith," I answered, sounding like Gino in spite of myself. "Kenny wouldn't last a round with me."

"I don't understand."

"It doesn't matter. You're buying his record, and I'm telling you good-bye. See ya."

"Are you a musician?" she asked before I could get away.

"You can say that."

"Saxist?"

"Yeah."

"And I take it you don't like Kenny G."

"Look, I like everyone. I don't want to ruin your day."

"You won't," she said with only the hint of a Japanese accent. She had long shiny black hair that fell to her shoulders and a shoulder-strap Gucci attaché case. She was at least six inches taller than me, but I didn't mind. She didn't mind when I watched her pay for the Kenny G CD with a platinum American Express card.

"Whom do you play with?" she wanted to know.

"Whoever pays."

"For example . . ."

"I just got off the road with Royal Flush."

"They're big."

"Huge."

"But I take it that you're not crazy about their music."

"I told you, I like everyone."

"Well, I'd love to hear you some time," she said, giving me her card that read 'Sue Kawisha, Personal Manager.'

"Who do you manage?" I asked.

"Mainly actors and actresses, but I'm always looking for talent. I like to think of myself as a discerning promoter. Feel free to call."

I didn't feel free. I felt confused. I felt that I didn't want to go and she didn't want me to go and we really wanted to stay and talk and get to know each other. Maybe have a drink. Maybe go out and hear some music. Maybe drop by a club where I knew the cats would ask me to sit in so I could play and Ms. Sue Kawisha could hear that I wasn't bullshitting, that my sound was for real. But who had time to chase after another chick? Who had the heart for it? That was Gino's bag—impressing the ladies—not mine. Besides, I was being good. I'd been faithful to Kathy since the beginning of summer—nearly two months now—and there was too much on my mind to start thinking about picking up gorgeous dark-eyed Japanese ladies in record stores. Even if Sue Kawisha was a personal manager and a discerning promoter.

I walked back out on the street and started picturing a cardboard cutout figure of me. I was working out three days a week and looked pretty good, but, hell, I could hit it hard, I could start pumping seven days a week, I could get super-ripped, say, in just a couple of months. If I wanted to, I could be the Arnold Schwarzenegger of saxophones. But who needed that? Who wanted it? As a kid, I'd already gone through that shit. That was Gino's thing, not mine. Kenny G was making a fortune with skinny arms and no pecs. I wondered if he curled his hair. Mine is naturally curly. I've got these ringlet curls. Kenny's got a big honker, but my nose is even bigger. I've got a Roman nose. So if the record companies think big noses are sexy, I'm their man. Plus I got Gino's square jaw and thick neck and Mama's brown eyes and small mouth. "You got the best of both of us," Mama liked to say. "You're gorgeous."

But who cared about gorgeous? I asked myself as I headed towards the subway. I cared about music, I wanted to make the most beautiful, burning, get-your-feelings-out-of-your-gut-into-the-horn music in the world. Music was God's gift to me. "My gift to you," Gino used to say, "are my genes. You got strong genes." Okay, I look like the old man. I'm strong. But being strong is one thing and pumping yourself up into a muscle-bound freak is another. Gino was a freak. Charlie Parker was a god.

Arguing with myself—four or five voices were always talking inside my head at the same time—I hurried towards the subway. The streets were jammed and the sky was clouding up. It was muggy and sticky and just before I started going down the stairs, I noticed a pet shop. I had to stop.

Soon as I walked in I heard the birds. First jazz musician I loved was Charlie Parker 'cause they called him *Bird*. Bird was dead nearly twenty years the first time I heard one of his records in 1974. I was twelve. I saw this record called *Bird* and I bought it 'cause I'd just bought my first bird whose name was Sir Christopher. He looked like an Englishman. He was what they call a Border Fancy canary and looked like he was wearing a long coat, like a butler. I dug his attitude, which was very proper. For a canary, he had this low voice and a strange little song that sounded like he was singing, "Tea is served . . . tea is served . . ."

Bird the jazz musician nearly blew my head off. I never heard anything that fast. The cat burned. Sounded like he had fifty fingers, not ten, running up and down his sax. At the time I had a recorder and a flute—I was just getting started—and hearing Bird nearly made me quit. Until I remembered what Gino used to say: "Someone bigger than you is always gonna walk in the gym. The trick is not to quit, the trick is to turn intimidation into inspiration." Sure, Bird scared me, but he inspired me. He let me know that music's a rocket to the moon; he made me want to zoom.

Birds made me want to play music. That's because they talk music. Birds are chatty and I'm chatty, so we get along. We listen to each other. Birds teach me songs. That's how I came up with "Songbird" ten years before Kenny G. Now here was this salmon-crested cockatoo in the pet shop, this feisty little fellow who seemed to be crying, "Take me home . . . take me home . . ." I needed another bird like I needed a hole in the head, but this guy was still a baby, and I could teach him to cuddle under my hand and rub against my neck and maybe he'd get along with Lady Day who lately had been looking a little lost and lonely.

Riding downtown on the subway, holding the cockatoo in a tiny perforated carton over my head so he wouldn't get crushed, we were squeezed in like sardines, everyone hot and sweaty.

"Don't worry, pal," I kept telling the bird. "I got this gal at home you're gonna love."

He started singing and an old lady started smiling when a young dude turned up his boom box blasting out a hip-hop rap with a funky bottom that had the old lady frowning and me tapping my foot. The groove was grueling, the beat was bruising, but I kept asking myself—*Where's the melody? I can't hear no melody*—when I remembered reading that forty years ago the enemies of bebop, the new Bird music that changed my life, were shitting on Charlie Parker for the same thing. They said they couldn't hear no melody. That was different, though. The melody was there. It was just turned around. Nowadays the rappers weren't singers, they were talkers, preachers, teachers to the young. They sure as hell didn't care about playing pretty. The cats were expressing themselves. They had a right. They had shit to say, and they said it loud, and here on the subway, everyone had to listen. Me included:

> *If you follow your heart and shake your fear*
> *You, my man, are gonna get somewhere*
> *So even if society ain't too willin'*
> *Kick back for a minute and do some chillin'*

There was a message in the music. It was a little like Gino's home-grown gym-jive philosophy. The point was—*go for it; and if the timing isn't right, wait a sec before you strike.* That's what I'd been doing with the arena-rock thing. I'd been waiting for my turn. Waiting for my chance to come. What was wrong with that? Here I was learning more from the rappers on the subway than Doctor Shrinkhead in his tweedy carpeted office. The rappers understood what it was like to be sitting on a volcano about to explode. My own music was about to explode. But what music was it? Straight-ahead jazz? Kenny G Muzak elevator jazz? Fuck no. Raunchy rhythm-and-blues? That was more my speed, but wouldn't I be selling out? I could work the studios and play a little of everything, but it was tough getting on that circuit, and even if I did, those gigs never gave any satisfaction. I was stuck.

The train was stuck. It jerked to such a sudden halt I nearly dropped the bird, but I managed to hold on. The lights went out and you could feel the panic in the jammed car as the homeboy's boom box blasted on, the black voice rapping right through the dark:

> *If you're too uptight 'bout making mistakes*
> *It's tough to know what road to take*
> *It's easy to make the right decision*
> *Soon as you cop an attitude 'bout winnin'*

The little cockatoo got the message. He wasn't scared at all. He started singing over the rap when the lights came back on and the train jerked forward. The train started moving, the cockatoo started wailing and I decided to call him Happy. Maybe I should quit the shrink. Maybe I should just buy more cockatoos and rap records. What the hell was the point of analyzing, analyzing, always analyzing? I was just too uptight about making a mistake. I needed to act, not analyze. Shrinks like Mueller got off on analyzing.

I got off at Sheridan Square. Walked up Seventh Avenue, stopped at Al's Newsstand to buy a new *Down Beat, Musician, Rolling Stone* and the *Village Voice*. Just 'cause I didn't graduate high school doesn't mean I don't read. I've read a zillion books on birds, plus biographies of Charlie Parker and John Coltrane and an old novel I found at a used-book store called *Young Man With a Horn*. I loved it. I also read this story by Harold Robbins about Hollywood producers who get blowjobs from the stars, which was pretty good, and I started some histories of jazz but they got a little dry, even though my pal Drew keeps bugging me to read more. I tell Drew I learn about jazz with my ears, not my eyes, but Drew's a scholar, Drew's big on the written word. Drew writes for the *Voice,* which is why I buy it—to read his stuff and find out who's playing where and the other magazines tell me about the new instruments and maybe I'll read an interview with Wynton

Marsalis or Miles Davis 'cause cats like that are always arguing shit.

I walked up to our little rent-controlled apartment on Jane Street, the magazines in one hand, Happy in the other. In the distance, I heard the rumbling of hot thunder. Rain was coming. My apartment was in a rundown building that Kathy had fixed up soon as she moved in a year ago. That's one of the things I loved about Kathy: her taste. She painted the walls white and put up classy posters from European jazz festivals and moved in some butcher-block tables and wicker chairs and lots of green plants and made my mess look light and happy like Happy the cockatoo who started singing up a storm the second I walked through the door.

"Hey, baby!" I shouted, looking for Kathy. No one home.

I took Happy into the second bedroom, which was my aviary, my gym and my studio. Kathy never even bothered to straighten up in here. It was hopeless, it was so crowded with bird cages, barbells, dumbbells, a half-dozen saxes and a funky old Fender Rhodes keyboard that I used to play the blues. I ain't a half-bad piano player. Naturally, I'm self-taught, like everything else I ever learned except for Gino's bullshit on bodybuilding.

"Happy," I said, "meet Lady Day."

I put him in the cage to see what would happen. Birds are like people. You never know whether they'll coo, kiss or kill each other. These two seemed pretty cool. They struck up a nice little duet while my other birds—there must have been twenty in the room —chirped in.

"Vinnie?"

Kathy was back. Her voice told me she was in a good mood. Kathy was a schoolteacher at a junior high where all the students loved her.

"Come meet Happy," I told her.

She walked in my room smiling. Kathy's beautiful. She's shorter than me, which is pretty short, with short hair so red you'd

know she was Irish the minute you saw her freckles and her emer-
ald-green eyes and her snappy little figure that caught my eye
when she caught me playing one night last summer at the Bottom
Line behind the big blues singer Etta James. It was just a pickup
gig for me, I was a last-minute replacement, but I was having a
blast 'cause Etta blows up a storm, and Kathy loved her blues and
loved me that same night like I'd never been loved before, saying
that she knew everything about me just by the way I played my
horn.

"This is the first time in my life I've ever gone to bed with
someone this soon," she'd said, embarrassed by the speed of the
whole thing.

"I believe you," I'd told her.

"I trust you."

"Don't."

"Why?"

"I'm a musician."

I tried warning her, tried warning myself, but me and Kathy,
we fell in love. It was the first time for both of us, and maybe I
wasn't ready 'cause I had to keep testing it. Kathy caught me only
once—hurting her hurt me almost as bad as it hurt her—but I
told her, even after she moved in, I said, you can't change a leop-
ard's spots. "I was the first guy to ever wear leopard-spotted bikini
briefs in the contests," Gino must have told me a hundred times.
"It was posing in those leopard-spotted bikinis," said the old man,
"that got me so much action."

"I've got great news for you," Kathy told me after meeting
Happy. Her baby-blue Danksin top was so tight I could see the
outline of her sweet boobs and her stiff nipples and I wondered if
this was any way for a woman to walk around New York City. She
also had on these spandex bicycle shorts which fit her fine fanny
like a glove. Kathy had more than a good figure. She also had

muscles which came about from going to the gym we'd joined on Eighth Street, the Village Health Club, which Gino hated 'cause it was trendy with Life Cycles and Nautilus machines and mirrors everywhere you looked. Kathy was one of the stars of the place, working out longer and harder than anyone, especially on the free weights. She wasn't put off by pain. When we'd play softball in Central Park, she could slug the ball further than a lot of the guys. Kathy was a killer jock, a champion runner at college up in Buffalo. Sometimes that would make me proud, and sometimes it wouldn't.

"What's the news, baby?" I asked her.

"I'm out."

"Out of what?"

"I'm through teaching."

Kathy has a high, happy voice. She's smart and perky and talks in quick spurts, the way I play my sax. Maybe that's why we got along so good. But maybe she was talking too fast tonight; maybe I didn't understand. "Say it again," I asked her.

"I quit my job. Summer school's over today, and I told them I'm not going to be back in September."

"That's crazy. The kids love you."

"I love the kids, but I've been telling you, Vinnie, my heart's not in it anymore. I want to try something else, something more physical."

"You can't do that. You don't have another job."

"That's the good news, honey. I got a job today."

"What kind of job?"

"At the Village Health Club. Last week they asked me if I wanted to be a personal trainer."

"Why didn't you say something to me?"

"Because you would've said no. Everytime we discuss the idea of my changing careers, you call me crazy."

"You *are* crazy."

"If it's crazy looking for work that makes you happy, then I'm crazy. Either way, I've taken the job."

"And what I think doesn't matter?"

"What you think matters too much. I'm too influenced by you, Vinnie, too ready to live through you, too anxious to make you happy."

"I like that."

"Well, I don't. I've had to make this decision alone, and I'm proud of myself for doing just that. After all, it's not like we're married."

"It *is* like we're married. We're living together. Besides, who in their right mind would give up a respectable teaching job to work in some gym where all you gotta do is make fat ladies lose weight."

"I just won't be working with women. I'll also be working with men."

"Who hired you over there?"

"Wilbur Guest, the owner."

"That yuppie lug? That goon?"

"I think he's a nice guy."

"He doesn't even know how to train. He's all arms and no legs. You ever see him work his legs? He's got no calves."

"You sound like Gino. Wilbur's a good businessman and you know it. He's tripled the size of the club in two years."

"He's jive."

"He's bought three buildings on Eighth Street, and he's getting ready to open a compact-disc store in SoHo."

"I'm sure he'll sell tons of Kenny G. Look, Guest ain't nothing but a spoiled rich kid. His father set him up. His father runs some scam on Wall Street."

"Wilbur's a smart marketing man, and he sees that I'm a natural teacher."

"You need to be teaching kids, not horny health nuts."

"I need to be challenged by something new. I'm tired of being around fourteen-year olds all day. My life is getting stale."

"Well, get ready to get ripped off. Gym owners are worse than club owners—they'd screw anyone."

"Wilbur charges his clients fifty dollars an hour for one-on-one training and gives the trainer thirty. I think that's fair. Right now he needs trainers. Business is that good. I'll easily wind up making twice as much money at the club than school. Wilbur also claims that the trend is for women to train men, especially with free weights."

"What the hell do you know about free weights?"

"Everything you've taught me, everything you gave me to read, plus a lot more. You always said I had perfect form."

"No one's perfect and it's plain nuts to spend all day in some gym. It's torture."

"For you, not for me. You're getting your past mixed up with mine. I love working out. Squeezing in two or three nights a week was never enough for me. Now I'll be able to work out for as long as I like, and for free, every day of the week. I love the idea of getting stronger."

"Do you know how many guys will be hitting on you over there?"

"I can take care of myself."

"I can see you now, running around all day in one of those skimpy little leotards. Personal training is like turning tricks. You gotta touch the guys and everything. I don't want you doing it, Kathy. I really don't. This is nothing but a lame-brain scheme. You don't know what you're doing. You haven't thought it through."

"I've been discussing it with Daphne for months now."

"That's what I thought. Daphne is behind this whole thing."

"She's behind my doing what's right for me. Daphne is the

most level-headed lady I've ever met. She never imposes her ideas on me. She just helps me to understand how I'm really feeling about myself. Can't you see that?"

"I can see she's a shrink who's only in it for the money."

"That's like saying you're a musician who's only in it for the money."

"You're hitting below the belt."

"You're the one who talks that way, Vin. You're the one who wants to make enough money to buy a house in the country. Well, maybe if I start making more money, we'll get there sooner."

"And you think that's going to happen by working in some gym?"

"When you start fulfilling your potential, the rewards follow quicker than you think."

"You're talking like a fortune cookie. That's the same line you fed me when you made me see the shrink your shrink recommended."

"I didn't make you do anything. You went because you needed to go, because you're hurting inside. And he's doing you good, isn't he?"

"He's doing me in, that's what he's doing. I'm quitting."

"You'll be making a mistake, Vinnie. Can't you see that you're artistically paralyzed? You haven't touched your horn in months. You're running out of money and you're getting scared. In order to go forward, you need to go back and see what caused the paralysis."

"Shrink talk."

"Straight talk. Talk you know is true."

"All I know is that you're switching up on me, and I don't like it."

"For weeks now I haven't liked living with you. It hasn't been easy. Even your own mother..."

"Have you been talking to my mother again?"

"I love your mother."

"I love my mother too, but I don't understand why you're always talking to her."

"She's my friend. Aren't I allowed to pick my own friends?"

"Look, Kathy, I'm starving," I said, wanting to drop the subject of Mom. "You wanna fix me something to eat?"

"No—and I resent you asking now."

"Why the hell can't I ask for something to eat?"

"Because it's a power play. It's your way of reminding me that if you're hungry, I cook—no questions asked."

"Have I ever been that kind of guy?"

"Not until now."

"Well now I'm hungry and I wanna eat."

"I love you, Vinnie," Kathy started saying, tears running down her cheeks. "I love you very much, but right now it's hard being with you. You don't know where to take your life and now that I'm about to change my life, you resent it. You're taking all your frustrations out on me."

"How?"

"By creating restrictions. By making demands."

My head hurt. I was tired of talking and hungry as hell. "Okay, let's just call a truce and go out have some dinner someplace."

"I can't. I have an appointment."

"With who?"

"With Wilbur."

"For what?"

"To go over some details."

"At seven at night?"

"The club's open till ten. Why don't you come along?"

"The last thing in the world I wanna do is watch Wally prancing around with that abstract art shit smudged all over his tank top."

"His name is Wilbur and that abstract design is the club logo."

"It's horseshit."

"Whatever it is, I like it. I think it's classy. I think the club is classy, and so is Wilbur."

"Then go *fuck* Wilbur if you like him so much!" I screamed. It was a dumb thing to say, but I already said it. Kathy is usually patient, but she's also got this Irish temper, and when she snaps, she snaps, and as soon as I said, "go fuck Wilbur," she slapped me across the face and I almost slapped her back, but I stopped myself and she called me an asshole and I called her a bitch and she wheeled around and ran down the hall and slammed the door behind her so hard that one of the police bars came off its hinges.

Okay, I said something stupid. Big deal. Big fuckin' deal. I was entitled. My girlfriend was going off her rocker and I couldn't stand by and pretend everything was cool. Besides, I hadn't eaten all day and when I get hungry I get angry. She should thank her lucky stars I didn't slug her and put her silly ass in the hospital. The only reason she hit me is 'cause she's a girl and she knew I wouldn't hit her back. That's chickenshit, that's cheating, and maybe she's cheating, maybe she's fucking Wilbur the WASP, Wilbur the blond pretty-boy owner who probably pops steroids 'cause I never saw him go through any real training routine. How else could he get those kind of muscles? He was way too big, way out of proportion, way out of line stealing schoolteachers from a junior high where the kids needed Kathy a lot more than the fat slobs needed her to help them trim their flab.

Fuck Wilbur. Fuck Kathy and her fucked-up ideas. I was pissed, I was hungry, and I was going out. I changed T-shirts. I put on the sleeveless one with Rico Reeds written across the chest.

I almost forgot to feed the birds who were screaming—it nearly killed them when me and Kathy fought—and now it looked like Happy wasn't getting along with Lady Day 'cause they was pecking at each other and I had to put Happy in a cage by himself.

When I hit the streets, I could still hear distant thunder. I saw streaks of far-off lightning. Sirens were screaming. The New York City cops-and-robbers game never stopped. Ambulances were racing to hospitals and cabbies were cursing kids on bikes. It was one of those nights when everyone was out. Maybe it was going to rain, maybe it wasn't. You see everything in the Village—guys holding hands with guys, girls holding hands with girls, drag queens in diamonds, poets with snow-white beards longer than St. Nick's, wide-eyed gurus selling mantras and gypsies selling beads. Usually I like the place—I moved there to get away from Mom and Pop, I moved there 'cause of the jazz, the Village is always jumping with jazz—but sometimes the Village is too weird for me. Like tonight. Tonight I had to get away.

Tonight the Village stunk of garbage worse than ever. Maybe it was the humidity. Whatever it was, I kept walking. I went all the way down Bleecker, past the jewelry shops and coffee houses and quaint brownstones, walking walking walking, trying to forget Kathy and the way she slapped me and the way she bugged me, just getting away, not knowing exactly where I was going but figuring I needed some peace of mind so why not head over to the old neighborhood where I was born and raised and felt good, especially good about eating pizza. I was dying for pizza.

Soon as I got to Mulberry Street I felt better. I was home. I love Little Italy, the barber shops and pastry joints, the candy stores and old churches. I love the smell of espresso and oregano and I especially love Salvatore Ungaretti who's been running the best pizza parlor in the city since I was old enough to hop up on a stool.

"Hey, Sal," I said, hopping up on the stool. "How you been?"

"Great, Vinnie. What'll it be?"

"A whole pie. And pile on the prosciutto. I'm dying of hunger."

"Coming right up."

While I was waiting, Sal asked, "Hear about your old man?"

"What about him?"

"Take a look."

Intentionally, I'd been avoiding looking across the street at Pop's basement gym. I was here for the pizza, not for Gino. But when I did look, I had to look again. I couldn't believe my eyes: There was the old shingle sign, lit by a single light, that had been there ever since I could remember, the one that said Gino's Gym with an arrow pointing down to the cellar. That part was the same. But where it used to say Men Only, it now read Men and Women. The Men and Women words were painted in bright red.

"I don't believe it," I mumbled.

"None of us do," said Sal, who at sixty had been on the street as long as Gino.

Sitting at the counter, I ate my piping-hot pie in silence. It was delicious, but I was still stunned by the sign. I kept staring at it, wondering what in the hell had happened. When I got through eating, I was still wondering. I paid for the pizza and jumped off the stool.

"Going over to see him?" asked Sal.

"I don't know what I'm going to do," I answered honestly. After fighting with Kathy, the last thing in the world I needed was a visit with Gino. On the other hand, it'd been a month since I'd seen him. What could have happened in a month to change something he'd swore his whole life he'd never change?

I had to know.

I walked across the street, past the sign and down the stairs. I pulled on the forty-pound dumbbell door handle. Inside, the smells hit me, just like they always did, flooding my mind with memories and smells of sweat, iron, leather and long workouts with Gino yelling they weren't ever long enough. The place was ugly, but it was also beautiful 'cause it was so simple and pure. It never changed. Until now.

I looked around and saw three people working out. Two muscleheads were taking turns spotting each other on the bench press. Nothing unusual there. But working the cable pulleys was a woman. No doubt about it. She was flat on her back and her chest wasn't flat at all. Her chest was out to here and her hair was bleached blonde and her pink-and-black leotard barely covered her crotch and all over her arms were tattoos of leopards and lions in full color. I couldn't believe it.

"Look who's here!" Gino shouted from the back of the gym where he sat on his stool and screamed orders to the world to work out harder. "The champ's back!"

The two guys and the gal looked up at me. I waved to them.

"The world-famous musician is back," said Gino in a New York accent thicker than the salami Sal sliced across the street. At sixty, Gino's hair was gray. He wore it long enough to make a ponytail, tied in a rubber band, that flowed down his back. He had these wild eyes and wide shoulders and of course a massive upper-body covered by a white sweatshirt with Gino's Gym written in red on the front and a drawing of the famous pose of Gino as Mr. Olympia of 1948 on the back. He always stood solidly, his feet wide apart. "If you can't think straight," he liked to say, "at least stand straight." For a man his age, it was a miracle that his face didn't have any lines or wrinkles. He looked great—Gino always looked great—except no one had seen him with his shirt off for the past ten years. Not even me.

"How did this ever happen?" I asked him, nodding towards the blonde on the pulleys.

"Before I tell you the story of my life, kid, I got people to train. If you wanna wait, I'll be through in fifteen minutes."

With Gino, nothing was easy.

"The way you two meatheads are bench-pressing," he told the muscleheads, "you might as well be home eating ice cream for all the good it's doing ya. Bring the goddamn bar down to your neck, not your tits. Your tits are big enough. Your tits are too big if you ask me. You apes need upper pecs, not big tits."

"But Gino . . ." one of the guys started to say.

"Ya gonna argue or ya gonna work?" Gino yelled. "If you wanna argue, take a walk. In here it's either my way or the highway. I ain't been training champions for the past fifty years to have some lug like you give me lip."

The lug clammed up.

"Let women in the gym," I remember Gino saying, "and the only muscle that'll get bigger is the one between your legs."

Yet here before my very eyes was Gino instructing a woman on the proper form for stomach crunches on the high bench.

Watching this blonde lift her legs—she couldn't have been older than thirty—I couldn't help but admire her firm thighs and low-slung ass. Naturally guys notice these things in gyms—gyms are nothing but raw sex—which is why Kathy's new job was still bugging the hell out of me.

Surprisingly, though, Gino was patient with this woman, a hell of a lot more patient that he'd ever been with men.

"You know my son over there, Brenda? That's Vinnie. Don't let his long hair fool you. He ain't no hippie. He just likes to imitate his old man. I been wearing my hair like this for twenty years, haven't I, Vinnie? Vinnie's a musician. Now I don't understand his brand of music. Me, I understand Puccini, I understand the operas of Verdi. I can sing every aria from *Trovatore* and *Aida*. Maybe not in perfect pitch, but I got the words memorized. See, that's my heritage. Vinnie, he goes with the colored. Don't ask me why. Ask him."

"He's cute," said Brenda, getting up from the bench and arching her back to display her wares.

"He's hard on me," Gino grunted. "He thinks I messed him up by working him too hard when he was a kid, so he doesn't come in anymore. He works out somewhere else, but at least he works out. You can see, can't you?"

"He's beautiful," added Brenda who spoke with a little lisp. "You should be proud."

"His mother should be proud. I tried to raise him right, but his mother got hold of him and . . ."

"Leave Mom out of this!" I shouted, angry that Pop was publicizing all this private stuff.

"And he's temperamental. That's the other thing. He's got this trigger temper . . ."

I turned to leave. I'd had enough.

"Hold on, champ," he said. "You came to talk, so'll we'll talk. After a few calf raises, Brenda's out of here anyway."

"Don't mind me," she said smiling. "You guys work it out."

Gino walked to the back of the gym, went behind his counter and sat on his stool, raising himself higher than me. When we talked, he liked looking down on me.

"You working?" he asked me.

"I work when I want to."

"That means you're not working."

"What does that sign out front mean?" I asked, switching subjects. "What's that woman doing in here? How the hell did this ever happen?"

"You got your girlfriend to thank for that sign."

"What are you talking about?"

"Kathy's been coming in. She's been talking to me."

"About what?"

"About you, about her, about training, about life, about everything. Can I help it if she likes talking to me?"

"She never said a word to me."

"Why should she? This was between me and her. Poor thing, she never had a mother or father. Raised in some foster home. It was tough on her, but she survived, she's a tough..."

"I live with this girl, Pop. I know her. You ain't telling me nothing new."

"I'll tell you this, Vinnie, and I'll tell it to you straight. Usually you got your head up your ass, but not with this gal. With this gal, you've struck gold. See, I been having some problems," Gino said, lowering his voice, "business is off. Real off. And then she starts coming around and saying things like I'm a natural when it comes to training women. The idea puts me off, but the way she says it makes sense. Fact is, she doesn't just say it, she shows me. She has me show her all these exercises, and you know something? She does 'em all perfectly."

"That's 'cause I've been training her."

"She never mentioned that. Anyway, the gal's a natural and I'll be damned if I didn't mind training her myself. Didn't mind at all. 'Look,' she says to me, 'I can't train here 'cause I don't want to get in the middle of your relationship with your son'—she's a smart girl, Vinnie—'but I just want you to know, Mr. Viola, that you have a great deal to offer women...'"

"She was coming on to you!"

"Are you nuts? Of course she wasn't coming on to me. She thinks you created the sun and the moon and all the stars in six days. She's a wonder, that Kathy. You better hold on to her."

"I'm through, Gino," Brenda broke in. "See you tomorrow night."

"I'll walk you out," I told her. "I'm leaving myself."

"Be careful of this guy," Gino warned Brenda. "He's practically married."

"Kathy and I busted up tonight," I announced.

"Why would you do something stupid like that?" asked the old man.

"She's your friend. Get her to explain it."

"There you go, champ," Gino groaned, "fucking up again."

"How can I fuck up," I asked my father, "when I know I got a guy like you in my corner?"

Outside, the clouds cracked open and the rain came thundering down. Lightning lit up the sky and me and Brenda, already soaked, ducked into a little espresso bar on Hester Street.

"Your father's wonderful," she said, sipping her cappuccino. "He knows tons about the human body."

Her body was driving me nuts, especially her stiff nipples jutting against her wet leotard.

"Gino's different," I said, tired of thinking about the old man.

"He's been showing me how to isolate my muscles," Brenda explained, pointing to her biceps. "He's teaching me mind-to-muscle." I could see that she didn't have the mind of a Fulbright scholar, but who cared? Kathy had been a Fulbright scholar and look where it got me.

"What are you training for?" I asked.

"I'm trying out for roller derby."

"I didn't think they had those things anymore."

"They're coming back. There's a rink out in Queens. Good pay, if I make it. Right now I'm driving a limo."

"You're kidding."

"It's fun. I get to wear a black suit and this cute red bow tie. Last week I took Dr. Ruth to the airport. You know Dr. Ruth, the sex therapist, the one from TV? I asked about orgasms. 'Why do I have so many?' I asked her. 'Because you're a lucky girl,' she said."

That's all I needed to hear. "Wanna go hear some music, Brenda?"

"Sure. I love music."

I figured I could have made my move right then and there, but why be hasty? Why not make a night of it? Who knew where Kathy had gone? Who gave a shit?

"I need to go home and shower and change," said Brenda.

"Don't bother. The rain's cleaned us off. Besides, this is just a neighborhood joint over in Tribeca. You look fine."

She looked incredible in the cab, her leotard under her raincoat. "You got so much definition," she said, running her fingers over my forearms. "But there's just one thing I really want to know."

"What's that, Bren?"

"How come your father never takes off his shirt?"

"That's just his habit."

"What does his chest look like? Does it look like yours?"

"I don't know anymore."

"Is he out of shape? Is that why he keeps his shirt on?"

"Look, Brenda, if you wanna go out with Gino, go out with Gino. But you're out with me so let's just have a good time and listen to some music. I'm not into muscles, I'm into music. Get it?"

"Jeez, you don't gotta be so touchy."

We got out of the cab at Warren Street. Through the rain, the twin towers of the World Trade Center, only a few blocks away, glowed like giant lanterns. You could hear the jazz from the street. The cats were just winding down. The club was called Intrusions.

My friend Drew Williams was sitting near the bandstand. He looked at me and Brenda real funny 'cause he liked Kathy and I could see him wondering what I was doing with a strange chick. Drew's a black guy my age I met in high school. Then he went to college at NYU. His old man teaches history over there and Drew looks like a professor himself. He wears big round gold wire-rim glasses, V-neck sweaters, tweed sport coats and knit ties. He's a tall, handsome dude. He's a little hung up on the Ivy League look, but that's okay 'cause he's taught me so much about the history of jazz I can't even tell you. He studies it during the day and goes out to hear it at night. Then he goes home and writes about it. He's writing a book. He calls himself a classicist when it come to jazz. It doesn't bother me that he's gay. Fact is, that makes it easier 'cause I don't have to worry about him and Kathy. She likes him too and sometimes they go to the ballet together. There ain't nothing I hate worse than the ballet.

I introduced him to Brenda. When she took off her raincoat, all the guys in the club gave her the serious once-over. Drew looked at her like she was a Martian.

"Brenda's famous," I told him.

"How's that?" Brenda wanted to know.

"Brenda's the first female member in the history of Gino's Gym," I explained.

"I've never been to Gino's Gym," said Drew—which is one of the reasons I liked him.

"You oughta see it," Brenda urged. "All these pictures of mus-clemen on the wall. Plus, Gino's a genius."

"Talking about geniuses—or wasted geniuses," said Drew who spoke like he was writing, "did you read the interview with Miles Davis in *Vanity Fair?*"

"No," I said. "What'd he say?"

"Miles is hopeless. Now he's praising Kenny G."

"Oh God…"

"He says, and I quote, 'The boy's playing pretty melodies that the girls like. What's wrong with that?' This is the great Miles Davis, the man who gave us Bill Evans, Cannonball Adderley, John Coltrane, Chick Corea, Herbie Hancock and Keith Jarrett, the man who is revered as the boldest innovator since Bird."

"And you think he's full of shit?" I asked Drew.

"I *know* he's full of shit. Miles isn't playing anymore, he's jiving. He's so into being a pop icon, so into being the magnificent and mysterious Miles, he's lost artistic credibility. Just last week I did an interview with Betty Carter—who, by the way, is singing as marvelously as Sarah Vaughan—and she confirmed my position. 'Miles broke Freddie Hubbard's spirit years ago,' Carter told me. 'He's trying to do the same thing with Wynton Marsalis now, but Wynton's too smart for him, Wynton's too tough.' Wynton, you see, believes in the purity, in the *sanctity* of jazz."

"Is jazz some kind of religion?" asked Brenda.

"To Drew it is," I answered.

"And Vince," said Drew, "is one of the most important young members of the church."

"You gonna play tonight, Vince?" Brenda wanted to know.

"What have you been doing with your horn?" asked Drew. "I haven't heard you play since April."

"Been going through some changes."

"What kind of changes?" Drew wanted to know.

"I don't know, man—musical changes, personal changes."

"He broke up with his girlfriend," said Brenda.

"You and Kathy split up?" asked Drew.

"We're having a hard time right now."

"Look, Vin," said Drew. "I don't want to probe. I just want to hear you play. Bob's playing alto tonight but he also brought his tenor. Why don't you borrow it and sit in? It's a mainstream group. They've been playing beautiful straight-ahead stuff, mainly Monk tunes. I'd love to hear you."

"Me too," Brenda chimed in.

I wound up playing "'Round Midnight." I wasn't up to par. It was a borrowed tenor with the wrong reed. The rhythm section wasn't relaxed enough; I wasn't relaxed enough. I was too anxious to impress Brenda—the truth is, I was playing to her pussy—but it still felt good, just to have the horn in my mouth. Just to have my breath blowing ideas over that cramped little club, just to feel keys against my fingers, to talk through Monk's melody, to ride over the rhythm, to explain that I was feeling a little low and lonely and fucked-up over Kathy and fired-up over Brenda and sad about love and glad that Drew was listening 'cause he was the one who saved me when Bird's alto overwhelmed me. He suggested I try tenor, not alto. See, it was Drew who introduced me to the titans of the tenor sax—Coleman Hawkins, Lester Young, Ben Webster, Don Byas, Budd Johnson, John Hardee, Ike Quebec, Illinois Jacquet, Dexter Gordon, Gene Ammons, Sonny Stitt, Sonny Rollins, Stan Getz, Zoot Sims, Al Cohn, Arnett Cobb, Lockjaw Davis, Johnny Griffin, James Moody, James Clay, Fathead Newman, Wilton Felder, Flip Phillips, John Coltrane, Wayne Shorter, Billy Harper, Ernie Watts, Clifford Solomon, all my idols, the guys whose pictures hung over my bed when I was a kid, their music tormenting my turntable, soft ballads like the one I was playing tonight, singing the songs like vocalists, digging deep into their souls for all the beauty and wonder in a world of hurt and harmony and horny pain. Just to get it out, to let it out, to release the heat. I wasn't at my best, but I had a voice, I was me, I was burning and Brenda was melting, I know she was, and Drew was moved, I could see it in his eyes, and Kathy was out there some-where, moving away from me, no longer tuned into me, turned off to my tenor.

"God, you turn me on," said Brenda. I was staring down at her tits. I wondered about all those animal tattoos on her arms, but it didn't matter. It made it interesting, the way the leopards and lions seemed to be prowling around her boobs. I dug in. I sucked my way to paradise. I saw how she was digging me, rubbing me down with skin cream, creaming all over herself, her beautiful black bush, her toned-up thighs, turning and twisting, there was no re-sisting her, no holding back, just letting her lick and sticking it hard. It wasn't about foreplay, it wasn't about romance, it was a no-wait get-down dance, raunchy rock 'n' roll, first on the bed, then on the rug, her snug and snappy snatch, her mind-blowing muscle control, an exercise in fuckin' sexual stamina, a crotch-and-cock ride 'round the planet, me giving her all I got, her moaning and groaning and grinning and grinding and grabbing me for more, me bouncing on her bones till I thought my boner would break. "Give me a break," I finally said. "I'm through."

In the morning when I woke up, I was hung over. We'd smoked some and drank some booze. I had to remember where I was. Her place was on Canal Street near Chinatown. A big two-bedroom apartment filled with roller skates and gerbils. I dug the gerbils. When Brenda woke up, she said, "Let's love some more." I liked her 'cause she was honest. The girl was no yuppie.

"I don't know your last name," I confessed.

"Weinstein."

"A Jewish roller skater?" I asked, surprised.

"My father's a fight promoter. Sports run in the family."

"You from around here, Bren?"

"Eldridge Street. Just like you—never known anything but the Lower East Side. Wish we'd met years ago. You know how hard it is to find a real man these days—a guy's who's into his body and really likes to love a lady? It's also cool that you don't make a big deal out of it. A good lay is like a good exercise, isn't it? You have to know how to do it right. You have to hook up with someone who understands bodies. You and your old man. Both you guys are really something. What do you say to another round?"

I wished she hadn't mentioned Gino.

"Your mother Jewish too?" I asked, turning the spotlight back on her.

"She's a chorus girl from Sweden. She was a waitress over there and over here she became a Rockette. Fabulous dancer. She and Dad just moved out to San Diego. He's promoting local prize fights. Also bullfights in Tijuana. Plus, he's opening a check-cashing store in Del Mar, wherever that is. I could've moved out to the Coast, but I'm attached to the city. I can't leave it. Besides, I'm making it on my own. You ready for another roll?"

I wasn't. I was groggy, thinking about the pep talk Drew gave me last night before we left the club. "You're keeping the faith, Vin," he told me. "When it comes to jazz, your karma is absolutely clean. You'll be rewarded. Because you're in the great tradition, things will start happening for you—soon."

"Soon," I said to Brenda. "I'll be there soon. Just let me drink some coffee."

She pranced around her place butt-naked, showing off her gorgeous body with such style that I never got to the coffee.

We bumped and humped our way through the morning. It

was amazing how we fit together. But Kathy was different. She wasn't this crazy, she wasn't this pushy, she didn't scream and scratch and carry on. She was soft and sweet, she radiated a different kind of heat.

But Kathy was history, because when I got back to my place on Jane Street I saw that she hadn't been home all night either.

I SAID, "I'M QUITTING"

"**Y**OU'VE SAID that before," said the shrink.

"This time I mean it."

"Then why are you here? Why didn't you just leave a message on my machine, or send me a note, or not show up at all?"

"'Cause I wanna tell you face to face that I think this is a waste of time."

"And what, may I ask, has happened in these past few days to provoke such antagonism on your part?"

"I don't know!" I barked, jumping off the couch and tearing up the designer paper towel he'd placed behind my head. I was standing in front of his chair, defying him to say another word.

"Did you see your father?" he finally asked, looking at me through his artsy antique specs.

"How'd you know?"

"You're awfully worked up over something. Why don't you sit down. You'll be more comfortable."

I sat down. I wasn't more comfortable. I was filled with feelings I didn't know what to do with.

"Are you angry at your father?" asked Mueller the meddler.

"It's got nothing to do with my father. It's Kathy."

"What about Kathy?"

"Kathy's a bitch, a goddamn crazy bitch. She wants to be a bodybuilder. She wants to be *me*."

"What brought all this about?"

"She's quitting her teaching job to work at the gym."

"Your father's gym?"

"No, but it might as well be. She's been hanging out with him."

"And you're jealous?"

"Fuck no, I ain't jealous. Kathy doesn't have a father, and she doesn't have a mother, so maybe Gino makes her feel good. What do I know? The thing is, she doesn't even know him, and here she is telling him what to do. And I can't believe he's actually listening to her, like she's his daughter or something."

"I'm still not clear. Which gym is she working at?"

"The hi-tech yuppie gym on Eighth Street, the Village Health Club. This goon, this Wilbur Guest, hired her as a personal trainer—not because she knows what she's doing, but because he wants to fuck her. I'm sure of it."

"So you and Kathy had a fight."

"She moved out. Now you'll know more about her than me, because you and her shrink Daphne are buddies. You and Daphne probably discuss your patients all the time."

"I can assure you that we most certainly do not."

"You can't assure me of shit. Look what all this shrinking has done to her—and to me. It's fucked up our lives."

"You also said you saw your father."

"I didn't say it, Doc, you guessed it."

"Why don't you tell me about it?"

In spite of myself, in spite of wanting to walk out the door and never see this creepy headshrinker again, I sat there on the edge of the couch and spilled my guts out, not 'cause I wanted to but 'cause, well, I just did. I told him about Kathy convincing Gino to allow girls in the gym, about my wild night with Brenda Weinstein, even about last night's dream where I got to the Mr. Olympia contest and I couldn't even pull open the door; I was too weak to even lift a pen to sign my name.

"And what name would you have signed?" asked Klaus. "Vince or Gino?"

"What the hell kind of question is that?"

"You tell me," he said, placing a fresh designer paper towel on the sofa pillow.

I leaned back and thought about it. "It doesn't make any sense," I said. "Gino was Mr. Olympia, not me. I don't give two shits about that muscle stuff. Don't you see, Doc, I don't have anything to do with him anymore."

"Yet, metaphorically at least, you shared a woman with him."

"You're nuts. You're the one who needs a shrink."

"You emphasized how Brenda kept comparing you to Gino."

"That was her problem, not mine."

"But what do you make of the fact that you were compelled to pick up the first female ever to train in your father's gym?"

"Nothing. Look, she's a horny girl in a city filled with fags, and I happened to be there, I filled her bill, and that's all there is to it."

"Last time you mentioned the woman for whom your father left your mother."

"Patty. She was nothing but a high-priced hooker. It didn't take her more than six months to dump Gino. Once she saw he didn't know how to make money, she was gone."

"Did your father discuss his other girlfriends with you?"

"Did he! He couldn't wait to see me so he could me tell me

about his ladies. That's why I quit hanging around him. I told him, I said, 'Pop, I don't wanna hear about your broads. It's an insult to Mom.'"

"Did Gino ever remarry?"

"No, and neither did Mom—that's the strange part. She always said she was devoting herself to make enough money so me and her could be comfortable. No men for Mom."

"I'm wondering if, at some point, you felt motivated to bring them back together?"

I was laying on the couch with my head on the pillow when I realized that Mueller, in his fancy English armchair, was looking down at me the same way Gino, sitting on his stool, liked to look down at me in the gym. I got up and started to leave.

"What is it now?" Klaus wanted to know.

"I don't understand what we're doing here. You're asking about stuff that's been dead and buried for ten years. This is jerk-off. This is bullshit."

"You're agitated, and you've been telling me why. You're getting some things off your chest. Why find fault with that?"

"'Cause I gotta pay you and I'm running out of money and I'm running out of time. I gotta get my life together and the last thing I need is to pay a shrink to hold my hand. See, I'm a jazz artist and I need to play jazz. That's my one and only problem. That's what Drew says, and Drew's right. Drew understands me. He's the one who knows my music and he got me to play the other night. He knows that when it comes to jazz, I'm pure."

"The way Gino is a purist in his gym? No compromising, no..."

"Jazz ain't exercise. Jazz is like when the birds sing, it's natural, it's..."

"Yet you described your playing as sexual foreplay. It was your way of seducing Brenda."

"Can I help it if girls go for muscleheads and horn players? If Kathy is out fucking someone else, why should I sit home sucking my thumb? If you wanna score, you better use what you got. Drew thinks jazz is king, but Drew's old man makes good money teaching college and his old lady edits books and that means that Drew doesn't have money problems. Sure, I could start a jazz group and gig around the city for peanuts. And even if I got a record deal, you know how jazz sells? Jazz doesn't sell worth a shit. So what's wrong with selling out? What's wrong with playing arena rock if it pays my bills? With Kathy gone, my rent just doubled. I'm a fool for knocking Kenny G when Kenny G is making a million bucks a year and even Miles says he plays pretty. Who's Drew to tell me what to play? I don't see him going hungry in the streets. What'd you call Gino, a purist? Well, purists are famous for starving to death. That's why he finally let chicks in the gym. It's his last chance to keep from going broke."

"What about studio work? You once mentioned musicians who earn a great deal of money playing the studios."

"Yeah, Michael Brecker, David Sanborn, cats who make a fortune playing every record date from Barry Manilow to Madonna. Then there are guys who do commercials. There's big money in commercials. And soundtracks. And computers. A lot of the cats are programming drum machines, synthesizers, synclaviers...all kinds of shit. They're sampling like mad, stealing the sound of a tenor or a dying moose in the middle of the woods. I could learn all that high-tech stuff, but it's not that easy for me, see, 'cause I never really learned to read music too good. I'm not mechanically minded. I play by ear. My ear's so good I can pick up anything, I can play whatever they want, but sometimes I feel a little funny when I first get in there and the producer starts yelling at me to do this and that. Fuck those producers. They just want me to turn tricks. And I'm too good for that. That doesn't bother you, Doc, 'cause it's a way for me to pay your bills. You're worried about your bills, ain't you?"

"I'm trying to understand what's worrying you."

"Well understand this: I'm a sax man. And I was raised to be one of the big boys—like Coleman Hawkins or Dexter Gordon. And believe me, those guys didn't compromise. Like me, a lot of those guys weren't great readers. They were dedicated mother-fuckers. They stuck to their guns. These were leaders, cats who always had their own bands."

"You've mentioned forming a band before, but you've never followed through."

"You know what it means to have your own band? It means you got other people looking to you for money, other people de-pendent on your ass for their livelihood. Meanwhile, I can't even pay next month's rent."

"Vince, I'm afraid our time is up."

"That's cold-blooded, Doc. I swear, you got ice water run-ning through your veins. I spill out my guts, and all you can say is, 'Sorry, bring in the next head for me to shrink.'"

"Time restrictions are always difficult. And making it even more difficult is the fact that we won't be meeting again until September first. I'm sorry, but I'll be vacationing till then."

"A month! Whoever heard of a month's vacation?"

"It's normal procedure for psychotherapists."

"What a racket you guys got going! Well, that's perfect, just perfect, 'cause it makes it easier for me to break this thing off. Don't look for me when you get back."

"In case you need to reach me while I'm gone," said Mueller, handing me a slip of paper, "here's an emergency number. I'll re-spond as quickly as possible."

"You think I'm going need you in the middle of the night? You think I'm about to crack up?" I asked, putting the number in my pocket.

Regina's House of Beauty was celebrating its tenth anniversary. There was a blue banner out front: Anniversary Special, Wash and Blow Dry, $10.50. Regina is my mom. Regina Viola never changed her last name, even after she divorced Gino. When you walk into Regina's place, it's weird to see a picture of Pop as Mr. Olympia of 1948 hanging over the cash register next to a snapshot of me feeding my birds. The whole shop is a little weird.

Regina's House of Beauty is in Long Island City, right under the El after you get off the Queensboro Bridge. It ain't a pretty neighborhood, mainly factories and warehouses and old apartment houses, but the clientele is loyal and Mom makes a good living. Better than Pop. Which, frankly, is why I went by. I needed money.

Kathy had been over to the Jane Street apartment when I wasn't there to pick up her things. She'd left me her key and a note saying it'd be better if we lived apart for a while, but she loved me and wanted me to know she cared. She didn't leave a number or nothing, so I was feeling pretty gloomy riding the subway over to Mom's. I thought at least me and Kathy could have talked it over, but I knew how she felt. She was scared I'd talk her out of her new job and she didn't wanna be talked out of nothing. She was stubborn and I was pissed. Let her lift weights like a goddamn man. Let her see how far that would get her.

I arrived at Regina's feeling foul. Mom was at the cash register counting bills when I walked in. She looked up and smiled. "The light of my life," she said. "You look terrible."

Mom had her own look. Maybe it was out of fashion, but she

liked the beehive style. She teased and sprayed her black hair, swirled with silver streaks, until it stood up on her head like a crown. "Regina means queen," she liked to say—and she meant it. She was taller than me and Pop, and she liked lots of powder blue eyeshadow and black eyeliner and that sweet Joy perfume was her favorite. "It costs a fortune," she'd remind me, "but I'm worth it." Like Gino, Gina had a high opinion of herself. Only, she was right.

Mom thought of hairstyling as an art, and lots of other working women like her style, 'cause she made enough money to buy a little house in Seaford, Long Island that made me depressed—it had all these pink drapes and crushed blue-velvet couches—so I usually came to see her at her shop. The shop was always buzzing with buggy-looking ladies. Lots of them were fat—unlike Mom, who kept her figure—and they liked wearing stretch pants and sweatshirts from Atlantic City that said "We Got the Hottest Slots" and getting manicures by Marla, the black woman whose son Tyrone, a badass bass player, was one of my best friends. I got Marla the job. She was Regina's first employee.

"What do you mean I look terrible?" I asked Mom. "I been working out pretty regularly."

"Men and their muscles. I ain't talking muscles, sweetheart, I'm talking the look in your eyes. Have you been crying? Your eyes are bloodshot. What's wrong?"

"I'm fine, Ma. There ain't a thing wrong with me."

I went over and kissed Marla on the cheek. She was painting red polish on the nails of Mrs. Sebiski, who'd been coming there for years. Mrs. Sebiski was reading the *National Enquirer*.

"Tyrone just asked after you yesterday," said Marla who had apple cheeks and sparkling eyes. She'd once been a model, though now she probably weighed 200 pounds.

"What's he doing?" I asked.

"Formed a funk band. He's playing over at Skeesie's up on 145th Street. You oughta run up and see him, sugar. They might need a sax player."

"You stay out of that neighborhood," Mama yelled from the cash register.

"Don't mind your mama," said Marla. "You'll be among your own."

A little later, in the back room, past the row of pink-painted hairdryers—everything was painted pink at Regina's—me and Mom sat in her cramped office crowded with cartons of shampoo and conditioner, the air thick with peroxide.

"It's been a tough couple of weeks," I confessed.

"Why don't you come out to Seaford and stay with me for a while?" She took my hand like she used to when I was a kid.

"What good would that do, Ma?"

"At least you'd have someone to cook for you."

"So you heard about me and Kathy?"

"Kathy told me."

"When?"

"We talk all the time."

"She called you?"

"No, she told me when she came to Seaford."

"When was she out in Seaford?"

"Kathy's living with me in Seaford."

"What!"

"I thought you knew. I thought she called you."

"She called, but she didn't say nothing about being with you. That's crazy."

"What's so crazy? Where else does she have to stay?"

"With me—where she belongs."

"You tell her that."

"How could I tell her if I didn't know where she was?"

"Now you know."

"I'm not calling her, Ma. I'm not about to beg. Besides, she doesn't want to hear what I have to say."

"So why do you have to talk? Why can't you just listen? She's a lovely girl, Vinnie, with a mind of her own. You won't find better."

"Why does she wanna be stuck out in Seaford?"

"What's stuck? She rides in here every day with me. She loves my new Cutlass. It's a beautiful car. It's like riding a sofa to work. From here she takes the subway and she's in the Village in twenty minutes."

"I can't believe she's doing this to me."

"What are you thinking? How does it hurt you if she keeps me company?"

"It's nuts."

"It's only temporary until she makes up her mind."

"About what?"

"About where to live."

"And you're her adviser?"

"I'm her friend. I also gave her a perm yesterday. You should see. She looks like a little doll."

"You're dressing her and you're feeding her and you're fixing her hair," I said. "You finally got the daughter you always wanted."

Mom gave me a hug and a kiss, saying "You're my baby, and I love you more than I love myself. I'd give up my life for you, and you know it. But things are different for girls now. Girls are deciding for themselves. If I had started this shop when I was Kathy's age, I'd be a millionaire, I'd be living in Las Vegas."

"Who the hell wants to live in Las Vegas?"

"No humidity. I love the desert."

"Look, Mom, with Kathy moving out, I'm in a little jam."

"Come home with me tonight. Stay here till I close. Kathy

will be here and we'll all ride out to Seaford together, like one big happy family."

"It's not going to work like that, Mom."

"You're proud but broke."

"I don't need that much."

"How much?"

"Five hundred—just for a month."

Regina sighed, then reached inside her billowy blouse where she fished five bills out of her bra.

"Take," she said, handing over the dough. "But I want you to know something..."

The speech: I couldn't get away without the speech.

"You're twenty-five now, Vinnie, and it's time to think about making real money. I hate to say it, but you're too smart to make the same mistakes your pig-headed father made—always broke, always chasing some skirt. You wanted to play your music, okay, you played it. I gave you my blessing. You wanted to mix with the colored, so you mixed with the colored. But where are you now?"

"I'm trying to decide on some things..."

"You're too old to..."

"Mom, I've heard this speech before."

"I'm not giving speeches, I'm just a mother telling her son that she loves him, that she wants the best for him, and that she wants the best for his girlfriend."

"What does Kathy have to do with this?"

"Women respect men who make good money."

"Are you saying that if I was making more money, Kathy would never have left?"

"I'm saying you need to think about these things. I look in your eyes and I see a mixed-up little boy."

"All I know is music, Ma. All I love is music."

"Have you ever thought of teaching the saxophone? You play

so beautifully there must be mothers who want their kids to learn. Maybe if you put an ad..."

"I don't wanna teach. I wanna play."

"Kathy says you haven't been playing."

"Kathy talks too much."

"Take this money, Vinnie. I want you to have it. But I also gotta tell you something, I gotta be honest. I'm saving every piece of profit and spare change I can get my hands on. I have plans."

"What plans?"

"Expansion. I'm thinking of expanding into a new business."

"What new business?"

"I'm not like your father. I'm not going to brag about anything until the papers are signed and the deal is done. I'm just saying that I'm going to need my money."

"You're opening another shop?"

"Better than that. I'm thinking of investing in wrestlers."

"I don't believe this."

"It's a going concern. Female wrestlers. They're starting a new league. They're looking for sponsors. Cable TV is interested. It's something I could manage."

"Am I going crazy or are you?"

"Making money isn't crazy. And when have I ever lost money? Regina Viola is not a gambler, you know that, but neither is Regina Viola afraid of risks. I've been going to gyms, looking for the right wrestlers. I've been looking into this for months. Kathy's been helping me. She's..."

"I don't want to hear about it, Mom, I really don't."

"Don't bite off your nose to spite your face, Vinnie. Call Kathy tonight. She misses you. I know she does."

"Thanks for the money, Ma. I'll pay you back. I promise."

* * *

I promised myself I wouldn't think about Kathy for the rest of the day. Kathy had taken over; first she took over my dad, then my mom. Kathy was everywhere I looked except in my bed. Kathy was driving me crazy and I wasn't about to call her at Regina's house on Long Island or Gino's Gym in Little Italy or Wilbur's Village Health Club. Why should I call her when Brenda Weinstein was calling me every hour on the hour, begging me like I was the last man on earth?

Bren said, "Meet me at your father's gym at eight. I'm doing upper-body. We'll work out together."

"I don't like working out there," I told her.

"Then meet me afterwards."

"Maybe."

"You don't sound like you want to see me."

"I'm supposed to hear this band."

"We'll hear 'em together. Like the other night. The other night was beautiful."

"You're going have to meet me up at Harlem," I said, thinking that would scare her off.

"That doesn't bother me. After I'm pumped up, I could meet you on the moon. Don't you love getting pumped up?"

"Later," I told her. "I'll see you later." I gave her the address of Skeesie's and hung up the phone.

While Brenda was pumping, Skeesie's was jumping.

I got there early. I wanted to catch Tyrone's first set. I brought my ax, my Selmer Mark VI sax. With my tenor by my side, I was feeling a little better. The shit about Mom and Pop and Kathy was somewhere in the back of my mind. Up front were the sounds of Tyrone and his band, the Righteous Rippers.

Tyrone played bass. More than play it, he plunked it, he

funked it, he flapped and slapped it, he punished and popped the thing until you had to get up and get down. This was dance music, and the crowd at Skeesie's, a converted bowling alley, was on its feet, bumping to the beat.

Tyrone was wearing a red leather vest, no shirt, white sweatpants, and green Nike high-tops. He was only a little taller than me, on the chunky side, his hair all curled up and drooped down—Marla was his stylist—his smile stretching across his wide face, his dark eyes dancing, his fat fingers flying over the frets of a guitar that had just taken the place of his bass. Now he was singing and rapping and raising the temperature on an already steamy night, talkin' 'bout "Papa's Got a Brand New Bag," an old soul dish first fried by James Brown, then Otis Redding, and now my man Tyrone Newborn. He sang like he meant it—gruff, rough and gritty.

The band was all black, two horns, a keyboardist and Tyrone —he called me V and I called him T—switching between bass and guitar. T waved me up to the bandstand and, all modesty aside, I played my ass off, sounding like I'd invented fuckin' gut-bucket rhythm-and-blues. I played so nasty I thought they'd arrest me for disturbing the peace; I growled so loud I thought I'd blow a speaker; I arched my back and pointed my sax to the heavens; I heaved and honked; I gave 'em hell. When I looked down, Brenda was sitting right under me, her eyes eating up my body soaked in sweat.

"Damn," said T. "You're plugged in solid. You're connected to the main circuit."

I was still buzzing. Brenda was drying me off with a paper napkin. T was scoping out Brenda.

"I met Tyrone eight years ago," I told Bren. "We played a wedding together."

"Jewish wedding," added T. "Nearly caused a riot."

"I'm half-Jewish," said Brenda.

"These folks were all-Jewish," said T. "They wanted rye bread, not cornbread. V saved the day. He got out his clarinet and made like a rabbi. V can play like anyone."

"You guys got gigs, T?" I asked.

"Couple here and there. Meanwhile, we're recording demos. One of the brothers has an eight-track at home. Why don't you come by? There's no money yet, but..."

"That's the trouble."

"The bread will be there. It's just a matter of time. This time we're going for it, V. We're tired of fucking around, man. We're laying tracks hot enough to burn this city down. What do you say?"

"I say I'm going back to blowing straight-ahead jazz."

"Fuck jazz."

"Why do you say that?"

"I'm tired of that word *jazz,*" said T. "Like it's some holy shrine."

"See," said Brenda. "I told you it was a religion."

"It's a trick bag cats get caught up in. Like you, V. You think it makes you clean and free of sin. It's that holier-than-thou shit."

"It's beautiful music," I reminded him.

"Well, so is greasy funk-in-yo'-face. When I see people jamming, that's beautiful to me. When I see the green on the bill and the bill in my pocket, that's music to my soul. That's pocket music. Man, that's real. I know you, V. You hang out with your downtown Village Negroes, cats with too much college, cats interested in building monuments and opening museums. Soon there's going to be the Wynton Marsalis School of Proper Jazz Behavior, no farting in the halls, no talking back, no cold-blooded jams, no ethnic grooves—ain't that what Wynton calls this funk?—no niggers allowed."

"Wynton loves Duke Ellington. What's wrong with that?"

"I love James Brown. He's *my* Duke. What's wrong with *that*? Look, I am who I am. I don't wanna work at no Seven-Eleven. I don't wanna wait on no tables. I wanna make people dance. If I do it good, they'll pay me serious money, and I'll love it, I'll be the baddest mammajamma on the block."

"I got so much music running through my head," I told T. "It's hard figuring out what to play."

"If your daddy didn't own a gym and your mommy didn't own a beauty shop, you'd be doing just like me, playing what's paying."

It paid to stick around for the second set 'cause I didn't mind dancing with Brenda, watching her bump and thinking about her box and not thinking about Kathy, not thinking how I'd take Kathy to the garden in the Museum of Modern Art where we'd hear string quartets or acoustic jazz and I could tell her about the piano player and she'd know about the sculptors and the French guys who painted the fuzzy flowers.

"Your father wants you to call him," Brenda said in the cab downtown.

"Why?"

"Business."

"Business must be bad."

"Business is booming. Gino said five new girls signed up today. He needs a trainer in there besides himself."

"Let him get Kathy."

"He's pissed at her."

"What happened?"

"When she told him that she wouldn't leave the other gym, he got mad. Now both of you guys are pissed at Kathy. That Kathy must be some bitch."

I was glad Gino and Kathy had fallen out, but I didn't like Brenda calling Kathy a bitch. I did like Brenda giving me a blow-job, though. She did it in a way where the cabbie couldn't see. With the city whizzing by and her tongue teaching me some tricks I'd never seen before, I had to admit it was exciting. Brenda was an exciting chick.

"Sometimes women wanna do crazy things," she whispered in her little lisp. "There's nothing wrong with that."

But what did Regina want with a league of female wrestlers? Wasn't that like being a madam? I asked myself after I returned the favor to Brenda back in her apartment, my tongue tasting my favorite flavor, one that ain't among the Baskin-Robbins thirty-one.

"You can sleep here if you want to," she offered.

Now Brenda was cool. Brenda was sweet. Brenda even had me playing the sax again. God knows she was doing wonders for my sex life. It was just that Brenda was so athletic. But so was Kathy. Kathy could beat me at bowling. But why did Kathy have to go live with my mother?

"I better go home," I said.

"Why?" she asked.

"I feel funny."

"What do you mean?"

"I need to talk to my birds."

There's nothing wrong with talking to birds. They listen. For example, Happy listened to me. I told him, "If you wanna get along with Lady Day, leave her alone in the mornings. She's a little cranky in the mornings." Me too. The mornings were lonely. It was the third week of August and by eleven A.M. the city was scorching. Since I had nothing to wake up for, I slept late. Most musicians do. The birds woke me up. Ever since Kathy left, I slept in the same room as them. I'd called Kathy a couple of times, but she never called back. So much for Mom's advice. The hell with Kathy. I'd rather talk to the birds anyway. The birds know my moods. They sing sad or merry, depending on me. If I have a headache—and I was having lots of them —they don't sing at all. The birds understand.

Understand, I wasn't feeling sorry for myself—it wasn't that. It was the money. I could go over and start recording demos with Tyrone, sure, but there was no money in it. There was no money playing at Skeesie's. I needed to start lining up studio gigs, but that meant lots of nasty no's on the phone, lots of snotty secretaries telling me the producer will call me, don't call him. Given my mental state, that was aggravation I could live without. I looked at the shrink's emergency number—he wouldn't be back for another ten days—but what was the shrink gonna tell me? He was gonna analyze me, and that's the last thing I needed. I needed money.

"I needed to talk to you."

I couldn't believe Gino was standing there at my front door. How'd he even know where I lived?

"Kathy told me."

"I thought you were pissed at her."

"Who told you that?"

"Brenda."

"You've been laying Brenda, haven't you?"

"This is what you came over to ask?" I asked.

"I came over to offer you something."

"Well, come in."

Gino was wearing a black sweatshirt and black sweatpants with the Gino's Gym logo up and down the left leg in big white letters.

"You got your own fancy sweatpants now," I noticed.

"That was Kathy's idea. She told me to do it last month. They've been selling like hotcakes."

"You want a cup of coffee?"

"Black."

"I know."

We sat in the kitchen. I had to admit it; with his long gray hair and his black workout getup, Gino looked tough. The old man had style. I guess I felt flattered 'cause he'd never come to see me before, not like this. Sitting across the kitchen table from him —and not looking up at him as he sat high on his stool at the gym—was a nice novelty.

"I know Kathy is pissed at you," he said.

"I thought you're pissed at her."

"I offered her a job."

"You told me. But she wouldn't take it 'cause of me."

"That was before. After you picked up Brenda, I offered her the job again."

"You didn't tell her about me and Brenda, did you?"

"I might have mentioned it."

"Might have!" I exploded. "Why the fuck would you do something like that?"

"Jealousy's the best medicine you can find. I figured she'd run back to you if she saw another dame in the picture."

"Well, goddamnit, you figured wrong. And besides, I'm not so sure you just didn't want Kathy for yourself."

"What are you talking about? She's a child."

"If you didn't wanna lay her, you sure as hell wanted to hire her. You just said so."

"I said I needed help. Women are flocking to my gym like you wouldn't believe. This is something I should have done years back. I'm charging them four hundred a month for one-on-one training —the whole four hundred up front—and they're paying, Vinnie, they're paying cash. They can't wait to start pumping. They say the old gym is sexy. They say it's got atmosphere up the ass. And then there's a whole new group of guys signing up. The guys are following the gals, and it's all been happening, it's been snowballing in the last few weeks. I'm telling you, the place is going crazy, except there's only one trainer—and that's me—and there's only one other guy who knows my methods, there's only one true heir to Gino's Gym and that's Gino's son and, goddamnit to hell, Vinnie, that's you."

My proud pop was practically begging. I didn't know what to do; I didn't know how to react. It was sort of satisfying, but also sad. I wondered what shrinkhead Mueller would have to say. It was a new wrinkle, but it was also infuriating that my old man was in the middle of my life, especially my love life.

"We'll work together," he said. "We'll be partners. I've got no one else. You were right about Kathy. She's turned bitchy. She's out there on the Island with your mother..."

Kathy with Mom and me with Dad. The girls versus the boys.

"I don't know what to do," I admitted.

"Your mother's right about one thing—you're lost, she said. And you don't need to be. You need to be in the gym."

"We went over this ten years ago, Pop."

"And we're going over it again, Vinnie, 'cause it's not going away. Gino's Gym is a fuckin' national institution. They talk about Gino's Gym in Toronto, in Tokyo. Russian bodybuilders write me letters, wanting to know should they lock out on the behind-the-neck shoulder press or shouldn't they?"

"I gotta think it over."

"What's to think over?" asked Gino. "I'm offering you joint ownership—we'll make a fortune together—and a chance to do what you do best. *I'm* the best, and *you're* the best, and never forget it."

I forgot what time it was—maybe three A.M., maybe four—when I called Dr. Klaus Mueller's emergency number. There was no reason except I couldn't fall asleep and all these creepy feelings were crawling over me, like the flu or something, except it wasn't temperature and chills, it was just nerves. My nerves were shot.

"Sorry to wake you in the middle of the night," I told Klaus. It hadn't even taken him an hour to call me back.

"You all right?" he asked.

"Just going a little nuts."

"Tell me about it, Vince."

"I'm not really going nuts, I'm just having a hard time going to sleep."

"You're alone?"

"Kathy's living with Mom. And Dad wants me to work in the gym."

"How did that come about?"

"I'm not sure. But he's got lots of women over there."

"For you and him to share?"

"We're supposed to train them."

"Like he was training Brenda?"

"Brenda ain't a bad chick."

"So you're still seeing her."

"She's keeping me company, she's got me playing the sax."

"You sound agitated, Vince, as though you're unable to settle on one thing."

"It's like I'm fifteen again and Mom and Dad are fighting for me and now Kathy's in the middle."

"And Brenda."

"Brenda wants to get stronger. So does Kathy. I can't blame her. I gotta accept this shit. If it's over, it's over."

"Have you been able to talk to Kathy, at least to discuss your feelings?"

"Why does it matter?"

"When relationships terminate, it's desirable that both parties have their say. It's good to clear the air, to ventilate your feelings, Vince."

"You think I should see her?"

"You sound like you want to."

"It's like you're Dear Abby or someone."

"You're hurting. I can feel that. You're in something of a crisis."

"I need money, Doc. Are you charging me for this phone call?"

"Do you think I should?"

"If I wake you in the middle of the night, I can't expect a freebie, but I'm worried. I need to work. Maybe I should help out Gino. What's wrong with that?"

"You'll have to tell me."

"I've been through it before."

"You may have to go through it again. I can't tell you."

"Then what *can* you tell me?"

"I can tell you that I'll be back in my office the first of September."

"Don't worry, Doc, I'll have it all worked out by then. I'm fine, I really am. I'm sorry about this."

"If you want to, call again. Sometimes getting through the night isn't easy."

"Thanks, man. Thanks a lot. It ain't serious, it's just that I haven't worked out in a couple of weeks. If I don't work out, I get crazy."

Kenny G's "Songbird" was playing over the loudspeakers in the Village Health Club. Thinking of the royalties he was getting for this song was getting me crazy. Stretched out on the floor of gleaming blonde wood, women in designer workout gear lifted their legs to the music. Everyone looked rich, everyone was toting liters of Evian water—young bankers and lawyers and ad agency guys and PR gals and housewives with polo players running around their $100 sweatshirts. The place was huge, creeping with shiny chrome and giant mirrors and machines so computer-complicated it took an engineer to explain them. In the month I'd been away, they'd gotten a slew of fancy new equipment. Naturally I was a little nervous looking around, since I expected to see Kathy any minute. I didn't tell her I was coming 'cause I'd decided on the spur of the moment. I'd decided to take Doc's advice about clearing the air.

"It's been a while, Vince," said Wilbur Guest, dressed in his too-tight tank top and oversized sweatpants. "You look a little out of shape."

"You been working your legs, Wil, or just hiding them under those baggy pants?"

"Baggy workout bottoms are what's happening. They're comfortable, and they're selling. We've starting our own line. Have you seen our little clothes boutique back by the juice bar?"

All I could see is that Guest overworked his chest. It was too big, way out of proportion to the rest of his body. It was just for show, for customers who didn't know no better, an easy way to impress women. For a guy six feet tall, he also had a deltoid problem. Okay, he had beefy biceps—I'll give him that—but his shoulders sagged. Gino would have made him do ten sets of ten bent-over dumbbell flyes—every single day—to strengthen and widen those deltoids. I could have told him, I could have helped him, but Guest was the kind of guy who had to do all the talking. He was also the kind of guy who went to tanning parlors so he could look even more like Robert Redford. I think he dyed his chest hair blonde.

"Has Kathy showed you the new machines?" he asked.

"No."

"Kathy's been doing a brilliant job. She gives you a lot of the credit for her training, Vince. She says you're quite a trainer yourself. I asked her if you'd be interested in working for me, and she suggested that I ask you myself."

This was getting good—two gym offers in one week.

"I'm a musician," I said.

"Lots of musicians like extra work. Plus, the hours are flexible. Let me show you these new machines, Vince."

Out of the corner of my eye, I looked for Kathy. She was nowhere in sight.

"What we're trying to create," said Wilbur, deep into his nice-guy routine which I didn't trust for a minute, "is an environment of unsurpassed ergonomic efficiency."

"Isn't that what they call snails in fancy French restaurants?"

He smiled and continued his spiel. "This row of Techno-Power machines is the latest in biomechanical design, utilizing a form of electromagnetic resistance. Get in and give it a try."

Why not? I climbed into the thing. It was like a spaceship. In front of my face was a computer grid with green, red and yellow lights blinking every which way. I put my hands on the levers and started to push.

"Wait," said Guest. "You need to punch in a program."

"Give me the max," I told him.

He hit the buttons and I started pushing. It wasn't easy, but when I finally was able to extend my arms all the way out, pushing through the pain of the electromagnetic resistance, I heard this voice from outer space saying, "I suggest, Vince, that you use a lighter weight."

"Who the hell said that?" I wanted to know.

"An electronically synthesized voice."

"How'd the motherfucker know my name?"

"I programmed it in. Each station, you see, is a humanoid, a personal coach. TechnoPower has memory and is able to recall your previous workouts. TechnoPower encourages you, but also chastizes you when you're not pushing hard enough. Then when you're through, a laser-jet printer spits out a complete evaluation of everything you've done. Workout, printout. Customers love it. It gives them a permanent record of every session."

"Then what do you need personal trainers for?"

"Some customers are still hooked on live human beings," he said as he led me to the weight room. "Take Ted. Ted's so hooked on Kathy he's booked her twice a day five days a week."

There was Kathy, her red hair all curly in a cute-looking Regina Viola perm, showing some meatball how to do a dumbbell curl. Even if her baby blue leotard had the Village Health Club abstract-art logo across her chest, she still looked good to me. I forgot how much I missed her. I forgot how much I wanted to hold her and kiss her and—

73

"Feel it right here," she was telling this Ted, taking her finger and running it over his bicep.

"You don't have to touch the guy to show him!" I shouted, all upset. "You can just tell him."

"Vince! I didn't see you over there. I'll be through in about twenty minutes. Why don't you . . ."

"You don't need to touch these guys."

"That's enough, Vince," said Wilbur. "You're disturbing—"

"Butt out, butthole. I wasn't talking to you, I was . . ."

"Okay, Vince, I'm going to have to ask you to leave." Guest's nice-guy routine was over.

"I'm not ready to leave."

"I strongly suggest you leave before . . ."

"Before what?"

"Before I throw you out."

Kathy and Ted had stopped what they were doing and were staring at me.

"I want you to come home with me, Kathy," I said. "You don't have to turn tricks for this pumped-up pimp."

The pumped-up pimp was faster than I thought. Wilbur walloped me with a left jab.

Kathy screamed, "No!"

I went down, but I was up before Guest had time to guard his gut. I slammed him hard with a right, smashing his stomach so strong he lost his breath. He was on his ass, and by the time he was halfway up, my fist was kissing his left eye. I wanted to murder this bum, and I was about to do it, I was about to finish him off when someone blasted me in the nose—it was the security guard, the same guy who had once asked me advice about ab exercises. The guard was getting me 'cause I'd gotten his boss and it was two against one, it was no fuckin' fair and I could feel that my nose was cracked, my nose was aching and my blood was streaming and Kathy was yelling, "Stop! Everybody stop it!" but I wasn't finished, I socked the security man square in the jaw but then Guest was back, paying me back, eye for an eye, he ripped me in the right eye and flipped me over his back. I landed with a thud but luckily put my foot in Guest's nuts before he could pin me down. He moaned like a dying dog. I was back on my feet but his man was up in my face, we were slugging it out and Kathy was crying and I landed a couple of decent blows and Wilbur got me good in the gut and I couldn't do it anymore, I couldn't fight 'em both. Guest and his goon had me by my arms and were carrying me through the club, my nose bleeding on their blonde wood floor, and everyone staring, past the bouncing aerobic bunnies, past the row of TechnoPower stations, out off the club, flinging me on the street like I was drunken bum or something. I landed on my ass.

Kathy ran after me, crying and wanting to take me to a hospital. I shrugged her off, saying, "You better get back to work before Wilbur gets mad."

"Why do you have to do this?" she wanted to know. "Why do you have to be this way?"

"You're the one who started this, not me."

She started to say something else, but words wouldn't come. Tears were streaming down her cheek. She looked so pretty *I* almost started crying. Instead I walked away.

My father was waiting for me. I don't know how he knew something had happened. Maybe it was just a coincidence. But he was pacing in front of the apartment building on Jane Street when I got there.

"What the hell happened?" he wanted to know.

"Don't worry. They look worse than me."

"How many were there?"

"Come on up, Pop. This is a story you'll like."

Naturally he loved my war story. He loved hearing about the talking weight machines in Wilbur's chrome-brained gym. He wanted to go back there and take them on himself. I told him that I wished he'd been there with me. He said he was proud of me. Pop had never said that before. He even helped clean me up, assuring me that my injuries weren't bad at all. I knew, though, that my nose wasn't right. I could live with the black eye but a doctor was going to have to deal with my nose. Gino agreed, saying, "I'll take you over to the hospital myself."

My father took me to the emergency room. He was there when the guy set my nose. "Not a bad break," said the doctor, "but a break nonetheless."

Gino walked me back to my apartment, even made me hot tea and lemon. By ten that night, we'd been together eight straight hours, the longest in ten years. When Mom called, half-hysterical —Kathy must have told her—Gino was even civil to her.

"Don't worry, Gina, the champ is fine. The injuries are minor. Right now he's sleeping," Gino lied. "I'll have him call you tomorrow."

"Tomorrow both your eyes are going to be black," he told me. "Your nose is still gonna be throbbing. Sleep late and don't come by the gym till afternoon. I'll be waiting for you. You'll do a light workout and maybe start training one of the women. What do you say?"

I said, "Okay."

I SAID, "I'M NEVER GONNA SEE MY CRAZY FATHER AGAIN"

"**T**HAT'S AN awfully strong statement," said the shrink.

It was the first day of September, our first meeting in a month.

"I mean every word of it," I told Mueller. "I told him and I'm telling you. I should take out an ad in the *Village Voice*, just to tell the world that this man is a maniac—a full-fledged, full-time maniac."

"I presume you went to work for him."

"It was impossible. He's impossible."

"Yet it was something you felt you had to do."

"He took care of me."

"Under what circumstances?"

I told Mueller about the fight at the Village Health Club.

"In the aftermath, then," Klaus contended, "there was a bonding between you and your father, a bridge."

"The bridge lasted for exactly one day. Then it blew up."

"How?"

"Does it really make any difference?"

"I can't tell you that, Vince. You're going to have to tell me."

I sighed. I was suckered into this shrink thing and there wasn't shit I could do about it. Like a guy on smack, I needed my fix. I had even showed up ten minutes early today. I wondered if they had Shrinkheads Anonymous for patients who couldn't get off the tit. I hated being hooked like this. When I told Mueller I didn't like myself for needing him so much, he said, "You're finding all sorts of ways to beat up on yourself, aren't you?"

"What am I supposed to say to that?"

"Whatever you feel like saying."

"I feel like I don't do nothing but tell you about me fighting with Gino."

"That last fight was ten years old. This one is new."

"This one wasn't really a fight. It was just me smashing a barbell against a mirror and getting the fuck out of there."

"And he didn't try to stop you?"

"He was too scared. He saw he'd pushed me too far, he saw I might do anything."

"How did it start?"

"Ask Regina. She married the guy."

"I'm talking about the fight."

"I know what you're talking about."

"And I know it's painful for you to relate the story."

"It's not painful, it's a pleasure, it's a pleasure knowing I'm never going to have to see him again. See, a guy like that feeds on a guy like me. He loves an audience. He needs a patsy. That's why he got me back into the gym. He's gotta be looked at or he ain't happy. Now with all these hot dames dancing through, he's going out of his mind. His ego is so big there ain't room for nothing else in the gym. These women like him, they really do. They look at him like he's a character. They think he's cute 'cause he's like their grandfather or something. All this is spacing me out, plus the fact that it's only been a couple of days since they threw my ass out of the Village Health Club and my eyes are still aching and my nose is still throbbing. After all these years, I'm back in Gino's Gym, and that idea is also making me a little crazy, back with the same smells and the same dumbbells—nothing ever changes at Gino's —and right away Gino's on me about putting away the weights and making sure all the benches are in place. It's like I never left, like I'm still ten years old. Why is it that I can never feel like a man in that gym? Anyway, when the first gal shows up, I see she's my age. She's nice. She takes a liking to me and I start training her, I start showing her different exercises when Gino starts yelling. 'Don't put her on the pulleys,' he says, 'start her off on legs, not arms. She needs legs.' Why argue? So I show her legs, and everything's cool until Gino comes over to tell me she needs sartorious, not inner thigh, so I give her sartorious and the next thing I know Vince is training her, not me. Fine. Except that happens with every chick who walks in the place. And the more they like me, the more Gino gets in my face. 'He's been away for a while,' he tells the girls. 'I'm still teaching him how to train.' But what the hell, it's my first day in the gym and I figure I'll lay low, I'll let the old man rant and rave, except it's hard 'cause he gets worse, he starts acting like I don't know what I'm doing. He's embarrassing me and making me feel dumb. It's humiliating to hear your father say shit like, 'You should have seen Vinnie when he was a kid, when he was really in shape, before all this colored music turned his muscles soft.' Finally, after four hours of this crap, Brenda comes bouncing in. She's all excited that I'm working with Pop and she wants me to work out with her. Before I know it, though, Gino breaks in. 'You got it backwards,' he says to me. 'You don't start her off with lat pulldowns, you...' 'You haven't given me a chance,' I tell the old man. 'Look, *I've* been training this lady,' says he. 'But now she wants *me* to take over,' says me. 'The hell you will! You'll never take over this gym!' Gino starts screaming. He's lost it, he's out of control. Gino's gone. Guys working out just stop and stare, but the old man couldn't care less, the old man can't stop screaming, 'You've taken advantage of her and you've taken advantage of me! This ain't no pickup joint—understand me?—this ain't no meatmarket, and I'll be damned if my own son is gonna use this gym to get his kicks and . . .' 'Shut up!' I finally yell back. 'Say another word,' he says, 'and you're out on your ass!' I don't say another word. I just pick up a barbell and throw it against a mirror and get out."

"What did Brenda do?"

"She followed me."

"To where?"

"What difference does it make?"

"You tell me."

"We went back to her place. We screwed. You happy?"

"It sounds like she was happy. It seems as though she found the father-son fight stimulating."

"Look, Brenda finds everything stimulating. She's a healthy gal. Except she's driving me crazy 'cause now she wants me to train her and I don't wanna train anyone, not even myself. I've had enough gym jive to last a lifetime."

"Well, where does that leave you, Vince?"

"Broke. I don't even know how I'm gonna pay you for this session. I don't know how I'm gonna pay the rent."

"You've given up on music?"

"Never! Music's the only thing that brings me to my senses. Music's the only thing in the world that makes sense to me."

"It doesn't make sense," I told Sue Kawisha, personal manager and discerning promoter. "Why should I have to take off my shirt? Don't you want to hear me play the saxophone?"

"Of course I do. And I will. But I also have an idea for immediate cash flow. That *is* your problem, isn't it?"

"Well, sort of."

"Last week a client of mine made fifteen thousand dollars modeling for a simple half-day session."

"I thought you represent actors."

"I'm extremely discriminating about whom I promote," said Sue, brushing back her long, silky black hair. She wore large thin-framed eyeglasses and a green silk dress. No doubt about it, she was a knock-out. Her Murray Hill office, with the teakwood furniture and black tiles, looked like a high-styled sushi bar. When she crossed her legs—Kawisha was over six feet tall—I couldn't help but look and listen to the swoosh of nylon. "I refuse to represent anyone," she said in her soft-strong way, "actor, musician or model, before I'm absolutely certain I can sell them."

"I've never modeled before in my life. Never even thought about it."

"Muscle men are much in demand now, especially those with a distinct ethnic look. Your face is fine. I just want to get a good look at your chest."

Something said this was bullshit, but something else said it was flattering. It's not every day a lovely long-legged Oriental lady asks me to strip. So I peeled off my shirt. I even did a little pose-down, a little light flexing.

"Superb," she said. "Simply superb. For someone who's never modeled before, you have a remarkably photogenic presence."

"When I was a kid, I won a few bodybuilding contests. That was years ago."

"Well, you haven't lost your touch," she said, touching my shoulders with the tips of her long red fingernails as she circled around me. "I like what I see, Vince. I think we can do business."

"About what?"

"I'm not sure."

"About what I'm doing here. To be honest, Sue, I had something else in mind."

"What was that?"

With her looking deep in my eyes, I tried to explain. "We met 'cause of Kenny G. Remember?"

"Of course I remember." She spoke with barely any foreign accent, enunciating like she'd been to the finest finishing schools.

"Well, that's what I was thinking of doing—being a saxophone superstar. It may sound cocky, but I know I got the chops, and now you're telling me I got the looks. Maybe I'd need a producer, or maybe I'd produce myself. See, I've been trying to make up my mind about which way to go—musically speaking—and I've decided to go all the way."

"I admire your attitude," said Sue, "and I couldn't agree with you more. If you play your horn as dramatically as you flex your muscles, Vince, I think we're talking mega-success."

"You mean that?"

"If I didn't, I wouldn't suggest the modeling route. The music, you see, will come later. First, let's get you back on your feet financially. Let's place your face in a national magazine or a network commercial. Let's get some dramatic shots of you—head shots, full body shots—and go from there. How does that sound, Vinnie V?"

It sounded great, but also scary. "I still don't know about modeling without making music part of it. I might feel weird. I might feel cheap."

"Not if I do the negotiating," she said through a beautiful smile. "If I cut the deal, you'll feel anything but cheap."

"This Mercedes doesn't feel cheap to you, does it?" Kawisha asked me as I slipped behind the wheel of her big black Benz parked in the underground garage. She wanted me to drive us to dinner. She had more to discuss. Did I have the time? I had nothing but time.

"The Mercedes feels like a million bucks," I told her, heady with the odor of heavy leather and light perfume.

"If you wouldn't mind," she suggested, "drive downtown to the Brooklyn Bridge."

Just on the other side of the bridge, we ate at a fancy joint flickering with candlelight and filled with fresh flowers. They had to loan me a sport coat that was so tight I felt like a fool.

"Don't worry about it," said Sue. "Look at the view."

Across the water, the skyscrapers shone like magic lanterns.

Two hours later, I had the same view from Sue's bedroom in Brooklyn Heights, only a few blocks from the restaurant.

All during dinner, Sue had questioned me about my past, but I'd turned the tables on her. I'd asked about her life. I didn't want to discuss Mom or Pop or any of the things that had me hooked on Mueller. I was trying to get unhooked.

"Would you unhook my bra?" she asked as she came over to the bed where I was sitting and staring out the window, looking across at the shimmering skyline.

I unhooked her bra. She stood right there, inches from me, naked and beautiful, bathed in the light of a full moon hung low over the river. She was tall and sleek, small-waisted, small-breasted, slender. She was also determined. At dinner she'd told me about coming to study at Smith College and staying to make her fortune which she didn't even need 'cause her father was a millionaire in Tokyo. He made copying machines. She said she'd copied American women; she believed in their liberation movement. "American women," said Kawisha, "have balls." She'd worked at a big talent agency for a year until she figured it out. "The trick," she claimed, "is learning to talk on the telephone. Telephone talk is everything."

Watching her bend down to unplug the phone, my dick was hard but my mind was muddled. I thought about what was happening. Sue was a winner. Sue had brains. Sue was good at getting what she wanted. And what she wanted was me. She let me drive her car. She paid for dinner. She took me over to her place and had me play my saxophone. I knew the score. I was playing for my dinner, I was playing for my future, I was playing for her pussy, playing "Stardust" and "Moonglow" and making up melodies that led straight to bed. Why not? Why not combine business with pleasure? Wasn't that the ultimate aim of life? Sue was getting me work. Sue was getting me hot. Sweet Sue even provided the rubber. So what was wrong? It was another great adventure, a wild and crazy fling, a high and a hoot. Why should I feel used?

Well, I did feel used, and I was just about to say something when she came over and put my hands on her legs. "Would you mind rubbing me?" she asked. I couldn't resist her legs. I got lost in her legs. Her legs were long and silky and soon she had me locked up inside her love, her legs around my mouth and my mouth on her mound—dark soft lovely mound, moist, and she was moaning softly, Sue was no screamer, Sue was a quiet storm, a tender tornado twisting me up and sucking me in, rising and falling, she swung me over the moon and hung me on the stars, far away from anything I've ever known, hardly a word, she kept me going, kept me up, kept me slamming and serving, every nerve wired, I couldn't get tired the way she tongue-teased, prolonging the pleasure of a long ride, an easy breezy bumpin' jumpin' joyride that stayed bright right through the night.

* * *

"In New York City," she said in the morning, "I haven't met many men like you. I hope I didn't wear you out."

Sue was smiling and wearing a white silk robe, moving around her elegant townhouse like a doe. I thought of Brenda and her tattoos and her funky flat on Canal Street. Brenda liked loud rock 'n' roll and flapjacks in the morning. Sue was serving me tea and toast with imported marmalade. Mozart was playing on the sound system. Kathy liked Mozart. In the morning, though, Kathy never listened to music. She'd grade her papers and read the New York *Times*. Kawisha was reading *Variety.*

We sat in her living room where I looked over a row of video tapes—Barbra Streisand concerts, Al Pacino movies—and one marked *Female Wrestlers of Japan.*

"You like that stuff?" I asked, pointing to the tape.

"Japanese are crazy about wrestling, and I've never quite lost my taste for it. Strangely enough, our women wrestlers are more aggressive than yours. We're much rougher, and I suppose I like it like that."

I was going to mention Mom, but decided not to.

"Would you mind driving me to work?" she asked after we dressed.

I didn't mind, except I thought it was a little funny when she sat in the back.

"It's easier for me to spread out my work back here," she said when I told her that I didn't wanna be no chauffeur.

When we got to her office, she made some calls to set me up with a photographer. "Don't worry about the costs," she said. "I'll deduct it from your future earnings." Her secretary was a guy, a nasty queen. He didn't like me.

It didn't matter, though, 'cause two weeks later me and Kawisha were in the first-class cabin, American Airlines Flight #5, on our nonstop way to the Coast.

"Let's talk about this trip you're about to make," said Mueller, the day before the plane took off.

"What's to talk about?" I asked. "I feel great. I've landed an agent. My dream's coming true. I couldn't be happier."

"That's not what I'm hearing."

"Then you're not listening, 'cause I'm fine. Things have turned around and now I'm cooking with gas."

"Are you and your agent lovers?"

"Why would you even ask such a thing?"

"You described her as gorgeous. And, well, you have a way with gorgeous women."

"You sound like you're jealous."

"You sound defensive."

"Even if we were lovers, what difference would that make?"

"You tell me."

"There you go again, throwing the shit back on me."

"I've already been through analysis."

"What are you saying—that you're cured and I ain't?"

"No. I'm saying that it's your money and your time. You're the focus here, Vince, not me."

"Well, this manager, this Sue Kawisha, she's focused on me. Not that she needs me. She represents this famous woman who acts on a soap opera, and a guy who starred in a movie last month, and a couple of models who make huge money. Plus, she's got family money of her own."

"So it's strictly your art? She's banking solely on your musical talent."

"Nothing's that strict. Except maybe Gino's Gym. And even Gino's Gym has gone bonkers. I used to think Gino was strict until he got involved with these women. See, these women are driving him nuts. The old man uses them. He's got them calling me. First Brenda calls to say he feels bad and wants me back in the gym. 'Fuck that, Brenda,' I tell her. 'I'm not going near that place. Ever. Tell him to forget it.' 'Well, when am I going to see you?' she wants to know. 'It's been nearly a week, Vince. Can you come to my roller-derby tryouts?' 'I'd love to, baby, but I've been practicing, I'm trying to get my sound back. You understand, don't you?'

"'I don't understand,' Kathy says to me the next day, 'how you could have done something like that.' 'The Village Health Club makes me crazy,' I say. 'I'm not talking about the club, I'm talking about Gino's. He told me what happened. He even told me to tell you he's sorry, but, Vince, it sounds like you were the one who lost control. You were the one who provoked your father. I know he's difficult, but deep down he's a good man. I've been working there as a trainer at night. Wilbur gave me permission—I'm just going to be there until Gino finds someone else—but really, Vince, your father wants you back, your father needs you.' 'Look, Kathy,' I say, 'why don't you keep your nose out of my family business because you don't know what the hell's going on.'

"'What's going on,' Mom says to me, 'is that negotiations for my wrestling league are getting serious. Kathy has been helping me every step of the way. She's a jewel, Vin, and she wants you to be part of this, just like I do.' 'Part of what?' 'Part of our family business.' 'Thanks, Mom, but no thanks. I got a business of my own.' 'You call music a business? Business is where you make money. Have you been making money from music?' 'My time's coming, Mom, my time's nearly here.'"

"I'm afraid our time is nearly up," said Klaus.

"Well, I'm not afraid of nothing. If Sue Kawisha can get me some coin in exchange for a little light modeling, what the hell is wrong with that?"

"So it's modeling, not music."

"It's everything, Doc. To hell with the field goal, I'm going for the touchdown. I'm going for the big score."

The big jet touched down at LAX. It'd been a nasty November morning in Manhattan, but it was an eighty-five-degree afternoon in California. A limo was waiting with a cute gal wearing a red bow tie and driver's hat behind the wheel. We wheeled our way out to Beverly Hills. "We'll have a leisurely dinner before going to work tomorrow morning," said Sue, her hand on my knee. Huge sunglasses covered her petite face; a tailored brown linen suit covered her body. Kawisha was in control. Outside, the city was light and easy, ocean breezes and swaying palm trees, freeways and Frisbees and billboards for suntan lotions. Last time I was here, with Royal Flush, it was raining. Besides, that was a heavy metal, white-lines, wired-to-the max trip, with no room for relaxation. I hated it. This time the sky was blue and Sue was talking about the Bel Air Hotel being one of the nicest in the world.

It was. They got swans and little bridges and flower gardens and Meryl Streep sipping tea in the dining room. They got terry-cloth robes for you in the bathroom and a fireplace in the suite with the walls painted pale yellow and outside the hills are green and up the street Quincy Jones is coming out his front door and waving like he knows me.

All this is cool, except Sue wants to stay in the room. She's got love on her mind. I don't. I want out.

"Where are you going?" she says.

"Gold's Gym," I tell her. "I feel like pumping up."

"You'll have time tomorrow morning. The shoot's not till afternoon."

"I'll see you later," I said, not bothering to argue, not wanting to get pissed.

I got pissed 'cause the cab down to Venice cost nearly thirty dollars and I had only a couple of hundred bucks in cash. Sue had paid last month's rent for me. Sue had advanced me money. Sue had convinced me that modeling for *Playgirl* for a quick $5,000 was a good career move. No nudity, she said, just tank tops and bikini briefs. I wouldn't be showing any more than Gino used to show at Mr. Olympia contests. Plus, I'd be playing my sax. That was the theme—a sexy saxist. "You do this," she argued after I argued that I couldn't do it, "and we'll have a record deal by the end of the year." I didn't argue any more.

Gold's was crowded with stars. Arnold S. was working his lats. Tommy Chong, from Cheech and Chong, was doing chins; I was surprised the cat was so strong. Glen Frey from the Eagles and Joe Piscopo from TV were doing cable pulls with Lee Haney, Mr. Olympia himself. At first I felt a little strange, maybe a little intimidated, but hell, I had this great gig tomorrow and God blessed me with a good body and even though Gino was a prick, Gino was a great teacher 'cause I could do any of these exercises with picture-perfect form and cold-blooded control. And I did. I worked legs and back and shoulders and arms, I pushed and pulled and crunched and curled 250 pounds over the preacher stand with a wide grip. I carried on like I owned the place, like none of these fancy movie stars mattered. I strained through the pain and went for the burns and stripped down to my tank top that said Gino's Gym and a couple of the guys came over and asked if I actually knew the legendary Gino Viola. "He's my old man," I said matter-of-factly, knowing he was known by every serious bodybuilder in the world. Word got around and soon even the movie stars realized that the son of a heavyweight celebrity was making his mark.

"You living out here?" asked one of the big boys.

"Just flew in to do some modeling," I answered, finally feeling good about tomorrow's gig as I looked in the mirror and saw the definition on my calves and the way my back rippled with the right stuff. Inspecting my rock-hard pecs, I could see why Kawisha had a pretty easy time selling me to *Playgirl*. "You should be proud," she said. "For every man they shoot, thousands have been rejected. Besides, they're buying more than your body. They're buying your overall look and the image you project."

In the shower, I was projecting about tomorrow's shoot. After a two-hour workout, I was feeling fine. Rich red blood was running through my muscles; my adrenalin was kicking in. I was plenty pumped.

"I'm taking you to Spago tonight," said Sue back at the Bel Air.

"I'd just rather have some pizza."

"That's just what they serve."

Except their pizza was covered with goat cheese and duck. I ate it anyway, looking around the room at Tom Cruise and Tommy Lasorda. Welcome to Hollywood. Outside, the L.A. basin looked like a giant bathtub filled with strings of yellow lights. The sky was crowded with jets and stars. Kawisha paid. "Let's go to bed early," she said. "I want you to be fresh for tomorrow."

I didn't mind making love to her, except I couldn't concentrate on her legs. I was thinking of Kathy's green eyes and Brenda's crazy tattoos. Afterwards, I told Sue I was going to get some ice, but instead I went to the lobby to use the pay phone.

"Kathy's out," said Mom, who loved the idea of my modeling. "She's working two jobs—at the Village club and for your father.

I'll tell her you called. We're all excited for you, Vince, we truly are."

A man answered at Brenda's. Who the hell was I to get jealous, but I was. "He's just a friend from roller derby," Brenda explained, all excited. "We made it together."

"Made what?" I wanted to know.

"Made the team."

"Congratulations."

"I told him about you," said Brenda. "I told him you're going to be in *Playgirl*. Everyone thinks that's terrific. I even told my father in San Diego. Will you call him while you're out there, Vinnie?"

"If I have time."

"You're a doll for calling me. I miss you, baby."

I could hear the guy telling her to hurry and hang up. I knew he was waiting to bang her. Kawisha was waiting for me. Kathy was probably with Wilbur.

"Where's the ice?" Sue wanted to know when I got back to the room.

"I'm not thirsty anymore."

We made love again, with me thinking about Kathy and Wilbur and Brenda and the guy on the phone.

In the middle of the night, shook up by a nightmare where barbells were falling on my chest, I couldn't go back to sleep. Instead, I tiptoed out of the room, back into the lobby. There was this cute little orange-winged pytilia sitting in a gold-painted cage. I could tell he was a friendly guy who knew I was going through a rough time. I would have talked to him—I would have told him what was on my mind and listened to him sing—but the night clerk on duty would have called the loony bin. Instead I called Mueller.

"What do you make of me and all these women?" I asked him.

"You require a great deal of attention, Vince."

"You're pissed because I woke you up."

"You're agitated because tomorrow you'll be photographed. Ultimately, you'll be the center of attention of millions of women. It's a dazzling fantasy."

"Then why don't I feel good about it?"

"Part of you does, and part of you doesn't. Different voices are saying different things."

"But what are you saying, Doc?"

"We'll sort it out when you get back to New York. For now, just try and hang in there."

"Why do I have to look hung?" I asked Sue, who was with me in the dressing room at the *Playgirl* photography studio.

"It's the style. Every magazine has its own style."

"But it's ridiculous. Who the hell ever heard of padded bikini briefs? Look, Sue, I'm perfectly normal, maybe even a little more than normal. I sure as hell don't need no puffed-up crotch. It's humiliating."

"Don't fight them on this, Vince. It's not worth it."

"Says you."

"Says the contract. We're locked in."

She came over and patted me on the head, like I was a dog or something. "Be good. On shoots like this, attitude is everything."

She handed me these leopard-skin built-up bikini briefs, but I refused to put them on. Instead, I grabbed my tenor sax and started to play. My big sound filled up the room, making me feel better. I was warming up, still wearing my sweat pants and sweater; I wasn't ready to strip down.

Then someone knocked on the door.

"We need him now," a gruff-voiced woman demanded.

I ran through some more scales, playing long and loud. I didn't want to take off my clothes.

"For God's sake," said Kawisha, "you're acting like a little boy at the doctor's. You're a grown man with a beautiful physique. Face it. Flaunt it. Go out there and show 'em what you got."

I sighed before finally stepping out of my pants, peeling off my sweater and putting on the briefs. They were nothing more than a G-string. The foam rubber surrounding my dick was at least two inches thick. I hated it, but I picked up my sax and went out there anyway.

They were all women—the director, the photographer, the lighting crew—and that kind of excited me, the way they were eyeing me, the way they moved me around the room, looking for the right angles. It was a nightclub setting, and the other members of my make-believe band were also women—a drummer, bassist and pianist. The chicks were dressed to the teeth; they were wearing tuxes while I was nearly naked. I wasn't happy, but I was there; somehow I'd make it through.

"Get on your back for the first shot," said the butchy director, who was taller than Kawisha and talked like a drill sergeant. She was even wearing a khaki pants suit.

I didn't wanna get on my back. I hated the idea. "How am I going to play my sax on my back?"

"You aren't going to play your sax, sugar. You're going to play this."

She marched over and handed me a trumpet. I wouldn't take it. "I don't play trumpet," I told her.

"Pretend," she insisted.

"I don't pretend nothing."

She laughed at me, trying again to hand me the instrument. I wouldn't take it.

"Sue," I said, "tell her that I don't play trumpet. I play sax."

"For the shoot," the director explained, "we decided trumpet was sexier."

"It shouldn't make any difference to you," said Sue, trying to smooth things over.

"Just get on the floor," the director demanded, "arch your back, spread your legs and stick the goddamn horn in your mouth."

That was it; I'd had enough. "Stick it up your ass!" I shouted.

"Vince!" Kawisha stomped her foot like a schoolteacher. "What in the world are you saying?"

"I'm saying I'm a saxist, not some cheap whore. I ain't stuffing my crotch and I ain't playing no trumpet and I ain't getting on my back no matter how much money they pay."

"We have a contract," said Sue. "We have a deal."

"Deal me out, baby. I'm gone."

Just like that—with the director shouting at me and Sue—I went back to the changing room. It was hard to tell who was more pissed, me or Kawisha.

"You're being ridiculous, Vince. You're being silly and immature and—"

"Look, Sue, you're a nice chick and I feel you want to help me and I appreciate all the favors and the money and I know you're on the ball but goddamnit, I ain't about to show up in no magazine with blown-up balls and some strange horn that I never played before in my life when everyone knows my thing is the sax. Don't you see?"

"I see an extremely headstrong man who's about to lose a lucrative career."

"What lucrative? What career? I got nothing to lose except my self-respect."

"You call it self-respect. I call it being short-sighted and stubborn. I thought you and I had something real here—an understanding, a common purpose, a mutual respect, a deep affection that—"

"Maybe we were just using each other."

"Speak for yourself, Vince. I was sincere—sincere about all of this..."

"I ain't no Chippendale's pin-up..."

"What you are is confused. And confusion is something I don't have time for. You've embarrassed me—"

"I embarrassed *you!* How about *me?*"

"You're on your own. I've made a mistake in judgment and, believe me, it won't happen again."

Kawisha wheeled around and walked out the door. I thought about following her, but figured what the fuck. Let her go. Let her find another fool. For the first time in weeks, I felt free. Maybe I had only $120 bucks in my pocket, but I had my dignity and I had my sax and I threw on my street clothes and marched out of that Hollywood photography studio with my head high even though I didn't know where to go or what to do.

I just walked. I walked down Sunset past the Motown building where maybe I could have gotten a contract if I'd played my cards right and flashed my ass, walked by the Famous Amos chocolate chip cookie store, past the hot-sheet motels where the working girls were hanging out and heaving their miniskirts so high you could see they were naked underneath. One winked and I wanted to wink back, I wanted to say, "Yeah, baby, I know how you feel, I been through the same shit," but I just kept on walking, walking past poster stores and porn shops, walking so I wouldn't have to think about who I'd been screwing or what I'd been doing, walking just to get this heavy stuff off my mind and find a little L.A. mellow, except the smog was yellow and my eyes were burning and tears were running down my cheeks and inside I felt all torn up from the mixup with Sue and the lousy shoot and the way everything had fallen apart.

I decided to stop walking when I saw a sign for a music store called The Horn Connection. Music stores always make me feel better. I went in to buy a reed. New reeds always make me feel better. Standing at the counter was Scott Hamilton, a great tenor saxophonist, a white guy who, still in his early thirties, plays like the black masters of the 1940s.

"Hey, Scott," I said. "Remember me? Vinnie Viola. We once jammed together at the Vanguard."

"Sure thing, Vinnie," said Scott, a beautiful cat who looks like a mouse but plays like a monster. "I'm playing out in the Valley tonight, at Alfone's. Why don't you come by and sit in?"

Doc Severinsen was standing at the bar. Benny Carter and Harry "Sweets" Edison were sitting at a corner table. And I was up on the bandstand, shoulder to shoulder with Scott, blowing my blues away. You should have heard us. We jumped out in front of the rhythm section on "Jumpin' at the Woodside"; we floated over "Easy Living"; we did a tongue-in-cheek thing, à la Sonny Rollins, on "Wagon Wheels"; we wept all over "Willow Weep for Me"; we got deep into "Laura" and leapt into "Lester Leaps In." Suddenly, from the back of the club, Billy Eckstine walked to the bandstand, shook our hands and called for "Sophisticated Lady," molding the melody with his voice the way Ben Webster would have sculpted the song with his sax. It was beautiful. He might be in his seventies, but he sounds timeless. Before he left the stage, he whispered to me, "Keep playing pretty, son."

Now I'm not saying I'm a mainstream master like Scott Hamilton or Billy Eckstine, but I hung in there with them, I got in my licks. Letting the music mellow my heart, I remembered I could still do something well in this world; I felt like a human being again.

"This boy's still in his early twenties," Scott told the audience, patting me on the back, "but he's got that timeless feeling, don't he, folks?"

The folks applauded.

"Where you off to now, Scott?" I asked him after the set.

"Europe."

"You don't need a tenor sidekick, do you?"

"Wish I could, but the money's not there, Vince."

"Talking 'bout money," I said, swallowing my pride. "I'm in a little jam. I'm stuck out here without the plane fare back to New York. If you could just loan me—"

"Sure," said the saxist, a prince among men. Least I wouldn't have to call Mom.

"I'm calling you, Mom, just to let you know I'm at the airport in L.A. I'm on my way back."

"When's the magazine coming out with your picture?"

"It's not."

"What happened, honey?"

I told her.

"Oh God," she said when I was through. "It's your father all over again."

I got mad. "What do you mean?"

"Pride. Gino's genes are filled with pride. Poor baby, you fell right out of his nut bag."

"Ma, you really want to see me running around some woman's magazine in my jock strap?"

"You're a good-looking boy, Vinnie, and good exposure never hurt anyone. Exposure is just what I've been trying to get for my wrestling league. Kathy will tell you. It's murder getting free publicity."

"You're making me feel bad."

"You shouldn't feel bad, *caro*. You live, you learn. I know you. You'll be back. Maybe it's all for the good. Maybe it means you'll start helping me and Kathy with the wrestling league. Have you ever thought about wrestling, Vinnie?"

"Are you kidding?"

"You'd be wonderful at it. Bodybuilders have a built-in advantage. Everyone says so. I've been talking to trainers. I've been learning the ropes. Just the other day Kathy was saying how—"

"Does Kathy ask about me?"

"All the time. She moved back to the city. She's got a place of her own, but we talk every day. You'll call her when you get back. She's got something to tell you."

"What is it?" I asked Kathy, a day after I was back in my Jane Street apartment.

"I'd like you to come with me to see Daphne."

"Your shrink?"

"Yes."

"Why do I need to see your shrink?"

"There's something I want to tell you."

"You're pregnant."

"No, I'm not pregnant, Vin."

"Then whatever it is, why can't you just tell me?"

"I'd feel more comfortable telling you in Daphne's office."

I missed Kathy, I wanted to see her, but I wasn't sure. "Let me think about it," I said.

"Ask your shrink what he thinks," she suggested.

* * *

"What do you think?" I asked Mueller who, wearing a dark pin-striped suit, looked like a rich banker today. This was the first time I'd seen him since I'd got back from L.A.—nearly two weeks ago. I'd been holding out. I didn't need him anymore. I would have stayed away except for Kathy.

"What do *you* think?" asked Klaus.

"Goddamnit, that's why I hate coming here. You don't got answers. All you got is questions."

"It's not improper, if that's what you want to know."

"How well do you know this Daphne Edwards?"

"She's a colleague, and an excellent therapist."

"You send each other business. You're in cahoots."

"From time to time we recommend one another, if that's what you mean, just as she recommended you to me, through Kathy."

"It's like everyone's in bed together."

"Is that a fantasy of yours?"

"You think I'm queer for you?"

"Are you?"

"There ain't a queer bone in my body. Look, Doc, I love Brenda—that's what I was trying to tell you before. I'm in love with this girl. I'm even thinking of moving in with her. When I got back from L.A., Brenda was the only one waiting with open arms and no questions. What's wrong with that? See, Brenda takes me the way I am. She ain't trying to change me."

"Does Kathy know about Brenda?"

"Why would she?"

"Then perhaps the session with Dr. Edwards might be a good place to tell her."

"What would the point be?"

"Easing your mind. Relieving your guilt."

"I don't have any guilt until you mention guilt. Now I feel worse than when I walked in here."

"Sometimes you need to feel worse before you feel better."

"I feel like Brenda's the right girl for me. She ain't no genius, but she's steady. If I told her I went to a shrink, she'd laugh. Maybe she didn't go to college like Kathy or Kawisha, but you should see her roller-skate. She's terrific. The way she whizzes her way around the rink is amazing. She's got great balance. I'm happy with Brenda 'cause Brenda appreciates me. She liked what I did in L.A. She says I got balls. Whatever I want to do is fine with Brenda. She doesn't even mind paying all the rent 'cause this roller-derby promotion company gave her a good advance."

"So you'll be living on her income."

"Did I say that!" I exploded, jumping off the couch. "I don't have to live off no woman! I can find work whenever I wanna!"

"Then you have nothing to hide from Kathy."

"But there's nothing I want to say to Kathy. What do I have to tell her?"

"One simple thing—whether you'll see her in Dr. Edwards's office or not."

DR. EDWARDS'S OFFICE

IT WAS getting to look a lot like Christmas. Only five shopping days left. New York was socked in with snow and ice and I'd been slipping around from one greasy gig to another. I'd been barely surviving—a wedding here, a bar mitzvah there, the kind of low-level jiveass jobs I'd promised myself I'd never do again. Not that I didn't have better choices. Tyrone, for instance, had stopped by to say the Righteous Rippers had a two-week gig in a funk club in L.A., and did I want to do it?

"I love you, T," I told him. How could anyone not love T, with his gold Hugo Boss sweatshirt pulled over his gut, his black paratrooper pants and his purple Puma high-tops. "But I can't see myself returning to the scene of the crime."

"What crime?" he wanted to know.

I told him about my *Playgirl* whirl.

He laughed. "So Tricks ain't walkin' no more. Is that it, V?"

"Suppose so."

"I still say come out and hang in Hollywood."

"Hollywood is Hollyweird to me."

"So what you gonna do, bro'?"

"Try to make a living playing jazz."

"The monk returns to his monastery."

"I could do worse than follow Thelonious Monk."

"Monk's kid played funk. There's all sorts of new monks now."

"Look, T, I figure I gotta play it straight. That's what I do best."

"You sure? You can burn up this dance shit pretty good. I've heard you myself."

"I'm just gonna stick around the city a while, T, and stay close to the nest."

That was in November, right around Thanksgiving. Reason I remember is 'cause Thanksgiving was the day I moved in with Brenda. Moved over to the edge of Chinatown where Brenda gave me her extra bedroom for my barbells, birds and saxes. It was crowded but cool 'cause she was easy to be with and downstairs it was like the Casbah with the junk stores and stereo shops and fruit stands and clothes racks on the sidewalk, Canal Street buzzing with busy buyers and sleazy sellers stealing and screaming day and night. It wasn't easy, but I managed to give up Jane Street and all the memories of me and Kathy. I even sold the bed we slept in. Who needed to hold on to the past? Let go, I told myself. Let Mom cook Thanksgiving dinner for Kathy and Gino, let them have their little family reunion in Seaford, Long Island. "The only reason your father accepted the invitation," said Regina, "is because he figured you'd be here. He's coming to see you, not me. Is that so terrible?"

"I didn't say it was terrible, Ma. I just said I wasn't coming. The whole thing's creepy to me."

"What's creepy?" Regina asked.

"The way Kathy has turned into your daughter," I told her.

"Why are you jealous?" asked Mom. "She's no daughter, she's a friend. And she's also a friend to Gino. You're too tough on Gino, Vinnie."

Since when was Mom talking nice about Pop? It was Kathy's influence. See, I knew Kathy was trying something I'd tried years before: she was trying to get Gina and Gino back together. It was a hopeless move. Maybe they'd get along for a couple of weeks, but then it'd fall apart. I didn't want no part of it. Besides, that wasn't my home anymore. My home was with Brenda. Brenda cooked me a turkey. Brenda made pumpkin pie. Brenda brewed fresh coffee. She never questioned where I went or what I did. And as far as the guy from roller derby who answered the phone when I called from L.A., she promised he meant nothing. Brenda was devoted to me. She even guessed that I'd been banging Kawisha, but she understood that was business. She wasn't mad. Brenda had the healthiest outlook on sex I'd ever seen—the more we screwed, the more agreeable she grew. She wasn't worried about my wandering ways. She knew what counted is who you come home to, and I was coming home to her. We liked being together. We even found a cheap gym over on Lower Broadway where we were workout partners. We pushed each other. "I won't go to Gino's anymore," said Bren. "Your old man gets you too upset. You need to concentrate on your music."

I did.

A week after Thanksgiving, while Brenda was out skating, Drew Williams took me to a new jazz club over on Avenue A in a mean neighborhood where the owner had turned a hellhole into a high-tech hangout. The owner was a greedy yuppie who said he'd love for me to play—for tips only. No salary, no nothing, just a jelly jar for loose change. Bullshit, I said. I might as well play in the subway. If he's making money on booze, why shouldn't I get a cut?

"I ain't about to be exploited," I told Drew who looked good in a tweedy Scotch plaid sportcoat and English racing cap. We'd gone back to his folks' roomy apartment at the end of Fifth Avenue off Waverly Place across from the Washington Square arch. His parents were off lecturing in England and he had the place to himself. Everywhere you looked you saw bookcases loaded with volumes about history and art and every thing you could imagine. The apartment wasn't fancy, but real comfortable, like a college bookstore. The Williamses were eggheads. If Drew was such a brain, though, why couldn't he show me how to make a living playing jazz?

"Paying dues has always been part of the great tradition," he reminded me as we sat in his father's study sipping French wine while a log fire roared in the fireplace and the Modern Jazz Quartet flowed out of the big Bang & Olufsen speakers. "The audience that appreciates truly fine jazz—or, for that matter, truly fine art of any kind—is necessarily limited."

"Why?"

"Good taste is not a mass-market commodity."

I wasn't sure. I knew I needed money, and I also knew some good saxists—like David Sanborn and Gerald Albright—who were making it big.

"Glad you mentioned Sanborn," said Drew, puffing on a briar pipe. "I discuss him in my new article on Kenny G. Or better yet, my attack on Kenny G."

I loved the idea. I wanted to hear more about it.

"Let me read it to you," Drew suggested. He left the room and was back in a flash with a neatly typed manuscript. When he read, his enunciation was like someone on educational TV—fuckin' perfect. He started out slowly:

"'Kenny G bears as much relation to serious jazz as Norman Rockwell to serious painting.'"

"Who's Norman Rockwell?"

"The illustrator who did those sentimental *Saturday Evening Post* covers, the one who drew so-called Americana—little boys in barber shops and little girls in pigtails."

"I like that stuff."

"Let me go on, Vince. 'The sad superficiality of genuine jazz talents turned pop stars—David Sanborn comes immediately to mind—is an indication of how commercialism can drain dry the juices of this country's most vital art form.'"

"Sanborn's still playing good," I protested. "Have you heard him with Al Jarreau?"

"I deal with Jarreau later in the article," said Drew. "He's another sell-out, someone who wants it both ways."

"What's wrong with that?"

"You can't serve two gods. Let me read you the rest."

He read, but I spaced. His shit sounded so preachy I couldn't concentrate. I got bored and also a little mixed up. I knew I loved real jazz, knew I could play it, knew I felt it deep inside my bones, knew it kept my head together. I still felt warm remembering jamming with Scott Hamilton in L.A. When I paid back the loot he loaned me, I told him he'd saved my life. Maybe it was jazz that saved my life. But I also knew that jazz was only one kind of music. Just like I loved more than one kind of woman—I still thought of Sue, I still thought of Kathy—why couldn't I love more than one kind of music?

"Have you talked to Kathy?" asked Drew when he was through with his sermon.

"Not for a while. Have you?"

"Yes, and if you'll pardon me for saying so, I think you should meet her at her psychotherapist's."

"So you know all about that."

"I know you've refused, and I think you're being foolish. Kathy's a wonderful woman with a sincere interest in your welfare, Vince. You owe it to yourself to hear her out."

"What does she want to talk about?"

"I don't know. But I can tell you that when we were together last week, all she talked about was you."

"You didn't mention Brenda, did you?"

"Dear Vince," said Drew, taking off his hornrims and cleaning them with a neatly ironed white handkerchief, "surely you know me to be more discreet than that."

It was funny. The same way Kathy was trying to get my parents together, Drew was looking to hook me up with Kathy.

"I'm crazy about Brenda," I told him.

"Brenda's beneath you. Kathy has class."

"Kathy's turned into a musclehead. What's classy about that?"

"Whatever Kathy does, she does with creative flair. She has humor, originality and style. There are few women like her."

"Sounds like you're in love with her."

"I am. If she were a man, I'd propose in a minute."

I had to laugh. Drew was a fruitcake, but he was a funny fruitcake 'cause he was so serious.

"Look," I said, "I don't need no lovelife advice. I need work."

"Work will come. For someone with your natural talent not to be toiling the jazz fields is nothing short of criminal."

"I've thought of robbing banks. Then I could play all the fuckin' jazz I wanted."

"You're too honorable for thievery or musical compromise, Vince. You're one of the most honorable men I know. You're the living example of the integrity of a new generation of jazz greats. Remember—to play jazz is in and of itself an honor. It's a formidable skill ninety-five percent of today's pop musicians lack. It's a precious art form. And you, my friend, are an artist."

When Drew talked like that—sitting in this antique leather chair surrounded by all these books and the leaping flames in the fireplace and Lester Young's sweet sax painting "Polka Dots and Moonbeams" on the CD player—he made me feel that all was right with the world, that maybe he was right to call me an artist, that I was blessed to be born with the heart and ear to hear and play the music he held up as damn near sacred. Like Kathy, Drew was a class act.

"Will you call her?" he asked me, walking me to the door at the end of the evening.

"I guess it can't hurt," I said, thinking of how it'd been months since I'd seen her last looking at me with my nose bleeding from the fight at the Village club.

"Keep the faith," urged Drew. "If I had half your God-given talent for playing pure jazz, I'd be the happiest man in New York."

A man of taste, no question.

New York gets beautiful at Christmas. Maybe it's because the snow covers some of the garbage or some of the assholes get goodwill. I don't know. But something happens to the city. Folks get nicer. They don't shove you as hard, they don't scream as loud. The stores are decorated and the carols are playing and even though I know it's commercial, I like to think everyone's getting ready for Jesus' birthday party and maybe that ain't a bad thing.

Anyway, I wasn't in a bad mood strolling up Lexington Avenue around 72nd Street. I'd just had a double cheeseburger at Nick the Greek's coffee shop and was feeling full. Kathy's shrink wasn't far from my shrink. The whole fancy-shmancy Upper East Side is overrun with shrinks—someone called it Couch Country —which proves that money doesn't give you mental health. Take me. My mental health was fine but my money was funny. That's why I hadn't seen my shrink in a while. I couldn't afford it. Moving in with Brenda Weinstein had saved my ass. "Am I the best piece of ass you've ever had?" Brenda liked to ask—Brenda liked talking dirty—and I liked telling her she turned me on, 'cause with her tattoos and her biker's-old-lady-lay-me-good attitude, she did. I was coming here to see Kathy purely out of curiosity. I was coming here because Drew was a good guy and Drew thought it was a good idea and Drew actually got me a halfway decent-paying gig playing jazz in New Brunswick, New Jersey, on weekends. So I owed Drew, I told myself.

Maybe I was a little nervous 'cause I was ten minutes early and no one was in the waiting room except a pile of *New Yorker* magazines. Drew said his dream in life was to write jazz criticism for the *New Yorker* 'cause the guy they got was jive; he'd been writing the same stuff for three hundred years and when he interviewed black guys he made them sound white. None of the jazz musicians in his articles ever cursed. I tried reading his column but didn't get too far.

I was feeling uneasy so I kept on my jean jacket and looked through the ads and when the inside door opened I looked up and there was the most beautiful black woman I'd ever seen in my life. She looked like a cross between Diahann Carroll and Vanessa Williams. She couldn't have been older than thirty. She wore a cool brown flannel business blazer and skirt and ivory satin blouse, but her eyes were on fire, her skin creamy rich, her legs strong and long, her hair parted and swept to one side, her smile dazzling, her teeth perfect white like cultured pearls. She had a slight southern accent that made her even sexier.

"You must be Vince," she said. "Looks like Kathy is a little late. I'm Daphne Edwards."

She reached out her hand for me to shake. Her grip was firm, her skin was warm. While we were touching, Kathy walked in the waiting room.

"Just in time," said Daphne. "Vince and I have just met."

Kathy looked taller, or broader, or stronger—I don't know which—but she looked good. She was wearing a long white coat that tied around her waist and when she took it off I could see her body had changed 'cause the tight black corduroy jeans showed her thighs were thicker and her ass was firmer and her waist was trimmer and her red hair was cut so bangs covered her forehead and she had a cute little ponytail in the back that reminded me of Gino's ponytail except Gino didn't have gorgeous green eyes and Gino didn't smell of jasmine perfume like Kathy. Kathy said, "Thanks for coming, Vinnie. I missed you."

My heart melted. I was too choked up to answer. I was already fighting back tears, and we hadn't even started. We went into Daphne's office, which was fixed up in lavender colors, with me and Kathy at opposite ends of a couch and Daphne sitting across from us in a chair and me noticing every time Daphne crossed her legs and her noticing when I took off my jacket so she could see my lumberjack flannel shirt was a little too snug 'cause I'd been pumping up my pecs pretty good.

"This won't be easy," Kathy said, looking at Daphne, not at me.

Daphne had a pen and pad for taking notes. Her pen was the same ruby red color as her fingernails. Behind her head, hanging on the wall, was her degree from Harvard Medical School. Next to the degree was this beautiful small sketch of Billie Holiday.

"We could talk about jazz," I said.

Daphne smiled, but only for a second. "I believe Kathy has her own agenda," she said.

Kathy was fidgeting on the couch. She still couldn't look at me. When she started talking, her words were still aimed at Daphne.

"I've gotten stronger," she began saying, "but in some ways being with Vince makes me feel weaker."

"If you could, Kathy," said Daphne, "I wish you'd address your remarks directly to Vince."

Kathy turned and looked at me, almost like she was pleading.

"Okay, I'll say it straight. You intimidate me, Vince, you make me feel like giving up all my plans and living only for you. You make me feel like loving you is the only important thing in the world, the only thing that'll ever make me happy."

"This is pretty heavy for openers," I said, my heart beating like crazy. "I walk in here and you hit me with this? I don't know what the hell to say."

"How do you feel about what Kathy is saying?" asked Daphne, sounding just like Mueller.

"I'm feeling like she wants to make up with me."

"I feel as though I've done nothing wrong," Kathy chimed in. "I have nothing to apologize for."

"I didn't say you did," I said.

"You make me feel that way, though."

"Is that my fault?" I asked her snazzy shrink.

"Kathy," said Daphne, "what is it about Vince that you find so intimidating?"

"The fact that my life could be so easily intertwined with his."

"But that's something you do, baby," I reminded her, "not me. I don't hang out with my parents like you do. I'm not in the middle of their life. You are."

"You sound angry about that, Vince," said Daphne.

"Here we go again," I snapped, "with shrinks telling me how angry I am."

"You *are* angry," Kathy said. "You've never gotten over your parents' divorce."

"What's that got to do with you and me?" I wanted to know.

"Everything," she told me. "Just the way your father made demands of your mother about what she could and could not be, you made those kinds of demands on me."

"I liked you as a schoolteacher," I admitted. "Is that so terrible?"

"It's terrible to hold a person back. Even your father sees that now."

"Leave Gino out of this. If you wanted to talk to Gino, you could have invited him here. I still don't know why the hell you invited me."

"To tell you something."

"Then goddamnit, tell me."

"I'm helping Gino remodel his gym."

"What?"

"With his help, I'm going to manage it. We're doubling the space. We're buying the place next door."

"Where're you getting the money?" I wanted to know.

"Wilbur's backing us. He's putting up the money."

"You mean my father's agreed to this shit?"

"He likes the idea. He likes Wilbur. Wilbur's sure it's a great investment."

"Why don't you get Wilbur to give money to Mom? I'm sure he's interested in her lame-brain women's wrestling scheme."

"He is. They're talking right now."

"Can you believe this shit?" I asked Daphne. "Can you sit there and tell me that my whole family hasn't gone bonkers?"

"What is it about Kathy's participation," asked Daphne, "that you find so threatening?"

111

"It's as obvious as the nose on your face. She's taken over. She's taken over my family. She's running it. And she's even got this meathead moneyman to bankroll the goddamn thing."

"I'm going to have fun with my life," said Kathy. "That's something you've not been able to do."

"What are you talking about? I have fun playing music."

"You're someone who's afraid of rejection, who's hiding out, who's doing everything to avoid putting yourself on the line because you're scared you won't make it."

"What gives you the right to talk that way? You don't know what the hell I've been doing."

"If I know you, you've been running from one woman to another."

"Well, you're wrong. I only got one woman."

"Today. What about tomorrow?"

"What about you? Tell me that you and this Wally—"

"Wilbur—"

"Whoever. Tell me that you and this goon haven't been bumping."

"I won't lie to you. I won't say we haven't—"

"See!" I screamed, "I knew it! I knew he was dying to get in your panties!"

"There's more to him than that. You should see how patient he is with Gino and Gina, how he treats them with respect..."

"Like I don't? Well, I don't, and I won't, 'cause far as I'm concerned you and them and him are all fuckin' nuts. You be the good daughter and he'll be the good son and the whole lot of you can go screw yourselves royally 'cause I've heard all the shit I'm gonna hear! I'm outta here," I said, picking myself up and heading for the door.

"You've never been able to deal with strong women," Kathy accused.

"You don't know what you're talking about," I accused back. "You and your shrinks got all these pet theories that ain't worth shit because in real life they don't hold up. In real life I got a girlfriend who skates at the roller derby and she's strong as all hell and she's got her own career and I ain't threatened and I don't tell her what to do and we're getting along just fine..."

"Is that why you moved out of Jane Street?" Kathy had to know. "Are you living with her?"

"What do you care?"

"You found another caretaker. Don't you see, Vince? That's the role women play for you. They cook and clean and care for you. They mother you. They keep you the way I kept you, the way you kept me in my place. Don't you understand that?"

"All I understand is that you got me over here so you could kick my ass and make me feel like shit."

"That's wrong. I wanted to tell you something." Now Kathy was also standing and looking me in the eye. "I wanted to say that I really love you, that I miss you, Vince, and that as far as I'm concerned a relationship is still possible, if only you could respect and acknowledge who I am."

"I acknowledge the fact that you're full of shit," I said, slamming the door behind me.

Outside the snow had turned to sleet and the sleet was cutting into my face. It hurt. This whole fucked-up business of shrinks and shrink talks and Kathy and Regina and Gino and Wilbur...it all hurt. But it didn't matter. I was drumming it out of my mind. I was forgetting it. I was making it go away. I wasn't going to any more shrinks—not mine, not Kathy's, not no one's. All the shrinks did was make it worse while making a million for themselves. I was going straight over to see Brenda. Never in my life did I feel more like seeing anyone. I wanted to be with Bren and tell her she was my baby and have her talk trash in my ear that made me feel

113

good, made me feel like I mattered 'cause I made her happy and she was always ready to love without a bunch of bullshit about relationships or feelings or any of the other crap.

It was 4:30 when I set out for Queens. Brenda would be through rehearsing at 5:00. I'd surprise her with a bunch of flowers and we'd head straight home and pump our way to paradise. I bought a copy of *Musician* to read on the subway and forget the past hour which was already fading out like last night's nightmare. I was standing in the F train, turning the pages of the magazine, when I happened to see a small item that stopped me cold. "Sexy New Sax Star Signed," read the headline. "Paolo P, called the Italian answer to Kenny G, recently inked a two-album deal with Epic Records, according to personal manager Sue Kawisha. The instrumentalist, Paolo Piacenza, of Buffalo, New York, has been featured with a number of national artists, including the touring bands of Engelbert Humperdinck and Neil Diamond."

I couldn't believe this! The bitch had copped my lick! The tiny photo of this guy—a curly-haired, big-nosed *paisan*—even looked like me. Who the hell ever heard of him before? Who the hell even knew if he could play? Talk about getting ripped! This cold-blooded Japanese chick had clipped me clean. She'd taken my idea and laid it on Paolo P. I wondered if she was laying him. She had to be.

By the time the train pulled into Jamaica I was madder than hell—mad at Kathy for taking over my family and fucking that pumped-up gym pimp, mad at Sue for stealing my sax-star idea. Everyone was using me. Kathy had used me to get a mother and father. My parents had used me to get the daughter they'd always wanted. Sue Kawisha had used me to get into the music business. But at least Brenda was honest. At least Brenda wasn't a user. Sure, she liked listening to the Sex Pistols, and sure, she could party a little too hearty, but Brenda wasn't using me. Brenda was giving, not taking.

In fact, Brenda was giving this guy a blowjob.

I know 'cause I seen it. I walked in on it. Now I know for a fact that Brenda enjoys giving good head, and I don't hold that against her, but when I went looking for her in the roller-derby rink and they said she was back in the men's locker room I started worrying. So I went back there expecting the worse and I seen the worse. I seen this bald-headed schmuck with a big schlong sitting on the bench while Brenda's going down on him, sucking on him like a lollipop. She don't even look up when I walk in. Him, he's smiling and groaning and wiggling his ass. He looks like he's forty or forty-five, and he's wearing his skating gear—his team is the Astoria Assassins with cross-bones and skulls all over the uniform—and I know he's the guy who answered the phone when I was in L.A. and I'm furious, I feel stupid, I feel like killing, I feel like I want to chew some glass and break some bones, and I go over there and pull her off him and she looks up and says, "Hey, Vinnie, meet Max Snider," like nothing's wrong. But there's plenty wrong, and when I call her a cheating lying two-timing bitch, he says, "Watch your tongue, asshole, you're talking to a lady," and he and I go at it but it don't last long 'cause he's got this bicycle chain which catches me on the jaw and knocks me cold where the pain puts out all the lights and I'm falling down this dark hole and I can't stop falling, deeper and deeper, darker and darker, colder and colder . . . I'm gone.

* * *

"The flight is half-empty. I can get you on." The woman's voice over the phone sounded so far away. Her Italian accent was so familiar.

"Who is this?" I had to know.

"Claudia."

"The stewardess?"

"Yes, Vincenzo, the stewardess."

I'd met Claudia a little over a year ago when she was working the coach cabin and I was touring with Royal Flush. The band was bonkers—smoking and coking in the bathroom—but I didn't do that shit, I didn't come on like a heavy-metal macho-monster, and maybe that's why Claudia liked me. She said I was a gentleman and naturally we had our common Italian heritage to help us break the ice. Then when it turned out we were all staying at the Hotel Forum across from the ancient ruins and down the street from the Coliseum, Claudia took me for a walk in the moonlight and explained about the seven hills and Romulus and Remus and later let me suck on her tits and rock her to sleep. She came to our concert, but that same night the band was off to Germany and a week later I sent her a postcard from Paris. We lost touch after that, though I never forgot her. During that miserable mind-bending ball-breaking rock tour, the groupies had left a bad taste in my mouth. They were silly and sad and, after one unhappy experience, I couldn't even look at them again without feeling for their lost souls. Claudia, though, was different. Claudia was real.

"I'm glad you remember me," Claudia was telling me on the phone. "Also remember Alitalia Flight 534. It leaves tomorrow night at 6:30 from Kennedy. Meet me at the gate just before departure. I'll come and seat you on the plane. We'll fly to Rome. We'll spend New Year's Eve together, flying over the ocean. Sounds nice, no?"

"How will I get back?"

"I don't know. You'll find a way. Or maybe you'll stay. Okay?"

What could I say? I didn't know whether I was awake or asleep? Was I dreaming? Was I imagining? What the hell was happening?

My jaw still ached, but the next night I dragged my ass over to Kennedy. I felt weird; I felt zonked; I felt like I wanted to get the hell away—far away. The only things I brought were a small suitcase and my tenor sax.

Waiting at the gate, I wasn't sure what would happen. I could have been sleepwalking for all I knew. All the passengers were already on the plane. The runway door was shut tight.

I was convinced this whole thing was bullshit, I was about to turn and walk away when the door opened and Claudia rushed out, all excited, wearing her tailored uniform and waving to me.

"Hurry," she said. "I can get you in first class."

WHEN IN ROME...

THE 747 took off with a tremendous roar. My head was roaring with thoughts and pictures from the past ten days. Ten days ago I woke up at the hospital and found Brenda by my side. I didn't want to see her, so I pretended to be asleep and waited until she left. The minute she was gone, I got out of bed, threw on my robe and caught a cab in the cold when I realized I had nowhere to go. See, I had no home, I'd given up my apartment and I sure as hell wasn't about to go back to Brenda on Canal Street. I hated Brenda. I also hated the fact I had no money. I couldn't go to Gino's Gym—Gino was the last guy in the world I wanted to see—so I had the cab take me to Regina's House of Beauty in Long Island City and Regina took me out to Seaford and put me to bed and made me minestrone. A few days later, while Brenda was out skating, I drove Mom's Cutlass down to Canal Street and picked up my birds, barbells and saxes. All this time, I never told anyone what happened—not Mom, not Gino who came out to see me twice, not Kathy who kept calling. Naturally they knew I'd been in a fight, they saw I was hurting, and they tried to cheer me up by telling me how Kathy and Gino were expanding the gym and how Gina was auditioning wrestlers. For the first time in years, Mom and Dad were actually talking to each other like civilized human beings, but I didn't care 'cause I didn't feel civilized. I felt sick. Sick and tired of feeling sick and tired. Here I was, nearly twenty-six years old, and back home with my mommy making me veal parmigiana like she did when I was ten. "You'll be fine," she said. "You've been a little upset. That's all."

During the days, she left me at home to watch "Sale of the Century" and "Wheel of Fortune" and I couldn't even listen to music 'cause music reminded me of what I wasn't doing. "You're just trying to recuperate," Mom assured me. "You've been a little nervous."

I don't exactly know what a nervous breakdown is, and I thought of calling Dr. Klaus Mueller and asking him, but I knew I'd never get an answer. Instead he'd just ask, "How do *you* feel about the way you're feeling?" So I didn't call. I didn't call Kathy 'cause I was still pissed at her for mugging me in front of her shrink; I didn't call Brenda who couldn't believe I moved out just 'cause I caught her getting friendly with a guy who wasn't anything more than a friend.

My real friends helped. Drew Williams called me almost every day, saying there was this resurgence of straight-ahead jazz action in the city—new clubs, record labels looking for groups, groups looking for saxists. Drew kept me connected; he kept the faith. He was teaching a course on bebop at the New School and he said, "As soon as your jaw heals, I want you to come to my lectures and demonstrate what I'm talking about."

Tyrone Newborn drove out to see me in Seaford, bringing along a batch of hot tapes. He was high on the nasty new jammin' producers—Jimmy Jam and Terry Lewis, the Calloway brothers, Teddy Riley, Mtume. We listened to Levert, Johnny Kemp, Keith

Sweat, "The Hardline According to Terence Trent D'Arby," Bobby Brown. "This is futuristic funk," said Tyrone. "It's shouting, 'Fuck art, let's dance!'"

Now this groove was dancing in my head as I sat on Alitalia Flight 534 listening on my Walkman to Prince singing "Strange Relationship." I looked out the window while the plane circled Manhattan Island with Central Park looking like a black postage stamp in the middle of a million orange lights, skyscrapers like Tinkertoys, the night clear and cold and me cuddled in first class with Claudia bringing me a hot toddy with a warm smile.

Claudia was young—twenty-two or twenty-three. She was pleasantly plump, with long, dark wavy hair. Her brown eyes sparkled. She had rosy cheeks and a personality like sunshine.

"How'd you ever find me?" I asked her.

"Remember you told me about 'Gino's Gym'? I called there and they said you're with Mama. They gave me Mama's number. Time to serve wine and cheese. I'll be right back."

Claudia was easy—the way she called me at Seaford was so easy and the way she got me on the plane was easy and the way I could fly out of New York and leave my nervousness behind. She brought me another toddy and then she brought me first-class food—veal and fettucine—and soon I was floating free, feeling fine, reeling in space, running out from my past but not giving a good goddamn 'cause I saw things getting better. Prince sang "Sign O' the Times" in my ear and I knew my time was coming. It didn't matter that his lyrics were about disasters 'cause his groove was moving, his groove was greasing and goosing this fat jumbo jet through the sky high over the ocean. I was moving a million miles away from Gino's Gym and Regina's House of Beauty, far from Canal Street and Bren's friendly blowjobs and Kathy's new apartment near Union Square where I never visited even though she'd asked me over just before Claudia called. There'd only been enough time to call Mom at work and tell her I was off for Europe and would she mind looking after my birds?

"What! Are you crazy?" she asked. "Have you lost your mind?"

"I got a free trip," I explained.

"How?"

"Playing the saxophone," I half-lied.

"When will you be back? You gotta be here for my first match at the end of the month. Then sometime in February Gino and Kathy are opening the new gym and..."

"I don't know when I'll be back."

"Have you called your father?"

"You call and tell him. You tell everyone..."

"I've told everyone," Claudia said, handing me a creamy choc-olate-sprinkled cappuccino, "that there's a famous musician on the plane."

"Who?"

"You. You're the famous musician."

"You only heard me play once."

"And I'll never forget it," she said smiling. "In the middle of horrible heavy metal, you sounded so pure. I could feel you didn't belong with them."

"I feel like I belong on this plane tonight," I told Claudia. "I feel like you've saved my life."

"Things were so bad in New York?"

"Things were very crazy."

"Too much heavy metal?"

"Too much everything."

"In Italy, we know real artists, we appreciate true musicians."

"I appreciate you, baby."

Looking around the cabin—there were only a half-dozen other first-class passengers—Claudia leaned over and whispered,

"Soon they'll all be asleep. Upstairs is the bar. It's empty. We can have our Happy New Year's upstairs."

It was quick but, oh God, it was happy. Somewhere around midnight, while the passengers snored and the jet jumped over the moon, I celebrated the start of 1988 with some fabulous finger-fucking. Claudia was funny. She worried about going all the way. Someone, she said, might come up the stairs in a hurry. So it was a little like high school, dry-humping and thumb-pumping, tongue-kissing and lots of licking. I liked it. I liked when Claudia said how much she liked my muscles. "You've gotten bigger," she told me. "You've gotten harder. No fat. It must be those weights you told me you like to lift." Suspended in space, I felt a big weight lifted from my heart. I held Claudia in my arms, kissing her earlobes and smelling her sweetness on the tips of my fingers. When she had to leave, she made the couch into a bed and covered me with a blanket. I slept like a baby.

When day broke and the dark sky turned pale blue, she was there with espresso and fresh pastry. She brought me hot towels. She served me eggs and ham and buttered toast. When the plane landed at Fiumicino Airport, she took me to a cab and together we rode into Rome. It was the same hotel where we'd stayed before. Our room overlooked the Forum. Claudia closed the shutters and closed her eyes and let me love her all the way down, calling me things in Italian that my mother used to say. *"Caro,"* she said, *"tesoro,"* she whispered, *"amore,"* she cried. We loved away our jet lag until I fell into another world, into a sleep deep enough to wipe out all worries. I dreamt I was a Roman emperor. Playing my saxophone, I led legions into battle. I was a conqueror who lived in a marble palace atop one of the seven hills that overlooked the Harlem River. When I awoke, I didn't know who I was or what century I was in. I pinched myself to see if I was still dreaming. Then I reached over to feel Claudia next to me. But she was gone, and the note said, "Sorry, must fly to Milan. That's where Peter and I live. Did I tell you I got married last year? Peter works for IBM in Milan. I'll call you when I return to New York, maybe in the spring."

I tried springing into action, but it didn't work. My body wouldn't move off the bed, my head wouldn't let me think. I fell back asleep. I dreamt of Gino's Gym, except it turned into a dungeon, with guys in chains and Gino screaming that no one knew the proper form for dumbbell curls. I dreamt I was in the bowels of a slave ship, rowing until my arms fell off. I was aching and sweating and then they stuck a sax in my mouth and made me play, except instead of a reed someone slipped in a razor blade, and when I bit down on the mouthpiece I cut my lips to ribbons and woke up screaming bloody murder.

Where was I? I looked out the window. Claudia was gone but the Roman ruins were there. I was ruined 'cause when the clerk called from downstairs, he said I'd need to pay for today's room in advance. Claudia had paid for only one night. That was big of her. In American money, it came to $260 a day, and that was pretty goddamn fuckin' crazy considering I had exactly four hundred bucks to my name.

"*Vado via,*" I told the cat. "I'm outta here."

And I was.

I hit the streets, my mind still furious and fuzzy from Claudia's note. What the hell was wrong with these women? What the hell was wrong with me that I attracted the kind of chick who liked to fuck me and then toss me out the window like last night's garbage? What was the world coming to? How the hell could someone sweet as Claudia be living a lie, lying to me and lying to her husband? And what was the point of her telling me—not face to face but in some nutty note lying on my pillow? Why couldn't she tell me, man to man, or woman to man? I hated her, and I had half a mind to try and call her old man in Milan just to say that his wife sat on my face last night and liked it, liked it so much she nearly suffocated me but I didn't care 'cause I liked giving pleasure and all I was getting was the shaft. Can you tell me why, Doc Klaus Mueller? Does it make any sense to you that a guy like me, a guy who the ladies seem to love, always winds up with egg on his face and rocks in his fuckin' bed? Maybe it's 'cause I got this build; maybe it's 'cause I just got a knack for picking nuts—Kathy the fitness freak, Brenda the skater, Sue the schemer, Claudia the flying lying waitress in the sky.

You're feeling sorry for yourself, I heard the shrink saying. Well, what else was new? I knew that. I didn't need no psycho-genius to tell me that. I didn't need no one. I had on my good wool over-coat. My suitcase was light. My sax was safely slipped into my gig bag. A clear winter sun was shining in the Piazza Venezia with fifty zillion Fiats running around a monument that looked like the big-gest white wedding cake in the world and me thinking—at least I didn't marry any of those wild women. At least I was still free— free to figure out this city 'cause I'd only been here once before, and only for a day, and you could spend a lifetime in Rome and not see all there is to see. What I saw today were gangs of gor-geous women, high-styled turned-out turned-on terrific-looking black-haired blonde-streaked stunning shapely sexy women. It was like New York, only the women were hipper. Walking down this bustling street called the Corso, past the fancy shops and banks and the churches with the paint peeling off, all the women looked like fashion models. The women looked like movie stars. Women were everywhere and everywhere I looked I saw faces I'd seen growing up in Little Italy—the shape of a nose, a certain walk, everyone talking with their hands. My grandparents, who never did learn English very well, taught me enough Italian to get by. I walked by an airlines office and decided I didn't want to use my money to buy a return ticket. Even if I had enough—which I didn't—I hadn't seen enough of Rome. I wasn't about to run home like a scared little boy. I was better than that. I was braver than that. Sure, Claudia screwed me, but she also did me a favor. She got me out of New York.

I liked Rome. I liked loading up on espresso at the coffee bar and listening to the guys bullshit. I could understand most of what they were saying. They were discussing pussy, looking at it and studying it as it slid by. They called pussy *fica.* That means fig. If you open up a fig and check out the insides, it does resemble the love canal. I could dig it. See, these guys were my roots. They were a lot like the guys I grew up with. Gino's parents were from Bari and Gina's folks came from a little town near Naples. I had a hundred percent southern Italian blood pumping through me. I could relate to Romans chit-chatting about chicks. I had a few stories of my own to tell, but now wasn't the time. Now was the time to eat. I wandered off the Corso into the back streets, my eyes eating up the antique buildings and the narrow stone alleyways and the motor scooters screeching like bats out of hell except this could be heaven the way the butchers had marble floors and their shops gleamed like art galleries. Everything—fruits, flowers, shoes, soaps, cheeses, cheesy magazines—was displayed like paintings. One guy had new toilet bowls lined up outside his shop like statues. Another guy was selling statues of armless goddesses and chubby cherubs pissing into pots. Water was everywhere, especially at the Trevi Fountain which sprang up in front of me like a dream. I threw in a couple of coins and wished for good luck and a better life in Rome. The fountain was crazy with Neptune in a chariot and water pouring out like music and marble sculpted like satin and the Japanese tourists snapping pictures and this one gal snapping my head back 'cause she had a figure sculpted like an hourglass and a tiny waist and huge jugs like Madonna. I waved to her but she wandered off which was fine since the last thing in the world I needed was another fatal attraction.

I was attracted to this trattoria down from the fountain. Sitting outside with the sun in my face and a forkful of tortellini in my mouth, who was I to complain? Sure, I'd been kidnapped and abandoned and left to rot, but what a way to go! The Frascati wine was so fruity and flavorful that nothing mattered except being in a city which, unlike New York, let you love life. I had my change of underwear and I had my sax and soon I was off to find a cheap pensione. I was surviving just fine.

On the Via del Tritone, right in the middle of town, this sign caught my eye: Pensione della Musica. That sounded right. The building looked like an old beat-up museum—a lot of Rome looks like an old beat-up museum—and the pensione was on the fourth floor, no elevator, take the stairs. To tell you the truth, I wasn't all that sure what a pensione was. I'd heard people talk about them, but all I knew is that they're cheaper than hotels. This place was nothing more than a big shotgun apartment with lots of bedrooms off a hallway, a sitting room at one end and big kitchen at the other.

"Musicista?" asked this fat man who had to be the owner. *"Musicista lei?"*

"How'd you know I'm a musician?" I asked him in my makeshift Italian.

"Many musicians are attracted here. We welcome musicians. Listen."

The sounds of a bombs-away opera were booming out of a cheap record player. Gino liked opera. I couldn't stand it.

"Do you sing?" asked the guy with a gut like a pregnant lady and a voice like thunder. He was way over six feet and wore a brown wavy wig that looked like Fabian in the fifties. He had to be sixty.

"I play," I said, pointing to my sax.

"Beautiful! I call myself Albertone. You must be American. We have a room that all the Americans love. There is a view."

The view overlooked a dilapidated church crusted with five hundred years' worth of filth. The bedroom was bare—one chair, one dresser, one naked bulb hanging from the ceiling and a mattress thin as a piece of soggy toast.

"Silenzioso e molto tranquillo," Albertone assured me.

We argued price and settled on a bargain—thirty dollars a day including lunch, the main meal. I figured I'd hang in here till I found work.

"Other musicians are here for you to meet," he told me. "You'll be happy, there can no be doubt."

I forked over the bread and tested out the bed. It was shit— the springs creaked and the pillow flattened out like a pancake— but what did I care? I was set up in the Eternal City, tired but happy as hell to be far from the folks back home. Mama Rome was my new home.

"Dear Mama," I wrote a week later. "I'm enclosing instructions about how to feed the birds. If you have any questions, ask Kathy. Meanwhile, things are cool. I like Rome. It feels homey. You see a lot of the faces you see in New York. It's my roots. Plus, they seem to like the way I play since I have good engagements and am getting paid good." (That was a lie, so Mama wouldn't worry.) "The owners of this pensione—Albertone and his wife Natalia— are beautiful people so you can write me care of them. I needed a change of scenery, and now that I have it, I feel better. I don't know when I'm coming back. So far, so good."

That was the truth. The room might have been gloomy— there was no heat at night and I was freezing my ass off—but

Natalia could cook and Albertone was the kind of guy who wouldn't let you get depressed. He loved Americans and said President Kennedy had really been Italian. He told the other guests at the pensione—mostly Germans—that I played sax for Frank Sinatra. Sure, Albertone was a bullshit blower, but he had spirit. He was a hustler, selling belts out of a suitcase and fake-leather suitcases out of the trunk of his beat-up Mini Cooper which he'd drive over to the Vatican where he'd set up shop in the shadow of St. Peter's. One day he took me along.

Albertone could bargain in all the main tourist languages— English, French, German and Spanish—and wasn't above short-changing customers. He also sold Pope trinkets and souvenir soccer balls. He was especially good with old women and young kids.

"Go see the church," he advised me, pointing to the basilica. "Get inspired."

I did. I'd never seen anything so big and beautiful. I'd never seen so much gold. All the art made me feel so small and God felt so big even though I knew it was the artists who'd made this big church, artists like Michelangelo who did this sculpture called *Pièta* with Mary holding Jesus who'd just died and looked so sweet that it broke my heart to think why anyone would torture and take out a guy who wasn't 'bout nothing but love. If that wasn't enough, I practically broke my neck in the Sistine Chapel where this same cat went nuts decorating a ceiling with scenes from the Bible that blew my mind 'cause of the fast-action feeling and the gutsy emotions in the eyes of the characters who looked real and ready to talk to me. The way, say, Charlie Parker drew pictures with his horn, Michelangelo made music with paint. I felt so inspired, felt like playing my sax, but instead I said a silent prayer for my mother, and I even mentioned my father and thought about Kathy and tried forgiving Brenda except I kept flashing on her sucking off that bum which isn't exactly what you should be thinking about in St. Peter's.

On the way back, at my request, Albertone dropped me off at a small gym in a nasty neighborhood called Trastevere which I dug 'cause of how it reminded me of home. This place was even funkier than Gino's. *Un sporco buco,* Albertone called it, a dirty hole. The weights looked like they came out of the Middle Ages and I couldn't wait to get pumping. It'd been weeks since I felt my blood blasting my muscles. The place was filled with a group of local muscleheads and I got a kick out of shutting them down. Pop would have been proud. I piled on the plates while everyone looked out of the side of their eyes. Soon they just came over to watch the show. Just like I needed the church to calm my soul, I needed a killer workout to get me going. After two hours of hoisting and heaving, soaked in sweat, I felt terrific, like I could take on the world. To get myself totally together, though, I knew I needed to play.

Back at the pensione, I grabbed my sax and went out into the early evening. The sun was setting a rich golden yellow. Albertone said this was the mildest winter he could remember. He also remembered a couple of jazz joints where I might find work. He gave me the names of the owners. When I stopped by, though, they weren't playing jazz but some soupy Italian pop shit. Besides, the owners hadn't heard of Albertone and didn't give a hoot about hearing me honk. I'd been feeling good all day, but now I couldn't help but start worrying about money again. After buying some clothes and paying for my room, I was down to $200. I needed work. Bad.

On the Via Veneto, near the American embassy, I saw a sign that said Steve Lacy, the dynamite soprano saxist, was playing at a club near the Spanish Steps. Maybe I could sit in. Turned out I couldn't even get in. The cover charge was crazy, so I stood on the pavement listening to Lacy loosen up on Monk melodies. He sounded great. During the break he came outside and I asked him about the employment scene. "Man, it's a nightmare here," he said. "You'll do better back in New York."

But I don't want to go back to New York, I thought to myself. I was too busy falling in love with Rome. I hiked all the way up the steep Via Sistina, past the ritzy Hassler–Villa Medici Hotel where, according to Albertone, sheiks and barons and billionaires stay. There I was, on top of the Spanish Steps, looking down on the city. The sky was filled with stars. Everything sparkled. Rooftops and church domes, looking older than time, were bathed in the silver light of a full moon. Looking over past St. Peter's, I could still feel the power behind all those paintings and sculptures. I was still pumped up from my workout. I was about to explode—I had to express myself, I couldn't hold back the beauty inside me—so I took out my sax and started to play. I'd never done anything like this before, but I didn't give a shit. I felt like I was playing to all of Rome. I played the most beautiful ballads I knew—"Bewitched, Bothered and Bewildered," "My Funny Valentine," "It Never Entered My Mind," "My Romance," "How Deep Is the Ocean," "When Your Lover Is Gone." My sound was happy, but it was also sad. I guess I was laughing and crying at the same time. My tone was so big that when I closed my eyes I saw the notes floating over the city on a cloud of melody. As I played, my heart sang the words. I was so deep into my sax I didn't even realize how long I'd been playing until this older woman gently touched my arm and I opened my eyes and saw she was dropping a bill into my gig bag. When I looked down, I saw there was a whole pile of bills. People thought I'd been playing for money—which wasn't even true—

but now the money made me play even more beautifully, 'cause I was being appreciated. I was playing for the city of Rome and the city of Rome was not only listening, but paying me back.

"You are quite remarkable," said the older woman who actually wasn't that old—fifty, maybe fifty-five. She had an English accent, a long black leather overcoat and wide-brimmed floppy felt hat which gave her a hip look. I saw a business card attached to the bill she gave me, but by the time I read it, she was already down the Spanish Steps and, like someone out of a dream, out of sight. *Vanessa Andover*, it said. *Fine Antiques.*

I counted the money—70,000 lire, about fifty bucks. I felt a little funny. I'd never played the streets before, and, honest to God, that wasn't my intention. I always looked on street players like streetwalkers. But I hadn't been turning tricks. I played 'cause I had to. I felt honest, like I'd really earned the dough.

I headed back to the pensione, looking to get a good night's sleep, when who should I see by the front door but Albertone.

"*Sei tornato un po' presto,*" he said. "Aren't you back a little early?"

I told him the story of my street success and he was all smiles. "Let me buy you a cup of coffee," he offered.

"To tell you the truth, Albertone," I told him, "I'm dead tired. I'm turning in."

"That's impossible," he said.

"Why?" I wanted to know.

"Because we need to get coffee."

"I don't want coffee. Coffee keeps me up."

"Then warm milk."

"I don't want warm milk. I wanna go to sleep."

"Don't go up now."

"Why?"

"I'll buy you a drink."

"Thanks but no thanks. I'm bushed."

I knew something was wrong 'cause when I went up the stairs Albertone followed and tried to stop me but I wanted to know what the hell was happening. When I got to my bedroom I saw what was happening—this little guy was fucking this big broad right there on my bed. They looked up at me and I looked over at Albertone who just shrugged. "Business," he whispered to me. "It's just business."

I was pissed. I knew Albertone was a hustler, but who the hell knew he was renting the rooms to hookers on an hourly basis. That was too much. The idea that I'd have to sleep on a bed where a couple of lowlifes had been screwing made me sick. There'd be cum stains and maybe even AIDS germs. I grabbed my suitcase and told Albertone I was getting the fuck out.

He followed me down the stairs, insisting he'd done nothing wrong. "We always change the sheets," he said.

"Yeah," I said. "But you lied to me. You said you ran a straight-ahead pensione, not some fuckin' whorehouse."

"With your knowledge of both Italian and English," he argued, "you could help me find a better clientele. We could go into business together."

"Are you crazy?"

"You have great charm, my friend, especially with the women. What would be wrong with working together? I've always dreamed of an American partner. Fifty-fifty. I give you my word."

He stuck out his hand, and you know what? I shook it. Not to close a deal, not to agree to pimp for him, but only to say good-bye. The goon was a greaseball, no doubt. I wasn't about to stay in his sleazebag pensione for another minute, but, with him standing here, smiling ear-to-ear and offering me a job, I couldn't stay mad. He was too goddamn likable. I had to give Albertone some skin.

"Ciao," he said, waving as I walked away.

I tried it again—an outdoor concert at the same spot atop the Spanish Steps—but this time it was drizzling and freezing cold. The mild winter had turned bitter. My teeth were chattering so bad I could hardly play, and besides, no one wanted to listen. The sky was dirty gray and the fog was rolling in. The magic was gone. My luck was turning. I played and played—played my guts out, played my blues—but didn't get one lousy lira.

I dried off while eating a wafer-thin cheeseburger at the McDonald's near the bottom of the Steps. I was feeling desperate. For the last few nights I'd blown big money on a decent hotel. I had to. The thought of seedy whores getting banged in my bed while I was out during the day made my skin crawl. The one bathroom at Albertone's had the kind of toilet which wasn't a toilet but a cement hole in the floor where you had to squat; it was downright disgusting. Fact is, only after I left Pensione Della Musica could I admit to myself how filthy the place had been. That's why I decided to splurge on a room with clean sheets and a private bath. For the past two days, I'd hardly done anything but take hot showers and buy good meals. Now it was nut-cutting time. I was down to twenty bucks and had to decide whether to wire home for dough. My pride said no. I could feel Gino and Gina and Kathy waiting for me to crawl back to them for help. But not me; I wasn't about to crawl to no one.

I had my little suitcase and I had my sax. Now I just had to find a super-cheap room and make sure it wasn't a whorehouse. But even if I could find a place for twenty bucks, how would I eat?

And what would I do tomorrow? Go begging? If the sun came out tomorrow, I'd go back to the Steps and sing for my supper. It worked once and it'd work again. Or would it?

Walking down the Via Margutta, ducking in and out of the rain, I was soaked to the skin. It was coming down in buckets. I was so chilled I was shaking. The cheeseburger wasn't digesting good. I wasn't feeling good. I was feverish and dizzy in the head. I was looking around for some low-rent pensione, but I realized I was in the wrong neighborhood. I had no business here in the high-rent artsy-fartsy antique district. I was so cold and shaking so bad I didn't know how much longer I could go on. I needed to find a bus—a heated bus—headed for funkytown. And just when I was about to turn around, just when I was about to drag my ass out of there, I looked straight ahead, blinked my eyes and saw that I was standing in front of this incredibly beautiful store, with warm lights and fabulous furniture, that said *Vanessa Andover, Antiquario*.

In the countryside outside of Rome, they have these incredible palaces called villas. They look like something you see in a storybook when you're a kid. By the first of February, I was living in a palace. I had my own wing. I had my own gym. I had my own servant. In the city, I had a twenty-four-track studio where I could record whenever I wanted. And I wasn't even fucking Vanessa Andover. I swear I wasn't.

IL DOLCE FAR NIENTE

"THE ITALIANS use the expression all the time," said Vanessa. We were dining in a small romantic restaurant that smelled like a rose garden. In the corner, a young woman ran her thin fingers over a harp while the veal piccata melted in my mouth.

"Il dolce far niente," Vanessa explained, "is the sweetness of doing nothing. It's the Roman ideal. Quite the opposite of your American work ethic. It takes a bit of getting used to. You haven't even touched your wine, Vince."

I was still too dazed to drink. It'd been four hours since I walked through the door of her store, only to have this clerk, this snotty Englishman, look at me like I was a piece of shit. Okay, maybe my clothes were dripping on the hardwood floor and maybe I didn't look like a guy fixing to fork over $30,000 for some fancy armchair from another century, and maybe I was so cold I was shaking, but I was an artist, and I knew the owner.

"I'm here to see Vanessa."

"Oh really?" said the snob. "You know Signora Andover?"

"She gave me her card."

"And your name, sir?"

"Vince. Vince Viola. Tell her I'm the musician, the sax player."

"Indeed. If you'll pardon me, I'll be back shortly."

He didn't offer me a towel or nothing, so I stood just there dripping, looking around at this place where everything—dressers, desks, chandeliers, tables, loveseats, mirrors and paintings—looked like something out of a museum. There weren't any price tags, so I figured everything cost a fortune. Classical music, which suited the furniture fine, was playing softly in the background while I wondered—what was I gonna tell this lady? At the same time, I also wondered—why had she given me her card?

"Of course I know Mr. Viola!" she said, coming out of the back room. She was slender and elegant-looking. She walked briskly, with perfect posture. She carried herself like a queen. She didn't have great beauty, but her eyes were sparkling blue. Her hair was cut short and stylish, black with gray highlights, like a woman who hires fashion models, like a lady in charge. She had on this high-neck gray dress with soft shoulders and a beautiful green suede belt, plus a pin that looked like a miniature African mask and loads of silver bracelets. Her smile was strong and sincere and she didn't hesitate to offer me her hand—and a towel.

"Gregory," she told the snob. "Bring Mr. Viola something to dry himself with. It's frightfully wet out there, isn't it?"

"I was just walking by."

"I'm so glad you stopped in. Might I offer you a spot of tea?"

Vanessa lived upstairs. Later I learned that she owned the whole building; in fact, her late husband owned a good chunk of southern Italy. He'd been a baron back in England whose father, an ambassador to the Vatican in the old days, had bought a bunch of Roman real estate for peanuts in the twenties.

Upstairs was even more spectacular than the store. There were marble floors and a gurgling fountain in the middle of the living room and a balcony the size of a basketball court that looked out on the rooftops and church domes of the city. The rain had stopped and the sky was breaking up—patches of blues were breaking through—while Vanessa had me follow her to the library, a room, she said, that had been her husband's favorite.

"The baron was a great enthusiast of American jazz," she said, "and something of a scholar. I found his love for the music quite infectious. Now that he's gone—it seems impossible, but it's been nearly a year—I've felt obligated to keep his collection in order."

The collection was incredible. The library was mammoth, with nothing but floor-to-ceiling dark wood shelves of records —78s, 45s, and thousands of albums and tapes. Like a real library, every shelf was numbered and labeled—"Kansas City Big Bands," "Early Louis Armstrong," "Billie Holiday on Decca," "Ben Webster, Small Combos, 1949–1952." And it wasn't just the old shit. The old man had been hip to Coltrane and Archie Shepp and had every album the Argentinean tenor terrorist Gato Barbieri ever made. His stereo equipment looked powerful enough for Radio City Music Hall. On the ceiling were paintings of angels playing harps and shepherds playing flutes. On the walls and in fancy frames sitting on the grand piano were photos of Baron Andover, a short handsome guy with a big barrel chest and a bushy mustache, standing next to Lionel Hampton, Erroll Garner, Oscar Peterson, Roy Eldridge, Art Farmer and Art Blakey.

"Many of these artists," said Vanessa proudly, "have played in this very room."

The collection had to be at least twenty times bigger than anything I'd seen over at Drew Williams' parents' apartment on Fifth Avenue.

"Is there something you'd like to hear, Vince?" she asked. "My husband had a particular fondness for the tenor saxophone."

"I love this guy Ike Quebec," I said. "His records are sort of hard to find."

Vanessa headed straight for the Ike Quebec bin where she produced a half-dozen albums in mint condition. "I adore the way he plays 'Blue and Sentimental,'" she said.

"Put it on," I urged.

Just as she did, a butler came in with tea and cookies.

"Would you care for a spot of brandy in your tea?" she asked.

"Sure," I said as Ike's huge sound soared out of the speakers. I looked out the window and saw a golden red rainbow arching over the half-black half-blue sky. I knew I was the middle of a miracle.

"I was struck by your presentation the other night," Vanessa told me. "Your style seemed so mature for one so young. You've obviously been nurtured on the masters. That's exceedingly rare among musicians of your generation, don't you find?"

"I have this friend named Drew, Mrs. Andover, and . . ."

"Please call me Vanessa."

"Okay, Vanessa. You'd love Drew. He taught me about the old masters. He played me all the records."

"If I might ask, how did you find your way to Rome?"

"It's a long story."

"Well, perhaps we should save the story for later. For the present, I've a guest room which I'm pleased to put at your disposal. There's also a closet full of clothes, some of which you may find suitable. I've meetings this afternoon, Vince, but I'd be delighted to have you join me for dinner tonight. By then you will have found time to unwind and freshen up. I'm anxious to hear more about you. I only wish the Baron were here to enjoy your company and extraordinary musicianship. You will play for me again sometime soon, won't you?"

"Sure," I said, still stunned. This Vanessa was something. She was about the nicest goddamn person I'd ever met. She knew I was on my ass, she knew I needed bread, but she handled it so smooth and cool that I didn't feel bad about accepting help. Fact is, when the butler showed me to this guest room fit for a king, I felt like the fuckin' luckiest motherfucker on earth. It had a canopy bed and a fireplace and the clothes, which must have belonged to the Baron, fit fine. Judging by his photos, he and I were about the same size.

With the fire lit, the flames crackling and Ike Quebec's honeysuckle tenor tearing through the bedroom speakers, I settled back in the sheets and had myself the classiest nap ever known to man. *Thank you, Jesus,* I said as I drifted off to a heavenly rest, *thanks for getting me into this joint.*

That night at dinner, I was still tripping, still pinching myself to make sure things were real. Meanwhile, things were only getting trippier.

"Tell me about your parents," Vanessa urged.

What was I going to say? Was I gonna tell her that Pop ran a rundown gym, and Mom owned a beauty shop and managed female wrestlers?

"They're working people," was all I admitted.

"What sort of work do they do?"

What the fuck, I figured, why not tell her the truth? I did and—guess what?—she loved it.

"I find that fascinating," she said, soaking up my stories like a sponge. I couldn't believe how easy it was talking to this lady. She wasn't judging me, wasn't feeling sorry or looking down at me. She liked me the way I was.

"The Baron used to say that beneath the jazzman's rhythmic drive was a sweetness unparalleled among all modern artists. 'Vanessa dear,' he would gently remind me, 'these are truly our lyrical poets.' It pained him to see your colleagues so woefully unappreciated in their own country. You see, the Baron was great friends with the expatriates Chet Baker and Dexter Gordon. Undoubtedly, these are difficult, complex men, but the Baron had a uniquely effective way of dealing with them. He treated them as luminaries. He extended them the respect they so deeply and deservedly sought."

I loved listening to this lady 'cause she talked like a book. Her English accent was smooth as silk; she was a goddamn class act. She kept talking about the Baron, but it was obvious as the little nose on her face that she herself knew tons of shit about jazz. How else had she picked me up? Listening to her talk, I could feel she was a lot more energetic than the average fifty- or fifty-five-year-old dame. Once you got past her perfect English manners and super-elegance, you could see this twinkle in her eye. That worried me. I couldn't help but wonder—after being shafted by Kathy, Brenda, Sue and Claudia the flying waitress—whether I was being set up for another fuckin' fall. Okay, she knew I blew tough tenor, but what did this dame really want with me? The more she talked, the more she sounded like a college counselor.

"Tell me about your plans here in Europe, Vince."

"I don't have any," I said, giving it to her straight. I told her how I got here and why I left New York. "The music scene sucked. Especially for jazz."

"And it's important for you not to compromise, isn't it?"

"I ain't good at faking."

"The mark of a true artist. But financially it would seem as though you're somewhat strapped."

"I'm flat-out broke."

"You speak as you play, Vince," she said through a warm smile, "from the heart. So let me be as candid with you as you've been with me. The Baron was a unique and wonderful man. For example, he allowed me to indulge my passion for antiques. He sensed it was important that I manage my own business, not simply for monetary gain, but also for my sense of self-worth. Ours was a childless marriage, and consequently, beyond our socializing and charitable work, I had a great deal of time on my hands. The Baron realized it was important that I realize accomplishments in my own right, and in my own way. In addition to my store in Rome, I have retail establishments and buying offices in Florence and London. Now this past year has been a difficult one for me, not only because I lost my husband—his sudden heart attack was a dreadful shock—but because, ironically enough, my business has nearly doubled in volume. Perhaps to escape my grief, or perhaps because I've little else to occupy my time—who can say?—I've worked far too intensely these past months. I've promised myself that I'd escape the city for at least two weeks. In fact, I'm leaving tomorrow. We've a place at Lago di Bracciano, a little town and a lovely lake forty kilometers from Rome. I find the solitude irresistible. If I might say so, I think you'll find it equally enchanting. Hearing what you've been through, Vince, I've a sneaking suspicion that you're in as much need for restful meditation as I. 'I have learned to look on nature,' wrote the poet Wordsworth, 'not as in the hour of thoughtless youth; but hearing oftentimes the still, sad music of humanity.' We both might be well advised to listen to that music. Wouldn't you concur, Vince?" she asked, softly touching my hand.

I said, "Sure."

I wasn't that sure. Sure, her place turned out to be a castle-palace on top of a huge hill looking down on this mirror-clear lake like something straight out of a picture postcard. And sure there were antiques up the ass and enough bedrooms for a small army and a staff of servants that didn't have shit to do except worry whether I wanted extra chocolate shavings on my morning cappuccino. My bedroom had a balcony that looked over the little village beneath us and I felt like a prince. Vanessa made me feel that way. Vanessa also made me feel funny. It wasn't that she came on to me—she didn't. At night, after we listened to music or I played some solo sax for her, she went to her part of the palace and she didn't show up in my room in the middle of the night looking for satisfaction like I half-expected. I knew she was real lonely. She said she had loads of friends but they were old geezers who bored her. She said she liked young people and I know she liked young men 'cause half the servants were well-built guys maybe younger than me and I wondered whether they were serving her in more ways than one. I wondered about lots of stuff. But what else are you going to do stuck out in the country? I wrote to Drew, telling him all about the Baron and his wife and their world-class jazz collection. I also wrote to Mom but I couldn't explain everything 'cause it'd sound fishy so I just said I was staying with a friend. I even thought of writing Dr. Klaus Mueller. I knew Signor Shrinkhead would get a big bang out of hearing about my Roman adventures, but I also knew he'd misunderstand everything and accuse me of being a motherfucker. But Vanessa wasn't nearly as old as my mom. She was five, maybe ten years younger. Besides, she acted young, like when we walked through the woods.

It spooked her to see that I knew about the birds. When I spotted this red-faced lovebird, for instance, and called it by its proper name, *Agapornis pullaria*, Vanessa couldn't believe her ears. Then I bent her ear about how I'd fallen in love with finches and canaries and had them flying all over my room when I was a kid, how the birds led to Bird and how nature music led to jazz. I told her how much I missed Happy and Lady Day and all my other little pals who'd kept me company and kept my heart filled with song. It was chilly as we walked down this path with the birds singing and Vanessa taking my arm and making me wonder how long it'd be before she'd make a move. If she did, I couldn't help but wonder—what would I do?

She ain't nothing like Mom, I heard myself telling Mueller. She's an Englishwoman and she's an aristocrat and mainly she's a jazz lover and yeah, maybe I am attracted to her 'cause who wouldn't be attracted to class? She ain't crude—I never heard her curse, not once—and what difference does it make if she's a few years older than me? I could see where someone like her would be a wild woman in bed, go apeshit and lose all her cool, especially since she's been without it for so long and her body is real trim and her personality is so sweet that the thought isn't repulsive, it's just different, and maybe it's even perfectly natural if that's what nature has in mind. At the same time, I ain't about to hit on her since she's my hostess and I'd never do nothing in the world to offend her, Doc, 'cause she figures me for a gentleman and, dammit to hell, I'm a goddamn gentleman if there ever was one.

"You often use your saxophone to seduce," I remember Mueller telling me when I told him about meeting Kathy, or Brenda, or Sue. Come to think of it, that's also how I met Claudia.

"Wouldn't Vanessa Andover," I could hear him saying, "fit quite neatly into your well-established pattern?"

No, I'd tell him. *Vanessa is this refined lady. She's different than the rest, she's by far the best.*

"You're talking about her as though she's already your lover. Is that your intention."

No, that's you making up shit again! That's you trying to read my mind!

I tried to read some books. There were thousands of books around the castle, but everything was in Latin or Italian or old-fashioned English. There was nothing I could sink my teeth into. The jazz books were back in the city.

"If you'd like to go back to the city," Vanessa said, "you've only to let me know and I'll have Pietro drive you."

"I'm cool," I answered after being in Bracciano for a couple of weeks. I wasn't cool, but what else could I say?

See, I still had no money. You couldn't exactly call me a captive, but at the same time where could I go without cash? I couldn't see myself asking Vanessa for money. That'd be too much like asking Mommy for my allowance. Besides, how could I complain? The meals were delicious and Vanessa had all these video tapes of jazz concerts all over Europe. It was a kick to see Ella Fitzgerald and Stan Getz performing at Albert Hall in London or the Montreux Jazz Festival.

"We'll go to Montreux in the spring," said Vanessa. "You'll adore the festival."

Fine, I thought, but what the fuck was I going to do for the next two or three months—watch the weather change?

"I think you should practice," Vanessa suggested, sounding a lot like a mother. "I think you should prepare for your first solo album."

"You're kidding."

"I've never been more serious. The Baron had an arrangement with a recording studio in Rome. He himself underwrote several record dates for musicians he deemed worthy. A good number of those endeavors proved quite fruitful. The tapes were eventually bought and distributed by major labels in the States, Europe and Japan. I strongly suspect he would have enthusiastically sponsored your efforts, Vince. It's something I certainly wish to pursue, if you're willing."

"Willing and able! I've always wanted to do my own album."

"Of course we'd have to be in agreement on the format. But I daresay we see the project in much the same light. I can't imagine you'd want to record anything but a mainstream album. I hear you playing the sort of time-proven ballads and standards which first attracted me to you."

"So you'd be the producer?"

"We'd select the songs together. It'd be great fun, don't you think?"

"I think I got something to say on tenor. I've thought that for a long time."

"Now you'll have a platform. I also hear you as the only solo instrument on the date. Naturally, we'd have to employ a rhythm section, and there, too, I have several people in mind whom I feel certain would complement you splendidly."

I was happy to be hearing all this—who wouldn't be thrilled at finally getting a record date?—but Vanessa's voice was so bossy it bothered me. Still, I played it cool. I wasn't about to blow the chance.

That weekend, as we spent hours together listening to songs, I noticed her nudging closer to me. She'd touch my knee, pat my back or squeeze my hand when I said I liked the same songs as her.

She even presented me with this tight white sweater she claimed would look great on me.

"You might try it on," she urged. This was Sunday night in front of the fireplace in the sitting room that looked like Robin Hood had lived there with the stone walls and the tapestries of knights on horseback and maidens with flowers in their hair.

"You want me to try it on now?" I asked, wondering whether I should take off my shirt in front of her, which I guessed was what she wanted. Maybe I was making it up, but I could feel her eyes all over me as I stripped down to my waist and pulled over the sweater. It was awfully snug.

"It looks terribly sexy," she said, which was the first time she'd used that word.

For the next hour or so, we kept listening to love songs and she kept telling me which ones she wanted me to play—"Lush Life," "Sophisticated Lady," "I Fall in Love Too Easily," "A Night-ingale Sang in Berkeley Square"—"to satisfy my English soul," she said—"You Leave Me Breathless," "No Moon at All."

I couldn't figure her out at all. I had a feeling she was going to grab my cock tonight, but no. After all the excitement of picking tunes, she simply excused herself and said she was going to sleep. I stayed and sipped a little more brandy, still waiting for the call to her bedroom when I noticed Pietro, her young driver and the best-built guy around—not counting me, of course—heading towards her wing of the palace. He was carrying a tray with a split of champagne. I decided to stay and see whether he showed up again. He didn't. He must be in there serving his mistress, I figured. But why him, when she could have me? And why had she been dropping by the work-out room when I was lifting? I knew she liked to look. I knew what she wanted. But maybe I was wrong. Maybe I was making too much of all this. Maybe she was just a rich middle-aged lady who just loved jazz and didn't care nothing about sex. Or maybe she cared a lot. Maybe she set up the whole thing with Pietro just to make me jealous.

I tried to make myself sleep that night, but it wasn't easy. I guess I was jealous, tossing and turning and thinking about how Pietro was probably pumping Vanessa. I was also excited about the album. Next week we were going back to Rome. Vanessa wanted me to see the recording studio, and she also wanted me to start rehearsing with the rhythm section she had selected. Whatever Vanessa wanted, Vanessa got. I dreamed she was a pit boss at a Vegas casino, giving out chips and serving up whores to the big-time gamblers. She had me playing in the showroom, only it wasn't jazz, it was circus music, and Drew was there in the front row yelling that I shouldn't be playing that shit, and my mother was on stage with her wrestlers, and Vanessa was saying, in her quiet strong-willed way, that my people would have to leave. She kicked out Mom and she kicked out Drew and said she was naming the hotel after me. It was Vinnie Viola's Palace from now on, except I'd have to play naked and I'd have to pretend that I was a lion and she was a lion tamer and she put me in this cage and she had this whip and...

I woke up when I heard a knock on the door.

"*Posta,*" said Pietro. "There is an express letter for you."

Almost like I was still dreaming, I tore open the envelope—it was from Drew—and could hardly believe what I read.

Dear Vince,

I'm answering your letter immediately and sending my reply via Federal Express. It isn't that I fear for your physical safety, although your mental health may well be at stake.

Yes, I have heard of Baron Bernard Andover. He was,

147

I'm afraid to say, a notorious figure. Yes, he was a legitimate jazz connoisseur and yes, he reportedly helped a good number of worthwhile artists. He was thought to be a friend of the music, but he was also an infamous pederast. This is not mere rumor, Vince, but something I know from personal experience. I happened to meet him during my junior year abroad. I was studying at Oxford when he came up for a lecture given by a well-known professor of American music. Apparently, the two of them had been lovers for years. They both also shared an appetite for young boys, something I saw first-hand at the private post-lecture party. The Baron made a play for me, but was not at all my type. My roommate, though, found him fascinating and later reported the particulars. I write this not out of maliciousness, but to tell you that my friend also informed me that the Baron's wife, Vanessa Andover, was present at the party, as both observer and participant. Apparently she and the Baron did this sort of thing quite often. And apparently she was the ringmaster. Over the years I've heard dozens of such stories. You should know that, for all her erudite charm, Vanessa Andover is reputed to be among the kinkier aristocrats on the continent. Her taste in antiques and furnishings is world-renowned, but so is her taste for orchestrating large and complex orgies. There are also stories linking her to Louise Chermont, the famous French opera diva. In that instance, I heard, it was the Baron who liked to watch. Others have said their taste involves instruments of light torture.

The exact configuration of their sexual arrangements is not the point. I couldn't care less. It's only that I know you, Vince, and I hate to see you being used. I see you as one of the straighter heterosexual men in recent history, so I must warn you that even though the Baroness has incredible wealth and a genuine appreciation of the music we love most, she undoubtedly has a hidden agenda. The word is that she's subtle, skillful and masterfully manipulative at arranging her pleasures. I'm sure she already has you sized up—quite literally—and is scheming your seduction even as I write. I just hope this letter reaches you in time, Vince; I hope I'm not too late. I care about you, my friend, I honor your tremendous talent, but in areas such as sexual deviation among the privileged rich, you're an innocent. It's not your crowd. So please be careful and, by all means, tell me what happens.

Your faithful friend,
Drew.

When I put down the letter, my hands were practically shaking. I was thinking about the cage and whips in last night's dream. It was almost like I'd seen the whole thing coming. I'd known something was up—I'd been feeling Vanessa's sex rays all along—but who the fuck knew that the bitch was a certified freak? Now I was pissed—pissed at her and pissed at myself. I'd been had again. Vanessa had made a fool of me. Now the last thing in the world I wanted was to jump in bed with her and her degenerates. That scene made me sick. I had half a mind to smash out all the windows in her palace and punch out Pietro and the other pretty boys busy licking their lady's asshole. I wanted out, and I was ready to leave right then and there.

But then I thought: I hadn't been fooled. I hadn't been had. I hadn't even been seduced. Drew had warned me in time. Sure, I could see how the Baroness was putting together her program, how she was pulling me into her web. I was right about the way she'd been using Pietro to make me jealous. She knew how to punch my buttons. But you know what? I could live with it; I could deal with her; I could handle her horseshit long as she gave me what I wanted: a record. Soon as I finished recording, I'd have me an album—and a hell of a good one at that. Once that master tape was in my hands, I'd be long gone. In the meantime, why not string the old bitch along? Let her think I was an easy target. Let her believe I was ripe for the plucking. If she was convinced I was gonna get in the pigpen and play with her, fine. But two could play this mind-fucking game, and I was fuckin' ready.

"I heard you received an urgent letter this morning," said Vanessa as we lunched on the glassed-in terrace overlooking the lake. The day was gray, but the lake was always gorgeous. Flocks of swallows and sparrows flew around it, dipping and diving in and out of the clouds.

"My mother," I lied, "said my old man ain't feeling well."

"Is it serious?"

"Naw. Mom's a worrier. The old man's strong as a bull. Sounds like the flu."

"I'm relieved. I wouldn't want anything to disturb our recording plans. Pietro tells me," said Vanessa, wearing an elegant black wool pants suit that showed off her slim figure, "that you've inspired him in the workout room downstairs. He claims he can now lift far greater weights than you. Isn't that true, Pietro?"

Pietro arrived with the coffee pot. Not knowing a word of English, the poor guy could only smile and pour. When Vanessa reached over and squeezed his biceps, he looked both embarrassed and pleased.

"Powerful men please me," she told me as she took a small bite of melon wrapped in paper-thin prosciutto. "Will it please you to return to Rome, Vince?"

"I can't wait to get started," I said, silently thanking God for Drew's letter. Without it, I'd be sunk; I'd be so strung out on jealousy I wouldn't know what to do. Now I did.

"Pietro," she said, switching to Italian. "Prepare the car. The three of us will ride back to Rome together."

"Dear Bro," said Tyrone Newborn's letter, waiting for me back in the city.

> Glad to hear you're chilling, but I'm willing to bet that you're still missing the music . . . least the kind of shit I've poured into this care package . . . check out the tapes . . . rap's ripping through NYC like a cyclone . . . Dig Public Enemy, Stetsasonic and Ice T . . . I know you've still got a jones for the golden oldies, so I'm sending something my mama said you'd like . . . it's King Curtis, the tough Texas tenor player who died too young. This tape was made practically before I was born, but I know you'll flip for the way the cat plays with so much greasy heart you'll start dreaming of ribs and black-eyed peas and cornbread with the butter dripping all down the sides . . . King plays so fine and funky you can smell his sax all the way over there in Spaghettiville. It ain't no straight-ass jazz, it's gut-bucket backdoor barnyard chicken-clucking down-and-dirty soul music, my brother, which is something you ain't ever going to forget, long as I'm here to remind you of the righteous religion, the one that preaches and reaches all the people, not just the snots and snobs. Italy's cool, but the street's the sure-enough school. We tore it up in L.A.

151

and now we're back home cutting up the Apple...looks good for a record deal...we're waiting to hear...but we could still use a heavy honky supersaxist sizzling on the front burner. Interested?

P.S. My mama says your mama got these female wrestlers running through the place. Says it's like working in the zoo. They got hairdos like porcupines and giraffes.

Wondering why I hadn't heard from Mom, thinking of how much I missed that positive pounding New York-sounding street music, I went to the Baron's library to put on the tape. Tyrone was right. King Curtis blew off the top of my head. Listening to that fatback tenor sound was like biting into a thick rare rib-eye. All prime meat. Man, I thought, wouldn't it be great to include some filthy blues on my album? Maybe cover "Soul Serenade," the Aretha classic that sounded so beautiful on King's Texas tenor.

"Does this sort of trash amuse you?" asked Vanessa who happened to walk into the room.

"It ain't trash. It's King Curtis."

"It's utterly lacking in sophistication. Surely you can hear that. It's just the sort of pseudo-jazz that the Baron detested."

"It ain't pseudo nothing. It's real as rain. This cat Curtis was super-bad."

"Are we being superficial today or merely silly?"

"I'm thinking of putting a song like this on the album."

"Never!"

She'd never raised her voice to me before.

"Wait a minute," I said, thinking strategy, "don't bust a gut. You can pick the tunes. You're still calling the shots."

A little smile broke out on her face.

"We'll meet the rhythm section tonight," she said, pleased to be in control. "Pietro will drive us."

Already the bitch was driving me nuts, so I figured I better go for a walk. I needed to get my head together and keep my cool. Needed to stay in control. Playing Vanessa's game, control was the key.

It was good being back in the city. I dug the wildlife in the country, and especially the free-flying birds, but being trapped out there with the Baroness made me nervous. Rome's a riot of traffic jams and motorbikes with a different kind of wildlife. Watching the working women wander around the train station made me think of Albertone, so I decided to pass by the pensione to see if I had any mail. I did. Albertone was out but his wife Natalia handed me a letter from Mom. I walked back up the Via Sistina, thinking of how playing my sax atop the Spanish Steps had landed me in the lap of luxury. Was that good or bad? I wanted my album so bad it had to be good. I'd make it good. It also felt good to be in the Villa Borghese sitting on a bench above the Piazza del Popolo, always poppin' with pedestrians, and reading the news from home.

Regina wrote:

> The news is good. The news is marvelous. My first wrestling card was a big hit. We held it out in Queens in the Corona Arena, and there was this big crowd and the girls were fantastic. I got six different girls now, and they're characters, they really are, real pros, Vinnie, starting with Marvelous Medusa who gets in the ring with snakes and Barbie who dresses up like the doll but fights like a tiger when she fights Tiger Lady and a new one named Sasha with tattoos all over her body. You've never seen so many tattoos.

I put down the letter and wondered—could Sasha be Brenda? No, impossible. Why would she leave roller derby to work for Regina? I went back to the letter.

We were on cable TV, and the ratings were good enough so they've asked me to work up another card for another date out in Jersey. If you can believe this, I personally cleared $5,000 for the night which is a tidy little profit. The beauty salon is still busy as a beehive so all I have is good news. Now your father and Kathy have news of their own, but he says he'll write you himself although I don't know if he will since he isn't much of a writer. I have to say that he's being very nice to me these days. Your father's a changed man. Anyway, I promised him I wouldn't ruin his good news so maybe you'll hear from him but don't hold your breath.

Now I'm a little worried about you because I called that number but the nice man said you'd moved out. Where to? Let me know right away with a postcard or a letter as I continue to worry about your health and wonder when you're coming home. Are you playing your saxophone? Are you getting enough to eat? I'm your mother and I have a right to know what's what with you. Write, *caro mio*, and keep me from worrying.

Mom

On the way back to Vanessa's I stopped at a newsstand to pick out a postcard. I wanted to mail it right away so Mom wouldn't have to worry. I'd written her from the country but the mail must take forever from out there. I was just about to buy this card of the Piazza Navonna, with all the gorgeous fountains sprouting water, when a new issue of *Time* magazine caught my eye. There was a bodybuilder on the cover and the headline said,

"FITNESS FANATICS—AMERICA PUMPS UP." I bought the magazine and, stopping at an espresso bar on the Corso, opened to the article.

My heart stopped. There, among many photos, was a picture of Gino with his arm around Wilbur Guest. They were both beaming. Gino's silver hair had gotten even longer and flowed down his back like a lion's mane. The caption read, "Merging past, present and future." There were also pictures of old-timers like Jack LaLanne and Joe Weider and movie stars doing ads for places like the Holiday Health Spas. I hurried through the article till I came to Pop's name.

New Age entrepreneurs like Wilbur Guest are aggressively marketing workout facilities in new and unique ways. Guest runs the most successful, highest-tech health club in Manhattan, frequented by Yuppies favoring spacy muscle machines with computerized voices. In four years, Guest has quadrupled his facilities and membership. He's also formed a partnership with elder statesman/strongman Gino Viola, Mr. Olympia of 1948, whose legendary Little Italy gym has been called the last outpost of stone-age bodybuilding. 'Gino's a genius," claims Guest. "He has a lifetime of knowledge about muscle growth, and, as such, has tremendous appeal to our clientele. They know he's for real. Unlike some, Gino's never overexploited his name. We're tripling the size of his original landmark gym, but keeping the historical ambiance intact. We're also preparing a major book by and about the master. It's about time Gino got his due." This Odd Couple—Guest and Viola—are predicting that the refurbished Mulberry Street gym, due to open next week with 24—hour service, will show a healthy profit its first quarter.

155

I threw the magazine in the trash and asked the bartender for a shot of scotch. I ain't much of a drinker, but I needed something to keep me from chewing glass. Or kicking over some cars. Or throwing a scooter through a store window. How was I supposed to deal with this shit? How was I supposed to feel about this fucked-up ass-suck son-of-a-bitch Wilbur Guest who first steals my girl and then steals my old man and gets his own grimy grinning picture for the whole world to see that he's so filthy rich and he's so fuckin' smart except they didn't write about how he inherited all his money and they didn't say nothing about how he don't know shit about bodybuilding and how he don't even work his legs and what the hell was wrong with Gino that he'd be taken in by this asshole? Gino was getting old—that was it—and Gino wanted money. Who could blame him? The old man had been a has-been until Wilbur came along. Through Kathy, Wilbur got the bright idea of re-treading Pops and turning him into a profit center. Would it work? Sure it'd work 'cause Gino was perfect for TV talk shows. Gino was enough of a character where he could jawbone with Johnny Carson and give the audience a few chuckles. He might even start working out again. Remember, Gino Viola was the best poser in the history of the Mr. Olympia competition. He liked people looking at his body.

Vanessa was looking at my body, but I wasn't sure I liked the way she was looking.

I was getting dressed to leave for the recording studio, about to pull on my pants, when she barged into my bedroom and there I was in my bikini briefs and her eyes ran up my legs and stopped at my crotch and she said, "I've brought you a present, Vince. I was at Gianni Versace earlier today and I couldn't resist this outfit. Please put it on, dearest. I'm terribly curious to see whether I chose the right size."

With her watching, I put on these shiny black parachute-fabric pants so tight my nuts nearly cracked and a black sleeveless T-shirt so small my pecs practically ripped the cotton.

"Perfect," said Vanessa just as Pietro walked in the room wearing the exact same outfit as me. She looked back and forth between the two of us—comparing cocks, I'm sure. Poor Pietro. He was this good-looking country kid, basically a decent guy who Vanessa had turned into her sex slave. The freakery was about to begin, I figured, but I wasn't about to bolt, not when the recording session was only a few days away. I was still determined to play it cool. I wanted that master tape.

I also wanted a little more.

"You know," I told the Baroness on the way to the session as we headed out to Parioli, a rich residential section of Rome, "if I'm about to record a new album I ain't sure that horn of mine is exactly ideal."

"There's absolutely no reason why you shouldn't have the highest quality equipment available. Early tomorrow, Vince, I'll direct you to the finest musical instrument store in Rome— they've been in business since the Renaissance—where you'll select whatever you wish."

"Thank you, Vanessa," I said, pleased my plan was working.

Her plan started unfolding when we got to the studio.

The rhythm section was already there, and they shocked the hell out of me: They were dressed exactly like me and Pietro— tight black bottoms, sleeveless black tops. What the fuck was this —the team uniform?

"I thought it'd be amusing to arrange a bit of sartorial har-

157

mony," explained Vanessa. "Don't you find it charming? We'll all be spending a great deal of time together, and it's important that we feel close to one another."

So this was the setup, this was the group, these were the puppets Baroness wanted to play with. I had to hand it to the old lady; she came up with a hell of a cast.

The pianist was a beefy blind Brazilian named Carlos. He talked like a girl and if he wasn't a fag my mama's a man. He had dark glasses and long slicked-back brown hair and huge hands which he ran all over me when we were introduced. That pissed me off. I stayed pissed till I heard him play. He was lyrical like Bill Evans and light-fingered like John Lewis and had great taste, plus he swung his ass off. I just wanted him to leave *my* ass alone.

The bass player was a tall Swedish blond named Inga whose hair was cut short like Peter Pan's. She walked and talked like a guy, with this deep-throated voice and shoulders out to here. The way she looked at Vanessa I would've bet they were bumping. Thumping the bass, though, Inga took care of plenty business. No doubt, Vanessa had taste in music and manly chicks.

It was the drummer, though, who destroyed me. She was India-ink black, only she didn't come from India, she came from London and she was about my age. Later she told me that her father was from Nigeria and her mother from Miami. She had rhythm written all over her. She spoke in an accent a lot like Vanessa's, all proper and finished and whisper-quiet. She was gorgeous and exotic enough to be on the cover of *Vogue,* with a flashing white smile and high cheekbones and her hair pulled back and piled in a tube on top of her head, large lips and broad mouth moist with light pink lipstick, small ears, big hoop earrings, work-of-art killer booty and oversized smart almond eyes taking in the scene like a camera. Where the hell had Vanessa found her?

"We met at Freddy Fitzgerald's party only last year," the Baroness told me. "Jasmine was playing percussion with a reggae band. She was quite marvelous. I wondered if she could play jazz as well as Caribbean rhythms. She assured me she could, and indeed she can."

Unlike Carlos and Inga, Jasmine didn't give out queer vibes, but under the circumstances, who knew who was doing who? For the time being, it didn't matter 'cause when we got to rehearsing in the ultra-modern studio the group clicked like a clock. Carlos was a sensitive accompanist. Inga laid down a ballsy bass line and Jasmine—her full name was Jasmine Otunju—handled her sticks like she was born in Birdland.

We rehearsed for about an hour, going over chord changes and tempos, with Vanessa saying, "A bit slower, please," or "A bit more lively, if you will." I could put up with her 'cause it felt so fuckin' good to be blowing my horn, releasing all the shit that'd been building up inside me. If anything, my sound had gotten bigger and I could tell Jasmine was into me by her cool little accents and the way she brushed against me, real subtle but strong. We were in serious sync.

Afterward, I went up to her and said, "You knock me out, you really do."

"Your style reminds me of the records my mother used to play me," she said softly. "I like romantic saxophonists who play the way singers sing. You're essentially a vocalist, aren't you?"

"Never thought about it that way. But this drum thing—how'd you ever get so deep into it?"

That's when Jasmine started telling me about her African daddy and Miami mama who ran a record store in London. "I was raised in a household of rhythm," she explained. "My parents are somewhat frustrated musicians. Looking at them, I suppose, I decided to avoid frustration at all cost."

I was frustrated as hell 'cause just as the vibes were heating up between me and Jasmine, just as I asked her out for a quick cappuccino, just as she was about to say yes, Vanessa stepped in talkin' 'bout, "Sorry, but there'll be no duets. Until the album is finalized, we'll relate to one another, musically and socially, as a quartet, or better yet, including Pietro and myself, a *sex*tet."

The way she said *sex*tet gave me the chills. The way Carlos was pawing Pietro and Inga was eyeing the old bitch made me think the moment of freakery was almost here. But the Baroness wasn't quite ready.

"'April is the cruelest month,' wrote the poet," said Vanessa. "To assuage that cruelty, I've scheduled the recording session for the first three nights of the month. After the third and final session, which, happily enough, falls on a Saturday, we'll award ourselves with a most private and original party. That will surely give us all something to look forward to." With that, she had Pietro peel off some bills to pay everyone, except me, for the rehearsal.

Carlos went off with Inga, but Jasmine hung back. Damn, she was pretty! I wanted to ask her how she'd wound up in Rome and why she was stringing along with Vanessa. But there wasn't time. Vanessa whisked me out of there so fast I couldn't even get the girl's phone number. I did get her smile, though. I thought her smile was saying, "Look, I'm not into freakery, I'm a musician, and I'm here for the sounds and the bread." I thought her smile was saying, "Save me."

"I'd like you to look over this contract," Vanessa said to me when we got back to her place on Via Margutta.

"It's in Italian," I said.

"You are Italian, aren't you?" she asked, letting out this sneaky little laugh.

"I can speak it some, but I don't read it real well."

"This document merely gives me the right to sell the master tape and, naturally, grants generous artist royalties to you."

"Great," I said, signing it and not giving a shit 'cause I knew what I was gonna do—contract or no contract. Balking would only tip off the old lady. I wanted her to keep thinking I was putty in her hands.

It was amazing remembering how just a few weeks ago I thought she was so nice; now she seemed like nothing but a conniving cunt.

"Tomorrow," added the Baroness, "you'll buy yourself a new instrument. Remember, my dear, only the finest."

I remembered, all right.

I picked out the most expensive sax in the shop—a Selmer Super Action 80. The thing lists for about $3,200 in the States, and I couldn't believe this guy was getting over $4,000. That's what you get for shopping in snooty stores. So much the better. See, I didn't really need a new horn. My old Selmer Mark VI was the best balanced-action sax you'd ever want. Truth is, the older horns sounded better; they were more resonant, they had more balls. But I had this plan.

I hung around the instrument shop nearly all afternoon. That way I was able to meet a couple of other saxists. I got their names and told them I might have something to sell them soon. Soon as the recording date was over, I was gonna ditch this new Selmer to the highest bidder, pocket the change, grab the master tape and bid the bitch fond farewell.

Concentration was the key. Didn't wanna think about Regina's wrestlers or Gino's new gym. Didn't wanna worry about

Wilbur with Kathy. The four of them—Mom, Pop, goony Guest
and his girlfriend—they were one big happy fuckin' family. The
last thing I needed was to see that group in action. Forget 'em—
that was my policy. Remember the job at hand—recording a dynamite album.

I was going good except for one distraction—Jasmine's booty.
And Jasmine's quick smile. And the way Jasmine dropped bombs
on her tom-tom behind me when I blasted through a barnburner
like Bird's bebopping "Big Foot," one of the two up-tempo tunes
Vanessa let me play. "Everything else," she insisted, "must be the
essence of romantic passion."

My passion was rising for Jasmine each time we rehearsed.
And each time I made a move, Vanessa was there to stop me,
reminding me there'd be time for "socializing" at the post-session
party coming up Saturday night. This was what the Baroness had
been waiting for; this was what she'd been saving me for. By now I
could read her mind. She figured I'd be so grateful for my record
I'd go along. Her hints were getting heavier. "I've been most patient," she said one night just before retiring. "But I sense you're
worth it, Vince. Everyone in the group responds to the enormous
animal excitement that you generate."

Okay, Doc Mueller, I'm an animal. Okay, I'm a hunk. Okay,
I'm using my brawn or my body or my sax or my sex or however
the hell you wanna interpret it as a way to win. You call it prosti-
tution; I call it survival. It's different than with Sue Kawisha and
the nude modeling 'cause here I'm playing jazz and I'm playing my
ass off. Here I'm making a real record.

After the first two sessions, I knew I had a classic. It'd taken a
little time to get used to the new Selmer, but I managed. I played
all the ballads with such feeling real tears were streaming down my
cheeks. My reading of "Lush Life" wasn't mushy but muscular and
lean. I leaned on "Sophisticated Lady" and made the woman come

to life. Blowing her portrait out of thin air, feeling Jasmine's gentle brushstrokes behind me, painting the lady in pastels, I was in heaven. I wasn't kidding when I played "I Fall in Love Too Easily." After two takes, even stern schoolmarm Vanessa was blown away. "Marvelous," she kept saying. "You're playing marvelously."

"Too Marvelous for Words" was the first up-tempo tune on the last set. It was Saturday night and the gang was going strong. This was the session—the final session—we'd been waiting for. This was Vanessa's shining hour, and she was dressed for the occasion, sporting this gold gown and bejeweled crown that made her look like a queen. She was also carrying a rhinestone-studded cane. (Or maybe they were real rocks. Who knew?) The old lady's little games were finally about to end, or start, depending on your point of view.

I was viewing Jasmine out of the corner of my eye and liked what I saw. The Baroness had insisted we wear our black-on-black outfits for the last time and this time I didn't mind 'cause of how those parachute pants clung to Jasmine. I was inspired. I was tonguing my tenor, tearing it up like a bear. I was growling, dancing over the changes so swift I didn't even know where my nifty licks were coming from. During the playback, I couldn't believe it was me.

"Non ci credo," I told Franco the engineer who'd become my pal. "I don't believe how good my shit sounds."

Final song was Bird's "Big Foot" and, man, I stomped all over it. The way Jasmine was burning back there, I had a feeling she'd gone to bed with her Mama's old be-bop records. Carlos and Inga were cool, but Jasmine was really ticking, timekeeping like no one's business. Even when Vanessa had me redo the thing four times—"I'm quite the perfectionist," she liked to say—I said, "slick," and kicked it harder each time around.

163

When I played the last note of the last take, I felt like a runner busting the tape at the finish line. I stuck my fist in the air and yelled "Yeah!"

"Keep that on the tape, Franco," I told my man.

It was ten o'clock and we were through. There was no big mix-down mess 'cause we'd played together, with no overdubbing, just like the old days, just like Vanessa wanted.

"The limo is waiting," she said. "Pietro is taking us all out to the country."

Before we left, when Vanessa wasn't looking, I whispered something to Franco. Then we were off.

The freakery started in the limo. The Rolls Royce stretch model barely squeezed through the narrow streets of Rome. Once we were outside the city limits, the Baroness brought out the blow.

"I know how you young people enjoy intoxicants," she said, passing around a vial of some of the strongest shit I'd ever sniffed. One small snort was enough. I didn't want no more, and I saw that Jasmine didn't take any at all. I was glad. Inga and Carlos were loading up and, much to my surprise, so was the old lady.

"Jasmine," said Vanessa, "I'm afraid you aren't entering into the spirit of the party."

"I'm fine," she assured her host, though I knew damn well she wasn't.

By the time we got to Bracciano, we'd also toasted a couple of jumbo joints which I'd only pretended to inhale. I wanted to keep my head clear. But the contact high was enough to make me paranoid. Except it wasn't paranoia; it was real. Once we got into the palace, Vanessa was really leading us down to the basement and really making us take these Ecstasy pills, a love drug I'd never done before. "Now," she said, "I am ready to lead our sextet in our most extraordinary performance yet."

She led us to the workout room which, since we'd been back in Rome, had been expanded. It was dark except for a couple of red lights which illuminated the hack slides and bench presses and preacher stands and cables. She had gone all out to create a real gym. Spooky-sounding church music was playing over loudspeakers.

"It's time to change, children," the Baroness announced, passing out our new costumes.

It was weird getting undressed right in front of each other. It was doubly weird to see everyone in black leather. I slipped into this black leather jock strap which looked like something she ordered from an ad in *Hustler* magazine. Pietro and Carlos were naked except for black leather vests with silver studs and Inga and Jasmine were wearing black leather garter belts with their bushes showing and I couldn't help but look real hard and heavy—Inga was so blonde and Jasmine was so black—and the Baroness was out of her gown and into big black leather boots and nothing else. To be honest, the old lady looked great for her age—I figured she was taking sheep-gland shots—except she was wielding this long nasty whip which was what the whole thing was about.

When I saw the whip, I wanted out. I wanted to kill Vanessa 'cause Jasmine was crying and saying this wasn't her scene, that she was afraid. "The drugs haven't had time to soothe you, my dear," said the Baroness. "I promise—new pleasures await you, pleasures you've never thought possible."

Soon she explained the setup: I was supposed to go around the gym, performing one exercise after another, dressed in nothing but this bare-ass jockstrap. "If I do not approve of your performance," announced the queen, snapping her whip, "I'll be forced to inflict a measure of punishment."

By now everyone was so high they didn't care what the bitch said. Carlos and Pietro were already all over Inga. They wouldn't give a shit if the Baroness blasted me with a submachine gun. Vanessa was starting to stroke Jasmine's thighs and I could see Jasmine was getting sick and I knew I'd seen enough. I'd be god-damned if this weird witch was gonna whip my ass while I pumped iron. I'd be goddamned if I was gonna stand for this sick shit another fuckin' minute.

Without even thinking, I grabbed the whip from the bitch and used it to tie up her hands so quick she didn't know what hit her.

"Best knot the Boy Scouts ever taught me," I said, kissing the Baroness on the forehead and whispering, "That's all you're get-ting from me tonight, sugar."

"Release me!" she screamed. "Release me *now!* Pietro, *Aiuto!* Help!"

"*Sta scherzando.*" I told Pietro she was just kidding, that it was all part of the game. Besides, Pietro was too deep into Inga to care. The coke and the smoke and the love pills had broken down the barriers.

"We're breaking out of here," I told Jasmine, taking her by my hand. We picked up our clothes and hurried out of the gym.

"You fool!" Vanessa's voice screamed after us as we changed and ran up the stairs. "You'll never get away with this! I'll burn your record! I'll destroy you!"

"Have fun," I yelled back, grabbing some blankets from the closet. We were out of that perverted palace in no time.

"Where are we going?" asked Jasmine.

"Away, baby," I answered. "Far away."

A coyote howled and Jasmine held me tight. We'd found a safe place in the woods to sleep, a little cove guarded by tall trees and bordered by bushes. It was a cool April night. The moon was silver-thin and there wasn't much light. The clean smells, though, were all over us and so were the songs of the birds. When I sang along and told Jasmine about my bird friends back home, she told me how she once had a lovebird who died. "I would have died back there," she said, "if we had done those hideous things."

"Forget the freaks." I tried to calm her. "That's all behind us now."

As much as Jasmine's behind still drove me crazy, I knew now wasn't the time to hit on her. We'd been through an ordeal. Now was the time to chill. Chilling, though, wasn't entirely possible since the Ecstasy love pills had kicked in and put a heavy dose of feely-touchy trippiness over our heads.

"I've taken it before," said Jasmine, "and it was wonderful. It's the only drug I've ever liked."

"I like it when you play brushes, and I like it when you play sticks," I said, thinking of her drumming. "You have this feeling."

"I'm feeling fine now, Vince. But what are we going to do? Where are we going to go?"

"We're going back to sleep, baby. That coyote ain't gonna get us and neither will the witch in the castle. Tomorrow we'll hitch back to the city. I told the engineer to expect some trouble, but also to expect an extra five hundred bucks from me for the master. I know Vannesa will clamp down on him, but he promises he'll give her a copy and she'll never know I've got the original. Once we get the tape and I sell my extra sax, we're gone. I already got my things waiting for me in a locker in the train station—did that this morning—so we're ready to roll. Where're you living in Rome?"

"In the back room of someone's flat. I've been somewhat

down and out. I've been wanting to go back to London. That's why I agreed to go along with Mrs. Andover. She promised me a plane ticket."

"Well, she delivered on her promise, Jasie. 'Cause I'm your ticket."

TICKET TO RIDE

I WAS riding high.

I'd cleared nearly three thousand banana skins for the Selmer Super Action 80, and a week after we ran out on the Baroness, me and Jasmine were on a bus to Fiumicino Airport, my new tape and old sax safely under my arm. We were off to merry ole England.

Jasmine made me feel like a hero. She kept telling me how much she appreciated me getting her out of Vanessa's grip, and maybe that's why she let me love her. I say let me 'cause it wasn't all that incredible. Maybe she was still recovering from the kinky night at the witch's castle or maybe I just didn't turn her on that much. Maybe I rushed her. See, I was fired up. Just looking at her all naked in this tiny little bedroom by the backwaters of the Tiber River made me crazy. And when we started holding and hugging and feeling and fondling, I was sure the screwing was gonna be spectacular. It wasn't. It turned out Jasmine was a little withdrawn. I was confused. Man, as a drummer she really gave it up, and I figured as a lover she'd do the same. I figured she'd be wild like Brenda Weinstein. No such luck. She was nice, she tried, but her heart wasn't in it. She never came. She loved more out of obligation than passion. Afterwards, I didn't wanna criticize her or nothing 'cause I didn't wanna hurt her feelings.

"It'll be better," she said.

"It's fine right now," I half-lied.

"I'm not quite accustomed to you," she added.

"If you'd rather go to London alone, I'll just give you the money for the ticket and..."

"No, no. You'll love the music over there, Vince, and the music will love you."

Despite the lackluster loving, I still dug hearing this foxy black chick talk with an English accent. She had all sorts of beady earrings hanging down and this beautiful high forehead. Her skin glowed, and so did her clothes. On the plane, for instance, she was wearing fluorescent pink tennis shoes, kelly green leggings and a snow white sweatshirt with "FREE SOUTH AFRICA" in big black letters.

In the coach cabin, we got some nasty stares from square businessmen and old ladies. Back in New York, I'd dated some Latin ladies before, but no one as dark as Jasmine, so I wasn't used to being looked at like a criminal. My first reaction was to shoot the shaft and say, "None of your fuckin' business," but naturally I didn't say nothing so as not to embarrass Jasmine. A few minutes later, the jet roared down the runway, taking off and tearing through a sheet of April showers. Much as I dug Mama Roma, I was happy to be bidding the old bitch good-bye.

What am I going to do in England? I wondered as the pilot turned off the No Smoking sign. I had no plans, but I did have this gorgeous guide. "Many musician friends of mine," Jasmine promised, "will appreciate you. Work will come quickly. You will see."

I had no eyes to go home. I didn't even want to know about

Gino and Guest and the rest of the gang. Thinking about them just made me mad. Besides, I liked London. The one time I'd been there, with Royal Flush, I was in and out in two days and didn't have time to see the sights. Now I'd have a real chance to catch the flavor of the place.

The flavor was spicy; the place was teeming with Africans and Jamaicans and all sorts of island people with dreadlocks down to their waist and the smell of strong sticky pot floating on air with the bluesy merry-go-round rhythm of Steel Pulse, Burning Spear, Jimmy Cliff, Ziggy Marley and Toots and the Maytals singin' 'bout "Funky Kingston" out of loudspeakers from the record stores.

"My folks' store is just around the corner," said Jasmine as we walked down Portobello Road in that part of northwest London called Notting Hill Gate. It was a market place with trinket stands and bead shops and cats playing steel drums and selling Bob Marley and Peter Tosh T-shirts out of plastic suitcases. I was buzzed. The aroma of sizzling rice and stews brewing on burners, steam rising from the street with the beat of black sunshine springtime in London ringing in my ear . . . man, I was still flying.

The Regal Record Shop featured all this African and Caribbean music, plus a healthy hunk of American funk. It was a small place and behind the counter was a big guy with burning eyes and bushy beard and not-too-happy expression on his face when he saw me walking in with his daughter.

I had a feeling it was my color he didn't like 'cause I hadn't opened my mouth. He and Jasie hugged—she'd been gone for three months—and when she introduced me, she said, "Vince is an extraordinary saxophonist from New York City. He helped me quite a bit in Italy, and I thought I'd introduce him to some of the musicians here."

171

The old man just nodded, but in his nod I read, "If I don't ever see this honky again, that's soon enough for me."

"Your mother's in the back," said Daddy Otunju.

Mrs. Otunju was American. She was a thin woman with good taste, like her daughter, in jewelry and hairstyle. She reminded me of a hip singer from the fifties that Drew had turned me on to—Eartha Kitt. Sitting at a table writing what looked like poems, she gave a salty, tough impression. When she saw Jasmine walk in, she beamed. When she saw me, she seemed confused. I think she was scared that I was about to be introduced as Jasie's boyfriend or, even worse, her husband. Jasmine quickly nixed the notion by making it clear I was just a musician acquaintance. The way Jasie was backing off me felt funny. After all, we had been to bed.

"You'll love these friends of mine," she said after we left the store. "They live in a commune and I know they'll have room for you."

"Does that mean we ain't staying together?" I wanted to know.

"We'll see each other, of course. It's just that I'll be staying at home."

So that's how it is. I save your ass in Rome and you dump my ass in London.

"Please don't think I don't want to be with you, Vince," she assured me. "I do. And I will. It's just that..."

"Don't sweat it, baby. I'm cool."

I was and I wasn't. I dug being in England, but I was starting to feel like this Notting Hill neighborhood might be a little hostile. At first, I thought I was among soul brothers, but now I wasn't sure. Maybe all that reefer in the air was getting me edgy.

I edged into this big flat on Lancaster Place that smelled like a pot farm. The cats were red-eyed and happy as hell to see Jasie, but I didn't get no big smiles. They had a reggae band and sure, they'd see if a sax could fit in, but no, they didn't have any extra room like Jasmine said they would.

"I have other friends who will be pleased to put you up," she promised me.

"Don't sweat it," I said. "Vinnie can take care of himself. Why don't you give me your number and I'll call you in a couple of days when I get settled."

"But how will you manage?"

"I play jazz," I reminded her. "I make it up as I go along."

"Sure I'll accept," said Drew.

"Sorry, buddy. I had to call collect 'cause my funds are a little short."

"What happened with the Baroness?"

"The bitch is history. No time to explain on your dime, but I cut the album and it's a motherfucker. Promise."

"Are you still in Rome?"

"London, England, which is why I'm calling. You know any-one over here interested in the European rights for a straight-ahead tenor album?"

"John Keningston. He has his own label."

"And he's into jazz?"

"He's a true believer."

"I truly believe," said John Keningston, "that there's some immedi-ate money for you in elevator music."

I couldn't believe my ears. I'd been in the guy's office for over an hour. I'd played him my whole album, all nine tunes, and he looked like he was loving every minute. At one point, he even said, "You have a lovely sound, Mr. Viola." He was a middle-aged guy in a coat and tie and thin little mustache and funny little eyes. Like all limeys, he was formal as a funeral. His office was in a town-house in the nice part of town around Hyde Park. On his wall were jackets of albums he'd made with Horace Silver, Joe Henderson and a host of other first-rate jazzmen. When my tape was over, though, he started singing a different tune.

"Drew was right to recommend you. Drew has impeccable taste. I so admire his thoughtful essays. I'm also glad to see that he's publishing in some of our British jazz journals. Truly, he's dedicated to the tradition. For a long while, Mr. Viola, I displayed that same dedication. But then, I'm afraid, cruel reality set in. You see, jazz is an extremely slow seller in the U. K. In recent months, in order to maintain my own economic health, I've had to diversify. In fact, I've recently purchased the Muzak franchise for metropolitan London. Although the music is necessarily bland, I currently employ a full-scale orchestra which records twice weekly. You indicated that you play soprano and alto as well as tenor, and I'm certain I could find you a slot. Would you be willing?"

Well it couldn't be any worse than getting whipped by a witch.

It couldn't, but it was.

It was torture. I told you how I can't read music that well anyway, so I knew the gig wasn't gonna be easy. It wasn't the reading part, though, that proved tough. See, John Keningston had put in a good word with the conductor, a nice-looking chick named Victoria who looked like a librarian and seemed to like me. She didn't make me do ensemble work, she let me play solos, mainly on a soprano sax which she provided. But the music was so syrupy and the solos had to be so soft it was more like snoring than playing. Worse, the other musicians kept telling me my sound reminded them of this American musician named Kenny G. Did I know him? No, I didn't know him, and no, I didn't like him, and please, let me just blow and go back to this bed-and-breakfast joint where I was staying not far from Piccadilly Circus and this dumpy gym where I'd been working out like a maniac.

Why is it, dear Doc Mueller, that I always wind up in dumpy gyms from bygone eras where the barbells are rusty and the customers are all meat-eating muscleheads? Don' t tell me I'm looking for my father 'cause I ain't. The truth is I'm looking to avoid my father and keep my brain together by keeping my gut tight and my muscles pumped so at least I can feel good about something 'cause I was feeling like shit about Jasmine and the way she used me to get back to London. Even though she was gorgeous and came on so sweet and shy, Jasmine was jive. And even though she was jive, I still felt myself drawn to her; I still called her from time to time to say where I was staying and playing, and she'd ask me out to her gigs at these reggae clubs in Notting Hill Gate, but I'd say no. I'd say I was too busy. "I hope you're not angry," she'd say. "I think you're a lovely person and a wonderful saxist, I really do." And I really wanted to cry, Doc, 'cause I was feeling something for this girl, but she wasn't feeling shit for me.

"I'm wondering if you see yourself as encapsulated," I heard you telling me again. You love that word *encapsulated*. When I asked you what it meant, you said "Trapped." Well, I ain't trapped. I'm free as a bird—that's how I was thinking. I wasn't thinking, just stinking mad about all these dames—that's why I wouldn't have nothing to do with Victoria the conductor when she started coming on to me, that's why I wasn't about to chase after Jasmine, that's why I was concentrating on staying in shape and seeing if anyone was interested in my jazz album.

No one was.

The plain fact was that I was alone. I had my Muzak gig and

my gym routine and not much else. I ran into Deon Estus, a brother from Detroit who once played bass for Marvin Gaye and George Michael and was recording his first album. He paid me good bread to take a short solo on a song, but it was only a one-shot deal. I auditioned for a fine English funk group called Loose Ends, but at the last minute they decided to tour without a saxist. I was at loose ends. Lavine Hudson, a great gospel singer, had me play at one of her concerts, but when she took off for the States, she went alone.

I was feeling alone and frustrated. It was mid-May, and this elevator music was frying my brain. I was burnt. I'd been going in every Tuesday and Thursday to do the Muzak thing, muttering under my breath how I hated it. I hung in for only one reason— pounds. The pay was good but the pressure was building. Also, the weather sucked. Spring got rained out. Every day a chilly drizzle dampened my spirits. The soggy English food didn't do much to help.

"We'll be doing a new song today," said Victoria the conductor. "Mr. Viola, you'll be happy to know you have a lovely solo over the bridge."

The song was "Sexual Healing."

Now it's one thing to play milktoast versions of "Bridge Over Troubled Water" or "You Are the Sunshine of My Life" or even Michael Jackson's "Man in the Mirror." It's painful to turn those tunes to pablum, but at least it's possible. To Muzakize Marvin Gaye's sexiest song, though, seemed a sin. You might as well de-ball a mountain lion. It was wrong. It was against nature. But somehow some birdbrain arranger had done it, or at least tried to do it, writing this sickeningly sweet string chart, slowing the tempo down to a drag-ass pitiful pace. I nearly puked.

"You're playing a bit too softly," said Victoria after my first attempt to solo.

"If I let go," I admitted, "I don't know what will happen."

"We'll see," she said. And she did.

I let go. In the middle of the mushmeal Muzak, I played the fiercest, most ferocious soprano solo in the history of elevator music. I squeaked, honked, farted and funked up that shit until Victoria had to scream at me to stop. But I didn't stop. I ignored her, I defied her, I kept jamming chorus after chorus, getting louder and looser, letting out my frustrations for having played this mindless music for so goddamn long. I couldn't stop soaring, wouldn't stop wailing, wouldn't take the horn out of mouth or shut down the stream of steaming ideas—sizzling "Sexual Healing" ideas—pouring out of me. It was probably the best thing I'd ever played in my life; Marvin would have been proud.

Ten minutes later, after the most soulful solo in Muzak history, Victoria fired me.

A day later, I was talking to Mom. We had a great connection; even with the ocean between us, she sounded like she was next door.

"I want you to come home," Regina said, "and this time I'm sending you a plane ticket. I don't want any excuses."

"What's so urgent?"

"We're having a party and we need a band. No one can play at this party but you."

"I don't understand. What kind of party is it?"

"It's a wedding party, darling. Me and your father, we're getting married."

"IF ANYONE HAS CAUSE WHY THESE TWO PEOPLE SHOULD NOT BE WED, SPEAK NOW OR…"

I WAS going to speak. I was going to scream out, "This ain't holy matrimony, this is some fucked-up crazy idea that ain't gonna work 'cause I know this man and I know this lady—I'm their only kid and don't tell me they're gonna get along and live happily ever after 'cause they ain't. They're both too selfish to put up with anyone else, plus, given half a chance, the old man never has and never will pass up any piece of pussy that gives him the time of day."

That's what I was gonna say, but I didn't. I just sat there in church. I'd flown in from London four hours earlier and was going nuts. I couldn't keep my brain from spinning. See, I'd made up my mind to attend at the last minute. I was about to return the ticket Mom gave me, telling her, "Thanks but no thanks." But I just couldn't do it. I couldn't treat my mother that way. After all, she was free to marry whoever she wanted—even my old man. I owed them both the decency of respecting their decision.

So when the priest said mass and my father, dressed in tails, said "I do," and my mother, wearing this blue satin gown with gold thread, said "I do too" and the people in attendance, like Kathy and Wilbur Guest, were sitting there smiling, including, if you can believe it, Brenda Weinstein who really *had* changed her name to Sasha and was wrestling for Mom, I watched and winced and gritted my teeth and tried not to lose my mind. It wasn't easy.

It was all happening in the Church of the Sacred Blood, the church of my childhood on Mott Street around the corner from Gino's Gym—excuse me, the *new and improved* Gino's Gym— where the reception was supposed to take place. Meanwhile, I was supposed to be thinking of how much I loved my parents, instead I was remembering when I was a kid how my old man refused to step in this place—he called it voodoo—and how he swore he'd never wear a suit. Never before in my entire life had I seen him in a coat and tie and here he was sporting this silly set of tails and blowing my mind 'cause he'd cut off his ponytail and dyed his hair black and, to tell you the truth, I didn't care.

I didn't care that, before the service, Brenda, her blonde hair all frizzed out like a wild woman, introduced me to her father, Jack Weinstein, a chubby, cigar-chomping guy with a white suit and a red polka-dot bow tie that bounced up and down his Adam's apple when he talked.

"Daddy's been helping your mother book Femmes on Fire on the Coast," said Brenda, lisping like nothing bad had ever happened between us.

"What's Femmes on Fire?"

"The wrestling card Regina put together. That's our team."

"Helluva gal, your mom," said Jack. "Her and me are gonna make my Brenda a star, you wait and see."

"Sasha, Dad—"

"Brenda, Sasha, whatever," Jack rejoined. "The point is, Re-

179

gina Viola's the only dame I know who's got the balls of a fight promoter."

Was this how I wanted my mother described?

I didn't care. I didn't care if she had balls or if she had Pop back or if she had Pop's balls pickled in a jar sitting on her cash register in the beauty shop. I didn't care if she'd adopted Kathy as her daughter and Wilbur as her son-in-law and I didn't care if those two were more part of my family than me. Fuck 'em all. I didn't give a shit if Kathy had let her hair—her beautiful red hair —grow long and curly down her neck. It didn't matter that she hugged me for a long time and whispered that she'd missed me. Her smell and her smile and the sweet way she talked like a school-teacher was bullshit 'cause she wasn't a schoolteacher anymore, she was the full-time manager of the Village Health Club and Wilbur, in his ocean-blue yachting blazer and chivey Ivy League I'm-a-college-graduate blue-and-green tie, Wilbur was chief operating officer of Guest Enterprises and everyone was operating big-time, everyone looked perky and prosperous and all I had was my tenor tape—the master tape from Rome—that I knew was to be my ticket to stardom.

The tape was the real reason I was back. The hell with the wedding. I wasn't about to get involved. The wedding had nothing to do with me. I was there only 'cause it was a hoot, it was a howl to see the old man prettied up, it was a kick to think back to my catechism where, in this very church, the nuns taught me beautiful chants and told me I had a beautiful voice. I liked this church. It wasn't the Vatican, but it was homey. Except deep down I wasn't feeling at home, I was feeling like it was a mistake to have ever flown back. Maybe it was the jet lag, maybe it was 'cause I hadn't slept in two nights, or maybe it was just the plain up-in-my-face fact that my parents were tying the knot and expecting me to play at the reception. I wasn't ready for that.

When I met my parents before the service began, I still thought I was dreaming. Mom had hugged me hard enough to hurt me. "You're here! You came! I knew you would! I told Gino, I said, 'Our boy will be here.'" Pop had just smiled and said, "You did the right thing, champ. You showed." He half-hugged me in a way that felt weird. He looked weird, like he was about to put himself in the electric chair but didn't have no choice.

I had a dozen choices. After the service, it seemed like dozens of dames were throwing themselves at me, dames who were wrestling for Mom or working for Pop. It was crazy. This one called Tiger Lady in a tiger-striped skintight dress with tits like Titan missiles started saying how'd she heard about me and couldn't wait to hear me play and she wanted the first dance and had I seen her publicity shots. There was another called Marvelous Medusa who had a fake snake wrapped around her hat. She was also a wrestler with wide shoulders and a backside big as the Bronx. The weirdest was Barbie, wearing all this white cakey makeup and dressed like a living Barbie doll with the platinum hair and the long legs and the little standup titties and a squeaky voice that said, "You're Vinnie! Oh, I'm so excited!" and she rubbed herself against me and I'm thinking that, counting Brenda—sorry, Sasha—I could probably fuck all the Femmes on Fire which is maybe what my mother wanted. Maybe that's why she sent the ticket. I was there to service her team.

See, after the service I was really getting crazy. I was losing it. When the whole wedding party walked over to Mulberry Street to Gino's new place, I was surrounded by these women wrestlers, almost like I was their mascot. By the time we got to the gym, I was feeling like I was in a dream. But even in a dream, Gino's Gym would never look like this. First of all, Wilbur had knocked out walls, buying the bakery on one side and the hardware store on the other, nearly tripling the size of the place. But it wasn't just the size, it was that the old equipment was gone—the beautiful cracked-leather benches and hack slides, the nasty old barbells and the dirty dumbbells—everything was replaced by shiny chrome weights and machines by Cyntex or Cybex or something that sounded like it belonged on the floor of the New York Stock Exchange, not on the floor of a gym. Even worse, the walls were painted California colors, turquoise and orange, with plush pale peach carpet that had nothing to do with gunmetal gray Gino. Except Gino wasn't gray anymore, he was black dye and I nearly died when I saw how all the great old bodybuilding photos had been remounted in fancy silver Art Deco frames. In a giant gold frame, high above the door, was the black-and-white shot of Gino as Mr. Olympia of 1948, colorized, his teeth gleaming white, his skin bronzed, his pose trunks painted purple. Thinking about how the joint used to look, I almost started crying. Ripping out the old gym, this goon Guest had ripped off my childhood. As he went around pointing out the features to everyone, I wanted to go over and rip out his heart except there wasn't no heart to rip out. There was just this goosey grin and hearty handshake and rush-captain pat on the back. "Glad you're back, Vin," he lied. "Business is so brisk, Gino could use another trainer. Have you met Terry? She's your dad's prize trainer right now. She's accepting applications."

Terry was pretty, toned-up and trimmed down in a slim silk dress and silver scarf. "It's an honor," she said, "to be working with your father."

"I was the first femme to ever work out in the gym, wasn't I, Vinnie?" asked Brenda, breaking into the conversation.

Before I had time to answer, the other Femmes had flown over and flocked around, almost like they were fighting over me. Champagne was flowing and mindless exercise music, worse than Muzak, was dripping out of giant loudspeakers. Gino once said he'd croak before he ever allowed music in his gym, but Gino wasn't Gino anymore, Gino was the shadow of the man he used to be, and it hurt me, it killed me to see my father—once the strongest, most prideful man in the world—now pussy-whipped and WASP-whipped by Mom and Wilbur. No matter, he was loving it, standing around getting his picture taken by publicity photographers hired by the great Guest.

"When are you going to play your saxophone?" Wilbur wanted to know.

"Get out of my face," I informed him.

"I'm trying to be civilized."

"Last time you had your goons around to save your ass. This time it's just—"

"Please, Vince," Kathy cut in, "it's your parents' wedding."

"You mean, *your* parents—"

"Hey bro', what's happening? Give T a hug and shrug off those bad vibes."

"Tyrone!" Man, was I ever glad to see him and his mom Marla! She was wearing this huge red tent dress and T was dressed up in canary yellow.

"I got your birds, man," he said. "Your mom gave 'em to us to keep for you. They're knocking me out. I love those tunes they play."

"We're so happy to see you, baby," Marla reassured me. "We're so happy you came home."

"Let's jam!" T insisted.

"I didn't know you were on the gig," I said.

"Who else they gonna get to play bass behind you? Look who I got on keys and drums—Squeak and Weasel. The Righteous Rippers are ready!"

They were, but I wasn't. I was feeling sick. Maybe it was the champagne I'd been guzzling—anything to get me through this thing—maybe it was the smelly cheese and salty caviar, maybe it was all those flaming Femmes falling over me or Mom telling the TV reporter about her upcoming matches.

"Yes," said Regina, the belle of the ball bursting with pride, "that's my son, Vince. He's a famous saxophonist. He'll be playing sax at the matches. You should hear him play 'The Star–Spangled Banner.' He also does a beautiful version of 'America the Beautiful.' Did you get a look at his body? Put the camera on him. Isn't he gorgeous? His father trained him. He's part of our team."

With the camera on me and Tyrone counting off a beat, I tried. Honest to God, I tried. But I couldn't play worth a shit. I didn't wanna play, I wanted to scream or cry or just run out of there and jump on the first plane to Mars. I wanted to die, my head and stomach were hurting so bad.

Play "Arrivederci Roma," requested Regina. "Your father and I want the first dance."

They got it. Barely able to breathe, I played the song, and they danced, and friends and relatives—Uncle Zito, Aunt Lorella, cousins Laura and Tony and Frank—everyone applauded them, the celebrity couple, and applauded me, the celebrity son, with flashbulbs popping and Wilbur grabbing Kathy and moving himself into the spotlight, dancing cheek-to-cheek—did that mean they were the next couple slated for marriage?—and then all these people I didn't know joining in, health-club members, healthy yuppie dimwits and dorks who made me want to puke. Which is exactly what happened.

Believe me when I tell you I tried to stop myself. I tried to get off the bandstand, but no one would stop dancing and my stomach wouldn't stop churning and I was feeling so faint that, I promise, I couldn't hold it back. It just happened. I couldn't hold it back, I just dropped my sax and fell to my knees, my brain reeling, crying for all the pain inside with my heart breaking for a million reasons I didn't wanna think about, couldn't think about, couldn't stop sobbing, oh my head was throbbing, eyes closing, falling flat on my face like some fool, disgusted, defeated, passed out.

Was that Happy I heard chirping away? Was that my beloved Lady Day? Where were my birds?

I wanted to find them, but I was lost in Candyland, climbing up chocolate chip trees and hurrying down peppermint paths. There was a gingerbread house surrounded by a picket fence of orange lollipops. The sun was a yellow gumdrop, and a big blue lake, made of taffy, reflected a mountain of vanilla ice cream. Atop the mountain was a giant red cherry. I wanted it. I started climbing, but got stuck in the goo. I couldn't get free, so I started crying. My mommy came, only it wasn't my mommy, it was a witch, and the witch had a whip, but Gino was a wizard, and he flew down in a big balloon, and he started screaming, only it wasn't Gino, it was Wilbur who started throwing forty-five-pound dumbbells, first at the witch, then at me. I ducked, but it was too late. Struck in the face, I screamed out like a baby falling out of the crib.

Marla Newborn caught me in time. She held me in her strong arms and wiped my forehead with a warm, wet towel.

"You been dreaming, baby," she said, lifting me back on the bed. "You been having nightmares."

"What happened?" I wanted to know, seeing I was surrounded by all my singing birds.

"Me and T, we took you home, honey. We thought you'd be comfortable staying with us awhile."

Slowly my mind slid into focus. I remembered the awful wedding.

"I got sick, didn't I?" I asked.

"You're getting better now. You need a little time to get yourself situated. Tyrone's already taken your saxophone to the repair shop."

"Did I mess it up bad?"

"Just bent a couple of keys. It'll be ready tomorrow. Everything's getting fixed up, don't you see?"

"Where are my parents?"

"Don't worry about them none. They're off on their honeymoon. I told your mom that I'd take care of her shop and I'd take care of you. Everyone's been a little worried about you, baby. In fact, someone's already called looking after you."

"Who's that?"

"Dr. Klaus Mueller. He left his number. Said Kathy told him to call you. Said he'd be happy to talk to you. Do you know who he is, honey?"

I nodded and closed my eyes.

I couldn't believe my eyes. Mueller had gotten big. Real big. He used to be this tall skinny blonde guy with no build, but now he was built up in the chest. When he took off his suit jacket—something he never used to do—I could see he had developed pecs and shoulders.

"What the hell you been doing," I asked, "going to a gym?"

"Something like that."

"You said you liked to ride bikes. When did this bodybuilding bullshit start?"

"Must have been around the time you left, Vince. Christmas of last year."

"You started 'cause of me?"

"That's an interesting way of looking at it. Why do you feel that way?"

186

"Here we go again. I ask a simple question and I get another question."

"The last time we spoke, Vince, you were considering seeing Dr. Daphne Edwards. After that, I never heard from you again."

"You must have heard what happened from Daphne or Kathy. Kathy called to tell you I was back. Did she also say I was nuts?"

"She said you were under great pressure."

"She didn't say nothing about Rome? Or London?"

"What about Rome and London?"

"I was there."

"Vacationing?"

"Working. I made a record. That's why I'm back. Now I just gotta promote it."

"That's wonderful. So I take it you had a productive trip."

"I haven't got my money yet, so I don't know how I'm gonna pay you."

"We can work that out later. Let's just call this a reacquaintance session. After all, it's been seven months since I saw you last. I'm wondering whether you'd be more comfortable on the couch than sitting in that chair. You might be able to relax."

"Maybe," I said, still skeptical, noticing how Mueller had replaced his artsy antique eyeglass frames with contacts. As he placed a sheet of designer paper towel on the pillow, I moved over to the couch, laid back and closed my eyes.

"So you really haven't heard about my parents' wedding, Doc?"

"To one another?"

"Then you have heard."

"I haven't."

"Then how did you know they married each other?"

"The way you put it, I surmised as much."

187

"Kathy didn't tell you? Daphne didn't tell you?"

"*You* just told me."

"And you haven't told me why you've been working out, why all of sudden you're taking off your coat."

"The air conditioning's on the blink."

"This city's murder in July, ain't it? I don't know why the fuck I came back."

"You said you had a record to promote."

"I have to sell it first."

"Will that be difficult?"

"A snap, Doc. The fuckin' thing is burnin'. My pal Drew—remember I used to tell you about Drew?—he's a jazz writer and a big brain and he says it's the best debut tenor album he's ever heard. He's helping me find a deal."

"Was it hard dealing with your parents' wedding?"

"Why would it be hard? Why would you even ask? Did Kathy tell you something?"

"I'd imagine that, from an emotional point of view, it couldn't be easy."

"It's their fuckin' business, not mine."

"So you didn't get too involved."

"I'm involved in staying uninvolved. I'm staying away."

"Living alone?"

"Does it matter?"

"I recall that you have quite a romantic history."

"What does that mean?"

"Women interest you."

"Lemme ask you something, Doc, and I hope to God you'll give me a straight answer."

"Shoot."

"What did Kathy say when she called you?"

"Simply that you might find it useful to speak with me, and would I mind calling you. I said not at all."

I sighed so deeply it felt like I passed every bit of breath out of my body. "Doc," I said, "I got some shit to tell you, but it's gonna take more than one session. Think we can work out an easy payment plan?"

"I think so," he said, smiling like he meant it.

Drew Williams, standing on the corner of 148th Street and Broadway, dressed in Brooks Brothers brown, was a strange sight to see. He looked a little nervous, and I didn't blame him. While the politicos were selling bullshit at their conventions—Dukakis had been nominated and the Bush man was next—cats in Harlem were selling crack like bubblegum. Around where Tyrone and Marla lived, traffic was heavy. Not that I was scared. I was used to it, and, besides, no one bothered me. The truth is that I liked Harlem. Most of the neighbors were hardworking and friendly. They knew I was a musician and treated me with respect. I felt secure. Right there on 148th Street, the Newborns had a big beautiful apartment with wood floors and thick walls and three giant bedrooms. One of those bedrooms was for me, my birds, my saxes and the weight equipment Mom had been storing. Earlier today, I'd moved the rest of my stuff out of Seaford. My parents had just got back from their honeymoon.

I'd been hoping Mom and Pop would be out, but they weren't. In fact, Gino was sitting under a hair dryer in the den while Regina was buffing his nails. When they looked up at me, I could feel the anger.

"I'm giving him a perm," said Mom. "He'll look a lot better with curls."

"I'm just here to get my stuff," I said, not wanting to watch my old man turning into a wimp.

"Where will you be living?" Mom wanted to know.

"I'm gonna stay with Marla and Tyrone a while."

"In Harlem?" asked Gino. "What, are you nuts or something? You gonna live with the colored?"

I didn't even answer. Mom turned off the hair dryer. Pop got up, his hair twisted into dozens of little red curlers, and sat down at the kitchen table.

"You owe us an apology, Vinnie," said Mom.

"I owe *you* an apology!"

"Yeah," said Gino, "for messing up the wedding."

"How 'bout messing up my life?" I wanted to know. "You gonna apologize to me for that?"

"You're your own worst enemy, Vinnie," said Mom, "and you know it. You have a wonderful girlfriend in Kathy, so what do you do? You throw her away. You have a wonderful career with your father, so what do you do with that? You throw that away too."

"My father got the partner he wanted—Wilbur Guest."

"Wilbur's a good guy," Gino jumped in. "He's doing good things for us, champ."

"Yeah," I said, "by turning you into a clown."

"I oughta belt ya in the mouth," Pop threatened, getting up from the table.

"You'd lose your curlers."

"Ya know, Vinnie," said Gino, walking over to where I was standing, "you're looking more like a loser every day."

"Least I haven't lost my balls."

Gino made a fist; I moved in closer.

"Go ahead, Pop," I threatened, clenching my own fists. "Try something."

"Both of you stop it!" screamed Ma, seeing how the old feud

had fired up. "Your father's a changed man, Vince, and you oughta appreciate it."

"What's to appreciate—that he sold out?"

"There's a difference between selling out and getting smart," she explained. "In his old age, your father's gotten smart. And he's also gotten honest. That's something we got Kathy to thank for."

"What are you talking about?" I asked.

"Kathy's the one who got him to the counselor."

"Gina," said Gino, "that ain't none of the kid's business."

"The hell it's not," Mom shot back. "If you were honest with me, you can be honest with your own son. Tell Vinnie. Tell him what you told the counselor."

"Goddamnit, Gina," grunted Gino, "I don't wanna discuss this now!"

"Your father's had a problem his whole life," said Mom. "It's something he's been hiding. It's the real reason him and me broke up eleven years ago."

"Regina!" Pop was screaming. *"Basta!* That's enough!"

"He'd tell you about his women," Mom went on. "I know how he liked to brag to you, but that was to cover up."

"Cover up what?" I wanted to know.

"Cover up what wasn't working."

"Now you've done it!" Gino yelled, pulling off his curlers and throwing 'em at Regina, who easily ducked them all. "I oughta bust you in the mouth!"

"You touch her and you're good as dead," I promised him, ready to belt him if he got near her.

"Shut up, the both of you!"

"Look what this asshole does," Gino grunted. "He comes over here and tears down everything we've been building up."

"You couldn't get it up! All that big shot talk just to impress some poor kid who didn't know no better—"

"I don't wanna know you," said Pop. "I don't wanna know you no more 'cause you ain't nothing but a goddamn mama's boy who can't do shit on his own. You've never amounted to nothing and you never will." With that, he stormed out of the room.

"He'll get over it," Mom promised. "He'll rant and rave, then he'll feel better. It's good that you know, Vince. The masquerade doesn't help anybody."

"It's hard to think about it. It's hard to believe that the old man, with all those muscles..."

"Yeah, but remember—the most important muscle is the one that can't be built up in the gym. Today, though, today they got remedies for everything. Me and your father, we go to this therapist. A sex therapist. Except it's a her, not a him. She's a wonderful woman and she has techniques. For forty years Gino's been going secretly crazy. Finally he's getting some relief. Can you understand it, Vince?"

"Mom," I said, completely exhausted, "all I understand is that I gotta get outta here. And fast."

That was the morning. By the time I arrived back at Marla's, the phone was ringing. It was Gino, about to bust a gut.

"All right," he said, "I hope you're happy. You've done it. I'm outta the house. I can't live with the bitch."

"Who you calling a bitch?"

"Your mother, that's who. You got her crazy today."

"Listen, Pop, don't call her a bitch and don't call me at all. I don't wanna hear from you."

"Now she's blowing her top, telling me how I'm incapable of telling you the truth."

"She's right. You wouldn't know the truth if it bit you in the balls."

"Look, Vinnie, I couldn't say nothing in front of Regina, but she's right about one thing—you're entitled to the truth. The truth is that I had to lie to her for her own good. She'd never accept the real truth."

"And what's that—that you're a super-stud?"

"Regina's the only woman I ever loved, I'll you that. But as far as pussy goes, I've had more than my share. You've watched me in action."

"What are you talking about? I've never seen you fuck anyone."

"You know Patty, the waitress from Crestini's. The way she had to have it all the time, she was a fuckin' animal. The wiseguys loved her, but she worshipped me."

"You can't live without boasting, can you?"

"I ain't boasting, I'm just telling you."

"Tell it to your sex therapist, Pop. Maybe she's buying your bullshit. I ain't."

"I'm doing it for your mother. Don't you see, champ? It's all for your mother."

I hung up in his ear. I hated to think such a thing about Gino, but at that moment I considered him slime.

"How could you use that word to describe your own father?" asked Kathy. She called five minutes after I'd hung up on Pop.

"'Cause I know him and he's a bum."

"What in God's name did you do out there in Seaford? For months your parents got along so beautifully. From all reports, they had a great honeymoon in Bermuda. Then suddenly you spend five minutes alone with them and they're at each other's throat. Regina just called and said she kicked him out. I've never heard her so upset."

"That's her business."

"You made it your business."

I'd heard enough. I was so pissed at these people I could have bent a barbell in half. "Look, goddamnit," I told Kathy, "if it's

193

anyone's business it's your business and it shouldn't be your fuckin' business except you made it your business. You and Wilbur. And his business. By putting his ugly puss in Pop's business he fucked up this whole business. And so did you. You're in the middle of a goddamn marriage that doesn't have shit to do with you. You love this shit, don't you? Well, *you* adopted them, now *you* deal with them. Just leave me the fuck alone."

I hung up before she had time to answer. I'd had it. I didn't want to hear another word about this crap. Let Mom murder him. Let Pop pop her with the curlers. They deserved each other. I deserved a life of my own. I had my career to worry about—my tape, my album, my music. I had to stay the hell away from these lunatics. Being in Harlem suited me just fine.

"Nice suit," I said to Drew, pointing to his Brooks Brothers brown. We were meeting for an early dinner. Coming in from Brooklyn, Tyrone was set to join us at six. Bringing my brothers together felt good. This was my true family, people who knew me best. They helped me forget Regina and Gino and their fake family with Kathy and Wilbur. Tyrone and Drew made me feel real.

"I'm really hungry," I told Drew who looked a little like a fish out of water. "Let's walk to Copeland's. It's just a couple of blocks down on 145th Street."

Broadway was bustling, blues blasting the air—dudes funkin' 'bout doin' "Da Butt," Latin rascals scratching up their sides with chile-pepper-poppin' grooves, working gals and pirate cabbies, students wandering up from Columbia, number runners and run-away chicks, hicks lost and looking to get back to midtown.

"I'm looking for some ribs," I told the waitress at Copeland's.

"You found 'em," she said. "What's your friend having?"

"Give him some ham hocks," said Tyrone, suddenly appearing

out of nowhere, "some candied yams, collard greens, cabbage, ox-tails and a mess of banana pudding for dessert."

T was wearing a chartreuse-colored tank top, white gym shorts and Popsicle-orange Airwalk high-tops.

"Drew, this is my friend Tyrone."

"Nice to meet you, man," said T, twisting Drew's handshake into the soulshake. "Heard lots of good things about you."

"Vince tells me you're a wonderful bass player," Drew told Tyrone. Everyone was on best behavior.

"Doin' my best," T replied.

"Have you heard the tape Vin made in Rome?" asked Drew, wiping his hornrims with a freshly pressed handkerchief.

"Yes, indeed."

"What's your opinion?"

"Cat can play anything," T told him between bites of a biscuit. "He blows and throws down in lots of directions."

"Did you play the tape for the guy at CBS?" I asked Drew.

By the agonizing way he put his glasses back on, I knew the news was negative.

"He heard it," said Drew, "and called me last night. He has a high opinion of your technique. He liked the selection of songs. He thought the drummer was marvelous"—(visions of Jasmine flashed through my mind)—"but had reservations about the bass player and pianist."

"And that's enough to nix the deal?"

"I'm afraid it's more than that, Vince. He claims straight-ahead jazz just isn't selling."

"It sold when people could dance to it," T broke in. "Wasn't there this cat called Count Basie?"

"That's *not* the point," Drew shot back. "The point is that quality music should find an audience regardless of commercial considerations."

"*Should,*" said T, "don't buy no groceries."

"Did you contact Concord?" I asked. "That's Scott Hamilton's label. He said he'd put in a good word."

"He did, but unfortunately they passed. They liked the music, but were also worried about recouping their investment."

"What about cats like Branford Marsalis?" I wanted to know. "He makes jazz records that sell."

"Only 'cause he gigged 'round the world with Sting," said T. "That got him a different following. Now the kids know him."

"Terence Blanchard and Don Harrison are great musicians," I said. "They have a deal."

"Terence," added T, "is on the soundtrack of the new Spike Lee movie. He's playing next to the funksters. You seen the movie, Drew?"

"I'm afraid not."

"It's about Wannabees. Blacks who wanna be white."

Defending Drew, I said, "You've got him wrong, T. Drew's a proud cat. He taught me the tradition. I promise you, he's down."

"Didn't mean no offense," T told us.

Drew wasn't buying.

I tried to survive the old man's phone calls, but it wasn't easy. I was still upset that Drew and Tyrone didn't get along, that I couldn't make peace among my brothers, and I sure as hell couldn't make peace among my parents. See, Pop couldn't stand the idea that, in my eyes, he was no longer a big man. He kept saying how I was being misled by Mom. The truth, he said, was that he had to lie. In order to remake his marriage, lies were a necessary evil.

"Are you lying to the sex shrink?"

"I'm trying to make your mother happy, champ. Is that so bad?"

"So you've moved back in?"

"I was only out for a night. I had to go back. Without me, she's a mess."

That was her version.

"Right now he'd fall apart without me," said Ma when she called, wanting to know when I was moving out of Harlem. "I'm worried about you up there."

"If Marla can take care of your beauty shop while you're out with your wrestlers," I told Mom, "Marla can take care of me."

"Aren't you a little old to need two mothers?" asked my mother.

"And what was your answer?" asked Klaus Mueller the next day.

"Motherfuckit," I said.

"What does that mean?"

"It doesn't mean shit, all this mothering business. It doesn't mean a damn thing."

"Yet just a minute ago, in referring to Vanessa Andover, you called her Regina."

"That was a mistake."

"A fascinating one."

"The whole thing was a mistake. Besides, I already told you, I never fucked Vanessa."

"But you allowed her to care for you."

"That was her doing. She picked me up."

"As I understand the story, she responded to your call. You sought her through your sax—the sax as an extension of your sexuality."

"I was just playing, Doc. It was one of those nights when I had to play."

"As I hear you describe the relationship, Vince, I wonder

whether the two of you weren't playing out roles—Vanessa as the sometimes indulgent, sometimes strict mother, and you as the sometimes obedient, sometimes rebellious son."

"She was a freak, I told you that."

"Didn't you once refer to your own mother, in her role as a wrestling promoter, as a freak?"

"I said she *hired* freaks. She's got these freaks working for her. And they're calling me, Doc, I swear they are. They're fighting over me. They're begging me to come out to see them."

"Are you interested?"

"What does it mean if I'm dreaming about women wrestlers?"

"It means you're interested."

Marvelous Medusa body-slammed Barbie Doll against the ropes. Medusa went for her platinum wig, but Barbie ducked, intentionally falling on her fanny where she karate-kicked Medusa, all 200 pounds of her, in the gut. Medusa moaned, groaned and reached out, barely able to touch the tip of Tiger Lady's six-inch-long yellow-and-black striped fingernail. Tiger flew into action. The tag team match was heating up. The crowd in the arena in Corona, Queens—smelling of cigar smoke and stale popcorn—was screaming bloody murder. "Kill the Tiger bitch!" they were yelling to Sasha, now spelling Barbie. Sasha was Brenda, of course, who'd dyed her hair the color of her tattoos—green, red and blue. Her body, lean and muscular, was in perfect shape. Quicker and stronger than Tiger Lady, she pounced and pinned her in a matter of minutes.

Watching Bren, I remembered the fun we used to have in bed. Her bodysuit was so brief I could hardly breathe.

"My baby's a genius," said her dad sitting next to me. "Look how she plays to the camera."

Jack Weinstein was wearing a lime-colored leisure suit, a Hawaiian shirt and white buck shoes.

"Where's your wife?" I asked him when the match was over.

"Back in San Diego. She don't like to travel. She don't like much of anything. Let's go see what Regina's up to."

Regina, wearing a rhinestone-studded baseball cap and a red-and-black Femmes on Fire sweatshirt showing shapely women wrestling over scorching flames, was being interviewed by the cable TV announcer.

"Next week in Jersey City," said Mom, "these same four gals are going at each other again. It'll be a hell of a grudge match. I know Marvelous Medusa and I can tell you, she ain't gonna take this sitting down."

Brenda ran into the picture. "We won tonight, we beat that fat Medusa slob, she's a fake." Just as Barbie came over to join Bren, Medusa ran up brandishing what looked like a live five-foot snake. "This ain't no fake!" bellowed Medusa who threw the snake in Barbie's face. Barbie passed out. Brenda slugged Medusa. The wiggling snake fell on the announcer's head, knocking off his wig. He cut to a commercial. The snake, of course, was just rubber.

"Beautiful," Jack congratulated Regina, putting his arm around her in a way that made me nervous. "Beautiful promo, baby."

"Where's Gino?" I wanted to know.

"He's on some radio talk show tonight," said Mom. "His book is out. I got a copy for you. Take a look."

Power-Pumping—The Master Speaks: Gems of Weightlifting Wisdom from Gino Viola. Pop was on the cover, curling a hundred-pound dumbbell, his biceps bulging, his newly curled hair shiny and black, his grimacing teeth recapped and pearly white. A sleeveless Gino's Gym sweatshirt was covering his chest, so I knew his pecs were still sagging.

"They're predicting bestseller," Mom says.

"When he's going on his promotional tour?" Jack asked, as if it was any of his business.

"Monday," Gina told him. "He'll be gone for three weeks."

"When you going back to California?" I asked Jack.

"I don't know. Your mom's keeping me busy. We're thinking about starting a Femmes on Fire sportswear line—leotards, lingerie, the whole business. We'll make a fortune."

"Let's make the late show at the Bottom Line," Brenda suggested to me. "Gato Barbieri's playing, and I know you love him."

Gato blows from his balls. He's got this gritty grunty tenor sound that makes me crazy. He's an Argentinian howler with the lungs of a lion. The cat's ferocious.

Brenda was purring. She was rubbing up against me, saying how sorry she was for what had happened before I left the country.

"It was just one of those things," she said. "I know I'm too wild, but it runs in the family."

Thinking about her father, I ran to the phone to call Regina. Pop answered.

"You hear me on the radio tonight?" he wanted to know.

"No. Is Mom there?"

"Not yet. They said I was terrific tonight."

"What do you mean, not yet? It's midnight."

"She had a match. She said she'd be home late."

I didn't tell him I'd been there; I didn't mention Jack Weinstein.

"You should have seen the broads at the radio station," said Gino. "This one gal nearly raped me. She was better built than my assistant Terry. You've seen Terry, haven't you? She's got the hots for me. Just like this honey at the radio station. She gave me her phone number and said if I didn't call her, she'd kill herself. She was eyeing me like I was Paul Newman or someone."

"Would someone like your father," I asked Brenda when I got back to our table, "ever be interested in someone like my mother?"

She looked at me funny and said, "They're grownups. They can do what they want. What *I* want, Vinnie, is you."

"What I want to know," Mueller said to me, "is whether you've ever experienced the problem before."

"Fuck no!" I was pacing around his office. "My dick gets hard just thinking about bumping broads, especially someone with a body like Brenda's. I'm telling ya, Doc, my dick's never gone soft on me before."

"Fascinating."

"Stop saying 'fascinating'! Maybe it's fascinating to you, but it's fuckin' frightening to me."

"It's fascinating—excuse me, it's *interesting* that this happened just after you spoke with your father."

"It wasn't my father, it was my mother. The thought that greasy Jack Weinstein might be plugging Mom wasn't real comforting."

"In identifying with Gino, in trying to protect and/or please Mother, you found yourself suffering from the very symptoms plaguing Father."

"That's gobbledygook, Doc. I wasn't identifying with no one. I was trying to fuck Brenda."

"You just said you saw Brenda's father and your mother—at least in your mind's eye—making love. You were obviously preoccupied. Gino's inadequacy—"

"Gino! Gino! Gino! I was doing better when there was an ocean between me and Gino."

201

"Were you? On the other hand, Vince, one might postulate that your complex relationship with Vanessa Andover indicates that your inability to separate Mother and Father is an internal problem. Your inner-father and inner-mother must be addressed separately from the real Gino and Gina. Your inner-parents, I would suggest, are the ones giving you the most difficulty and they, I'm afraid, will travel with you wherever you go."

"CANADIAN SUNSET"

AT THIRTY-FIVE thousand feet, flying through a bank of billowy clouds, I was listening to the song on an old tape by Gene
"Jug" Ammons, the master tenor player, and remembering what
Doc Mueller said about my parents traveling with me. I didn't
believe him.

I believed Jug. I believed he blew as fat and pretty as anyone
who's ever lived. When he played the melody, I could practically
hear the words—"a weekend in Canada, a change of scene." That's
what I needed.

"I ain't taking Gino and Gina on this trip," I told the good
shrink. "I'm getting away."

"Is it work, or is it escape?" he asked.

"I'll be working my ass off. I'm going out with the Righteous
Rippers. Tyrone's been asking me for over a year now, and I finally
said yes. They got a job in Vancouver and I'd be dumb to turn it
down. Look Doc, I'm out of money, and I feel guilty living rent-
free at Marla's. Meanwhile, not a single soul is interested in putting
out my tenor tape. Drew tried. He saved me once—by tipping me

203

off about the Baroness—so I thought he could save me again. Now I know he can't. It ain't his fault. It's just that Tyrone's right. The money's in dance music."

"Does that mean you'll be able to start paying my bill?"

"You worried?"

"We had an agreement, Vince. As soon as you found employment, you agreed to work something out with me. Your past due account already amounts to over a thousand dollars."

"I never stiffed anyone in my life, Doc, and I don't intend to start. I'll straighten out with you soon as I get back."

"When will that be?"

"Couple of weeks. End of September."

Now, at the end of a long day, with Jug jumping through my Walkman earplugs, I looked out the window as the plane broke through the clouds and circled Vancouver. It looked beautiful down there—islands, bridges, mountains and millions of pine trees. I was feeling mellow. I was happy to be getting away again. Not that Mueller hadn't helped me. He was a good guy to talk to, and given what I'd gone through—coming back to my parents' wedding, watching them get wackier by the day—I appreciated his being there. I appreciated him giving me credit, financial and otherwise. I figured the guy trusted me and, after all this time, I was starting to trust him. I was starting to feel like a whole human being again, especially after last night when I felt the urge to merge and met up with Rita Scavullo, an old girlfriend from the old days willing to wail for old time's sake. It was beautiful. She took me back to her place in the Bronx and rocked my socks off. My rod stayed stiff as a board. It didn't let me down until me and Rita made it to the finish line at the same time. Finally I could breathe easy and relax. Before she could ask for an encore, though, I was already getting dressed.

"What's the hurry?" she wanted to know.

"Got a plane to catch early tomorrow morning," I said, figuring it'd be best to leave on a high note.

"Certain notes," I remember Jug once saying in an interview, "taste better than others."

Jug played with perfect taste and no effort. With Rita, it was effortless 'cause I wasn't thinking, just tasting and not wasting my energy on weird wrestlers, not worrying whether my parents were worrying about me, not doing nothing but what came naturally. That was T's philosophy.

"Don't Worry, Be Happy," was this reggae ditty everyone was singing. Bobby McFerrin, a great jazz singer, was making a million on an easy-to-listen-to, easy-to-love little nothing melody that made you feel good and kept you from being discouraged.

Though the Rippers had been looking for a record deal for nearly two years, T wasn't discouraged. T kept on trucking—writing, finding gigs and finessing his funk until, as he put it, "the tunes turn bulletproof."

"If folks can't dance to our shit," he said, "it's only 'cause they're deaf, crippled or white."

We'd taken a bus to a seedy hotel on the corner of Pender and Columbia, smack in the middle of crowded Chinatown, and were sitting around jawboning—me; T; Squeak, the little cat with a high voice who played keys; and Weasel, the long-armed drummer.

"I like having a blue-eyed soul brother up front with us," T told the others. "Especially Vinnie. Vinnie's bad. Chicks like his looks, and his tenor gives us a whole 'nother dimension. The cat's deep."

T made me feel good. He made me feel needed and wanted, and when I worked out later that afternoon in a nasty little gym around the corner from the hotel, I pumped myself to the limit. I went for the burns, for what the body boys call "sweet pain." I wasn't thinking about nothing but mind-to-muscle—that was

Gino's mantra—and afterwards I felt like a million bucks.

The two-week gig was in a club that used to be owned by Tommy Chong, the Chinese comic from Cheech and Chong who I'd seen working out in Gold's Gym in California. During the hippie era, T told me, Chong played guitar and had a band called the Vancouvers with this soulful singer named Bobby Taylor. They even had some hits on Motown. Maybe that's why the club had such good vibes.

Man, it was good to be on stage. It'd been too long. I realized that recently my only performances had been on Mueller's couch. I'd been doing too much talking and not enough playing. Besides, even if by now Mueller knew something about Gino and Gina, he didn't know shit about music. He didn't understand how sometimes I thought I was selling out by playing funk, and how sometimes I felt foolish playing non-paying jazz. Sure, he'd nod when I told him I had artistic conflicts, but then he'd always bring it back to Pop.

"Purity," Klaus would say, "is something you once admired in your father, even if begrudgingly so. You described his old gym as a bastion of pure and unadulterated bodybuilding. Now you bemoan the fact that he's compromised and, in your mind, gone commercial."

"That's not about music, that's about weightlifting."

"But wouldn't it lift an enormous weight off your psyche if you could separate the two?"

"Who says I can't?"

"You worry about following in Father's footsteps."

"I asked you not to call him 'Father.' That sounds so stiff. He's just my old man, and there ain't a chance in hell I'd ever work in his gym again. Besides, it isn't even his any more. It's Guest the Goon who's calling the shots. Pop is just a dancing bear in the circus."

"Doesn't that describe your own apprehension about joining the Righteous Rippers? Isn't that why you've resisted the offer for so long? Aren't you yourself afraid of turning into a dancing bear?"

Fuck no. I liked dancing, and I liked watching people watching me dance. I could dance with my horn in my mouth like the old cats used to do—like Big Jay McNeely or Sam "The Man" Butera or Junior Walker—I could crouch and sway and swing my horn over my head, I could even leap off the stage onto the floor and jump on the bar and crawl on my knees and still kick ass. I could put on a show, playing just as mean as Maceo Parker—James Brown's saxist—sweating and getting crazy, bumping and grinding and sticking my big shiny sax out there like it was...well, Doc, maybe you're right, maybe when I'm on my game and ain't feeling tame I'm aiming to please the ladies by showing 'em that I can blow with the best of 'em—even harder, even longer—blasting T's funky brew all over the room, nonstop no-waitin' no-hesitatin' skatin' smooth, bumpin' big, humpin' heavy till all the tenderonis in the place—black, white and a couple of Chinese beauties—were all wanting to know where I was staying.

"He's staying clean," said T, sensing he had to protect me from the beautiful mob.

Back at the hotel, though, two of the more beautiful chicks—one was white, the other black—had found their way to my room. They were waiting for me.

"You Canadian girls are wild," I said.

"We want to experience you," said the white one, her arm around her dark friend.

"I don't know what it was, Doc," I told Mueller on the phone the next morning, "but I knew it wasn't going to work."

"What wasn't going to work?" he asked. "The experience?"

"No, my dick."

"What happened?"

"I played so hard back at the club I probably dropped ten pounds. I was exhausted. I was drenched. I needed a bath. It was one of those big old-fashioned tubs, and they jumped in there with me. They started soaping me up like Mom used to do."

"Until what age did your mother bathe you?"

"Who the hell knows, Doc? It wasn't last year, if that's what you're thinking. She'd wash me in the bathtub when I was a little kid, and I'd hate it, and I'd tell her to stop, and she wouldn't 'cause I think she liked it."

"Do you remember her touching you?"

"No! That's your perverted mind again. It wasn't anything like that."

"Sometimes mothers, innocently enough, enjoy exciting their infant sons. It's quite common."

"These gals were all over me with soap bars and washcloths, talking to me like a baby. 'Isn't he cute?' 'Isn't he darling?' 'Look at this and look at that.' They were driving me crazy, making me feel like a little kid, reminding me of Regina. No wonder my cock started shrinking, Doc. My dick felt like it was half an inch big."

"I understand how you feel."

"What good does your understanding do me? What am I supposed to do? After Rita, I was sure I was back in business. You should've heard me play last night. I turned the joint out. But now I'm so worried about my own joint I'm scared to even try again. Okay, maybe I had some problems before, but they were strictly mental. This here shit is real. I'm spooked. I need something. Some pills or—"

"It sounds far more psychological than physiological."

"That's what you say 'cause that's your line of work. But my old man's got some therapist, a sex therapist, who's doing him good. At least that's what Ma says."

"It's fascinating to see you following Father to his therapist."

"Stop saying 'Father' and stop saying 'fascinating' and stop saying I'm following him 'cause I ain't. I'm just saying that he's getting help. If I inherited this disease from him—"

"It's not a disease."

"It ain't normal. And until I started coming to you, I never even had the problem."

"You call me for help while, at the same time, you accuse me of hurting."

"I want an answer, goddamnit! Why is this happening to me?"

"It's complicated."

"It's bullshit!"

"Look, Vince, I can't prescribe pills over the phone, if that's what you're looking for. Often it gets darkest just before the light. You're experiencing dynamic changes. You're acknowledging feelings you've long repressed. I would have to say you're making progress, you're going forward."

"Tell that to my prick. It's going backwards. It's acting like a scared little worm who wants to hide inside my pubes. I'm gong nuts, Doc, I swear I am."

"You said your performance went well. That's an accomplishment. You have the admiration of your audience and your colleagues. On many levels, you're functioning well."

"I don't call not being able to fuck functioning."

"If you'd like to call later in the week, I should be available in the early evenings."

"What good does it do to keep calling you?"

"You'll have to be the judge of that, Vince, not me."

"Okay, I'll put it out of my mind, Doc. I'll just forget it. That's what I'll do."

* * *

But I didn't. I couldn't. Especially when, later that day, T showed up in my room with the afternoon newspaper.

"Take a look," he said.

On the front page of the entertainment section was a big picture of me on my knees, my tank top soaked in sweat, my muscles bulging, my sax raised in the air.

SEXY SAXIST SIZZLES AT CHINATOWN NITERY

Imagine Kenny G as a bodybuilder. Imagine Kenny G as a raunchy honker, not the genteel Pied Piper of the yuppies. Now you have some idea of the passion and power of a group of New York funksters—the Righteous Rippers—a black band that blew into town this week featuring an astoundingly athletic white horn player.

The article went on to talk about how the girls went nuts, and how someone said I reminded her of Bruce Springsteen with a horn in his mouth. "Oh no," someone else said, "he's got a better body than Bruce."

"You pissed that the paper didn't mention you and the other cats?" I asked T, worried I was getting too much attention.

"Hell, no, I ain't pissed. Man, I'm happy as a mud duck. This is what I was hoping would happen. We needed attention—any kind of attention—and you're bringing it to us, V. After this article, wait till you see what happens this weekend."

The weekend was wild. The crowds were lined up four blocks long. You couldn't get into the joint. The owner doubled the cover charge and was still turning away hundreds of people every night. On Saturday night, it got so crazy that in the middle of one of my solos this chick jumped me and tore off my tank top. Then a half-dozen other chicks jumped her, ripping the shirt to ribbons. Seemed like every hot chick in Canada wanted a piece of me. It got so bad we had to change hotels. T, Squeak and Weasel were getting their share, too. They were having a ball, but I wasn't. I wasn't balling at all; I wasn't sure I could. I was getting my rocks off by playing, not partying. I was turning down everything—toot, pot and pussy. Especially pussy. I couldn't handle it. My music was working, but my weiner wasn't; my weiner was still out to lunch.

"And to tell you the truth, Doc, I'm worried sick."

"When will you back, Vince?"

"Now I don't know. That picture of me—the one in the newspaper—was picked up and run all over Canada. Next week we're heading for the Blue Note in Toronto. It's already a six-day sellout."

"On some level you must be proud."

"I'm pumping every day. I'm working out like my life depends on it. I've never looked this good before."

"And the better you look the more you're adored, and the more pronounced your internal conflicts."

"On the outside, things have never been better. T gave me a big raise. He realizes what I'm doing for his gate, and he ain't stingy. But you're right, Doc, inside I'm going nuts. I can't tell nobody but you what's wrong with me. I'm ashamed. I'm too young to have this problem. What the fuck is happening to me?"

"You're being successful, Vince, and part of you—the sexual part of you—is denying that success."

"And what's that supposed to mean?"

"You feel big and small at the same time."

"It's water, water everywhere but not a drop to drink. A thousand chicks and me with the mindset of a monk."

"You'll rise to the occasion, Vince. It's only a matter of time."

"What's the matter, V?" asked T, a white-and-gold Roots baseball jacket zipped over his paunch.

"I hate it," I said.

"I don't understand why."

"I don't feel right playing a red saxophone."

"The manufacturer in Montreal says it's smoother than a Selmer. Just try it, man. The cat saw your picture in the paper and said you'd be a perfect spokesman for the sax. He's *giving* you the goddamn thing."

"I've never seen a tenor with a red enamel finish before."

"Fire engine red is a killer color, V. You're red hot, man, you deserve an ax like this."

"Lester Young, Sonny Stitt, John Coltrane—they never played red saxes."

"That's only 'cause they weren't around back then. Look at Miles, though. Ever seen Miles's red trumpet?"

"Drew calls it a gimmick."

"Screw Drew. Look what Drew did with your jazz tape. It's collecting dust. Out here, we're collecting bucks. Toronto's buzzing about us. Word's gotten back to New York. Someone just told me a big-time record exec is flying up from the city to see us tonight. I can't see the red sax hurting, V, can you?"

"I don't wanna mess up anything for you, T."

"It ain't just for me, Vinnie, it's also for you. You're the front man now. Don't you see what's happening? Look, I know I can play bass. Cats like Louis Johnson and Marcus Miller have told me I scare *them*. I know I'm laying down monster grooves. But one thing Tyrone don't ever do is bullshit Tyrone. And Tyrone ain't no singer, Tyrone ain't no rapper and Tyrone ain't no sex symbol. Same goes for Weasel and Squeak. You dig? We hook on some harmonies and we sing some leads, but we've never found the right singer. Until you. You singing that soulful shit through your sax is something else, and it's working like a motherfucker."

"If your father's fucking my mother," I told Brenda who called my Toronto hotel while Oprah Winfrey was getting ready to come on TV, "I don't wanna hear about it."

"Who said that?" she said. "I just said they were working together on this new clothing line. You should see the samples. I wanna model 'em for you, Vinnie. We're off this weekend and I was thinking about coming up there. What do you say, baby?"

"Not a good idea."

"How come?"

"I'm not up for it." On second thought, I wish I hadn't used that expression.

"You still worried about last time? That was just one of those things. From time to time it happens to most every man."

"I ain't worried about nothing, Brenda. I'm feeling great and I'm playing great but I just can't afford to get sidetracked. See?"

"I see you're scared of me."

"That's some dumb shit you're saying. Why the hell would I be scared of you?"

"Because maybe I really love you, like Kathy never would and Kathy never could. Maybe you're scared of love. And maybe you love me like you never loved her, except you're not over her yet and you're carrying the torch 'cause Kathy got this Guest guy and they got a new gym opening in White Plains."

"Where'd you hear that?"

"Your mother told me. She talks to Kathy all the time. Regina says she's sweet, but to me Kathy's a snobby little bitch."

"She's no snob."

"See, you're still hung up on her. That's your problem. That's why your cock's gone to sleep on you."

"Nothing's gone to sleep. And stop talking that way. Someone might be listening in."

"I'm down at my apartment on Canal Street, and I'm all alone. I wish you could see it. I fixed it up—new curtains, new couch, new king-size bed. I also bought a canary."

"No kidding. What kind?"

"The guy in the store said it's a border canary, a male. Males are supposed to be bolder and better singers than the females. The guy also said males hold themselves up straight while the females droop. I'm calling him Vinnie. He's a small guy, but he's got this beautiful chest. He reminds me of you, baby."

Thinking how much I appreciated Marla taking care of my babies, I told Brenda, "Be careful what you feed him. Canaries don't have any teeth in their beaks."

"You got teeth in your beak, baby. I remember how you liked to chew down."

Remembering those fine 69s I had with Brenda, my prick perked up for the first time in days. My prick was interested in what Brenda had to say. "No one ever licked longer than you, Vinnie," she told me. "No one ever did it better."

"Keep talking."

"I get hot just thinking about the things we used to do."

Now my rod was at full staff, rigid as a lead pipe. Brenda had done it. Maybe she *was* just what I needed this weekend. But just when I was about to say something, just when I was going to tell her to come up for the weekend, I heard Oprah introducing her next guest:

"He's just written a book on bodybuilding. He's a fascinating man, and his name is Gino Viola."

The lead drained out of my dick. "I gotta go," I told Brenda.

"What's wrong now?"

"Nothing. Gino's on TV. I wanna watch."

"I wanna tell every man and woman who's watching," Gino told Oprah, "that the key to sexual longevity—to long-term potency—is looking great and being in shape."

"Would you mind my asking your age, Gino?" asked Oprah.

"Not at all. I'm proud to be sixty-one and going on twenty."

Oprah approached the stool where Pop was sitting. He was wearing a black turtleneck and white jeans. I had to admit that, with the black dye job on his permed hair, the old man looked great, not a day over fifty.

"I've never requested this of a man before," said a smiling Oprah, "but I don't feel that the question—directed to you, Gino, a former Mr. Olympia—is inappropriate. Would you mind taking off your shirt?"

* * *

"Why don't you take off your shirt?" T suggested just before we went on the stage of the Blue Note. "The girls would go crazy."

"The girls are going crazy enough."

"I notice you've been ducking the foxes," said Squeak in his high-pitched voice. "What's going on?"

"I ain't used to this much spotlight," I answered honestly. "Plus, Pop was on Oprah Winfrey today, and *he* took his shirt off. That blew my mind."

"Wow!" said the lanky Weasel. "Is your old man one of those Chippendale cats?"

"Gino was probably selling his body-building book," said T, not at all surprised.

"Selling his body," I said, "like he was doing forty years ago."

"And the cat's still buffed?" Squeak wanted to know.

"His pecs looked pretty tight," I said. "For years he got lazy and his shit was sagging. But by the way he looked today, he must be back bench-pressing like a maniac. He blabbed on and on about stone-age nutrition and proper form. He even gave demonstrations curling dumbbells and lifting barbells. I've heard his spiel so many times before I could have said it for him. I could have done the demonstration better than him. But now he's got this guy Guest sponsoring him. Now the old man's got a national audience."

"V's daddy and mommy," Tyrone told the boys, "are different. They're like Vince. They're stars. It's a whole family of stars."

"Well, shine bright tonight, Mr. Vinnie Viola," said Squeak. "And lead us to a deal."

The ruby red sax didn't play as smooth as my old Selmer, but it worked. I'd never played a whole set without wearing a shirt, but that worked too. I did my knee-fall, my bar-walk and my bump-and-grind while the Toronto tenderonis took it to heart. They flipped out. They reached out just to stroke my red sax. They blew me kisses while I blew back the walls and tore off the ceiling.

I did a tenor version of Michael Jackson's "Bad" that was worse than bad. It was downright filthy. I was gone, honking my way to heaven with an original jam by me and T called "Captain Hornblower." I played just the way I felt, filled with frustrations, fuckin' furious mad but glad I had a way to wail, a way to let people see I had something to say. By the end of the second set they were standing on tabletops screaming for more. After the fourth encore, T whispered, "Up the back stairs, man. The record exec's waiting up there."

On the way up, someone threw a towel so I could mop off. From the top of my head to my toes, I was soaked in sweat.

"I ain't in no condition to meet no big shot," I told T.

"She'll love the way you look. She'll eat you up."

"*She?*"

"Vince Viola," Tyrone said as soon as we entered this private room, "meet Sue Kawisha."

"LEARN HOW TO TOOT YOUR OWN HORN"

THAT'S WHAT the ad said. It was in *Penthouse* magazine and it showed this picture of a curly-haired Kenny G holding something called the Casio DH–100 Digital Horn, this easy-to-play toy that can sound like a sax, clarinet, oboe or even trumpet. As the train pulled out of the Toronto station in the pouring rain, I was wondering how much Casio had paid Kenny G for being the spokesman. God only knows. Now the guy was getting even richer selling toys.

I was getting out of town. I decided to take a train to slow things down. I needed to be alone and think things over. Tyrone, Weasel and Squeak understood, especially after I told them what happened last year when I almost modeled for that magazine.

"When I came up here," Sue had told me back at the club with the boys listening, her legs looking longer and lovelier than I remembered, "I had no idea you were part of the band."

"Bullshit," I said. "I bet you saw my picture in the paper."

"I didn't. My Canadian correspondent called and simply said there was a hot band that merited attention."

Kawisha was wearing this white silk dress with her silky black hair flowing all the way down to her waist. With her little diamond earrings, sleek silver necklace and Louis Vuitton attache case, she looked like she was running the world. She was so beautiful it hurt. She'd also hurt me so bad last year I could hardly stay in the room with her.

"If you knew I was in the band," I said, "you wouldn't have bothered to come, would you?"

"Perhaps not. You see, I've started my own small label and can record whomever I please. After seeing this band, though, I must admit that my initial instincts about you were right, Vince. No doubt, you're a dynamic talent."

"What's this business with your own label?" I asked, still pissed and determined to resist her flattery. "Last thing I heard you'd stolen my sax star idea and peddled some guy named Paolo P to Epic Records."

"Epic's a division of Columbia and Columbia's now distributing my label. I know you've heard of Tamara, the teenage phenomenon. I discovered her in Maui. To date, her debut album is triple-platinum and still selling."

"And what happened to Paulo P?"

"Problems with chemical dependency. It was too bad. He had some talent."

"So you blew it with your sax man."

"Look," said T, breaking in, "if you two have this much bad blood between you, I don't see how we can make a deal with you, Sue."

"I don't wanna get in your way, T," I said.

"There are other labels out there," Tyrone assured me, Squeak and Weasel.

"But none as savvy or aggressive as mine," said Kawisha. "As you can see, I'm the first and only label who came up to see you.

From here on, you can be assured of personal attention. From production to promotion, I'll be with you every step of the way. Because my roster is small, I attend to every detail. Gentlemen, let me by frank: marketing muscle is what this business is all about. My track record with Tamara proves what the right label can do for a new artist."

"You've never handled a black act before, have you?" asked Squeak.

"You're not a a black act," Sue said. "You're an integrated act, a great act, a commercially potent act."

I cringed a little at the word *potent*.

"What do you know about our music?" Weasel wanted to know.

"I feel it. Right here in my heart, I hear its urgency and freshness. Beyond that, I don't need to know any more. You're obviously completely capable of writing and producing original material. You have a far sharper sense of the street than any overpaid A&R man. All you need is a first-class studio, a first-class engineer and a healthy budget to capture your sound on tape."

"You talk a good game," T told her. "But the way this group works, everyone's gotta be happy."

"Along those lines," she said, "I'm happy to offer the Righteous Rippers an advance against future royalties of one hundred twenty-five thousand dollars."

You could hear all four of us gulp at once . . .

Now I could hear sheets of rain slamming against the train. It was the day after the offer and the sky was dirty gray. A late summer storm was blowing like crazy while I was going crazy trying to figure my next move.

See, Sue was being cool. She'd called me this morning and said, "Let's not let the past destroy our future."

"You used me," I told her.

"You used me as well. Clearly, we used each other. And it didn't help that we became personally involved. We both lacked professional experience which, in these past months, we obviously have gained. But the truth, Vince, is that we were attracted to one another's talents. We needed each other—then and now."

"You're a hell of a saleswoman."

"You're a hell of a musician."

"You only saw me as a model, as a piece of meat."

"A beautiful body is an asset. Even with the Righteous Rippers, you exploit that asset well when you play barechested."

"That was T's idea, not mine."

"My idea is simply to make you and your colleagues an enormous amount of money by letting you play the music you love best."

"This isn't the only music I play, you know. I recorded a whole jazz album over in Europe."

"Your artistic agenda is something for you to work out with Tyrone and the others. I'd be the last to interfere, Vince."

Drew wrote me. His letters had arrived, along with a cassette, back in Vancouver, but this was the first chance I had to listen to it.

Paul Gonsalvez is one of the last great swing-era tenor players. Listen to the way he plays with the Duke Ellington band. I've been a little under the weather recently, and this music has done wonders to revitalize me. I always want you to remember that you're part of a glorious tradition, and there's no more glorious moment in our musical history than the American Jazz Festival in Newport, Rhode Island, July 7, 1956. It happened thirty-

two years ago. Duke wrote the piece in 1937, but his performance of "Diminuendo and Crescendo in Blue" at Newport is a
classic. Gonsalvez plays twenty-seven—count them, Vin,
twenty-seven—choruses of sheer improvisational magic! Surely
it deserves to be ranked with Coleman Hawkins's "Body and
Soul" and John Coltrane's "Giant Steps" as some of the most
inspired work ever played on the tenor saxophone. Meanwhile,
I think of you always. I regret not being able to help you more,
Vince. My inability to find a label for your tape continues to
trouble me. I trust, however, that a talent as large as yours will
not go unheralded for much longer. Meanwhile, I wish you well
in Canada and impatiently await your return. Whatever else I
have to say to you, Paul Gonsalvez can say it better.

Your friend,
Drew.

I put on the tape and plugged the phones in my ear. Duke
sounded great. His guys grabbed me and pulled me along, like a
locomotive. There's something about the swing beat that goes
with a train. Maybe that's 'cause the cats always traveled in trains
back then. All I know is that I forgot all my problems and put
my head in the fast-moving heartbeat of this big band kicking
up a storm, even as the wind was howling and the rain was
slamming, this Gonsalvez cat was blowing and going wild, on
and on and on, the crowd going nuts, shouting and dancing—I
knew they had to be dancing—and I was feeling better 'cause it
showed me that even Drew's great Duke was doing what I was
trying to do, getting folks off their ass and on their feet, while
Gonsalvez was blasting through, chorus after chorus, never running out of ideas, staying strong and playing hard, making me

feel like music and love were one thing, and that one thing was long-lasting, beautiful and good.

"I was feeling good for a while," I told Mueller. It was my first day back in the city and I was back in his office. "But the good feeling didn't last."

"Let's try to sort out your feelings, Vince."

"I feel like Sue won," I told the shrink.

"How so?"

"She was trying to sell me as a sex symbol. Now she's got her wish."

"The relationship between your sexuality and your saxophone has always been tricky."

"I ain't turning no tricks, I ain't no whore, if that's what you mean. I sure as shit ain't doing what Gino's doing."

"Which is what?"

"Selling out."

"I thought you were prepared to accept the money offered you by Sue Kawisha."

"You'd like me to take it, wouldn't you, so I can pay your bill."

"I want you to understand what you're feeling."

"I'm feeling funny about you, Doc."

"Why?"

"For the first time since I been seeing you, you ain't wearing a suit. The sweater you're wearing looks like it's too tight on you. I guess you're getting pecs, so you wanna show 'em off."

"Is that your projection?"

"What do you mean?"

"Things you feel about yourself you project on me."

"Sometimes I feel like you're jealous of me," I told the shrink.

"You say similar things about your father."

"The old man *is* jealous of me. I'm younger, I'm stronger, I can do shit he can't."

"You're still feeling pressured by him."

"Pressured by everyone."

"Who else is pressuring you?"

"You're pressuring me for money. T and the cats are pressuring me to cut the Kawisha deal. Now that Mom and Dad are so fuckin' successful they think I'm a bum and I feel pressured to show 'em I ain't. Plus Brenda and all these groupies are pressuring me to screw 'em."

"And Kathy?"

"Kathy's gone."

"Are you sure?"

"She don't call me and I don't call her 'cause we don't care no more."

"She called me," Mueller announced.

"About what?"

"About you."

"What about me?"

"She said she'd like to meet with us both. Since you were good enough to meet with her that time in Dr. Edwards's office, she wants to return the favor."

"Tell her not to do me any favors. Tell her the answer is no."

"Tell her the answer is yes," I told T.

"You don't sound like your heart is in it, V. If this bitch still bothers you..."

"I'd be an asshole to turn down the bread. I owe you, T. I

owe you more than you'll ever know. You and your mom gave me a home when I needed one. Living here has been a lifesaver, man."

"But that doesn't mean you're in favor of this Kawisha chick."

"Kawisha's a hustler. And she's damn good at it. Let her hustle for us."

"She wants some personnel changes."

"She wants me out, doesn't she?"

"Now you *are* being an asshole, bro. Of course she doesn't want you out. She just wants to bring in some chicks."

"What for?"

"For the look."

"What are they going to do, strip?"

"Backup vocals. While you're playing sax lead, they'll be singing behind you. What do you think?"

"My mom's got a bunch of beauties working for her. Why doesn't Kawisha call Regina? Or better yet, how about female mud wrestlers? They can be slapping each other around in the middle of the song. The crowd will love it."

"Look, V, I told you, if you don't like the deal, don't take it."

"Do salaries for the chick singers come out of our advance?"

"Sue said she'd foot the bill for them. When I told her our lawyer had meetings lined up with other labels, right away she called him and kicked up the advance to one hundred fifty thousand—if we sign this week. The way I figure it, I'll take fifty thousand, lay fifty thousand on you and split the last fifty thousand between Squeak and Weasel."

"Why am I getting so much?"

"You're my front man. You're the reason we got the offer."

"So she's buying us."

"If it ain't her, it'll be someone else. That's the music business, man."

"And chick singers don't bother you?" I asked.

"Bother me? If I had the money, I would have hired a few foxes long ago. They can't hurt nothing."

"He's hurting, Vince. And he doesn't want to tell you."

"If you've got something to tell me," I told Kathy, "why does it have to be at the shrink's?"

"Vince, I'm not talking about us. I'm talking about Drew. He's sick."

"Is that why he hasn't called me back?"

"He hasn't called because he's in the hospital. That's why I'm calling you."

"What's wrong with him?"

"I don't want to say it. I don't even want to think it. But I'm afraid. Please go see him, Vince. He's at NYU Hospital over on First Avenue. Go see him soon. You're as important to him as anyone in the world. He...he loves you, Vince...he loves you more than you'll ever understand."

I didn't understand until I looked at Drew.

I'll never forget his look. I'll never forget the day, Election Day, the first Tuesday in November, with me hoping both candidates would lose. Far as I was concerned, you could put Bush and Dukakis in a rocket and send 'em both to the moon for all the fuckin' good they'd do us. I was in a rotten mood. It'd been a long rotten day.

It had started out good. Me and Marla were riding the subway from Harlem to Long Island City, on our way to Regina's House of Beauty. Since Regina had devoted herself to wrestlers and gym togs, she'd just about turned over her shop to Marla. Like

Tyrone, Marla was making some real money. Also like Tyrone, money didn't change her loyalties.

"I know your mama," she told me as the train rattled down the dark tunnel. "I seen her strengths and I seen her weaknesses, but I'm here to tell you I like the woman. Sure, she can be testy, but not in no mean way. From the beginning, she worked hard to get what she's got—and without no man to help her. I respect any woman who's made it without a man—including Regina, and including me. We've helped each other through thick and thin. That shop does a steady business, and that's because she's steady in her dealings. She worked long years to get what she got. I'll tell you, Vinnie, she's plenty generous with me. She's just splashy, that's all. She's a character. And the shop, well, the shop just wasn't enough for Regina. She wants to make her mark. She's a lot like your daddy that way. Maybe that's why they never could get along."

"This new marriage of theirs is a bust, isn't it, Marla?"

"He hasn't been around much. With his new book and everything..."

"And Mom and this Jack Weinstein—"

"Listen, Vinnie, one of the reasons I get along with folks is 'cause I let 'em be. I don't pry, don't spy, don't ask and don't guess. Your mama's a grownup gal and what she does is her own business. All I know is that she's an honest lady, maybe a little crazy, but she loves you, I know she does."

"This gal," Pop wrote in a letter from Australia that was waiting for me at Regina's House of Beauty, "says she loves me. I'm sending you a snapshot of her and me to show you what she looks like. What do you think, Vin?" I thought she looked like a slut with peroxide hair and Spandex hot pants and a silly smile spilled across her face. Plus, she couldn't have been younger than forty. "She says she's twenty-five," wrote the old man, but I think she's younger. Anyway, I can't get rid of her. She loves bodybuilders and she says since I'm king of the bodybuilders she can't let me go. To be honest with you, champ, she's turned me into a tiger. I ain't had sex like this in thirty years. Her name's Holly and she's an Aussie and she's going with me next week when I fly from Sydney to London. Everyone in Australia has heard of me and Gino's Gym. Bodybuilding's big over here and my reputation is so big I can't believe it. The book's selling like hot cakes and someone said it was on the *Daily News* bestseller list. If you see it mentioned in the paper cut it out and save it for me since I'll be getting back in December and wanting to see all my clippings. Naturally don't say nothing to your Mom about this Holly but by now you've figured out that between me and your Mom it ain't no good and never was. That's okay since I got my life and she's got hers and I can respect what she's doing even though she's a ballbreaker, Vin, I swear to God she is. Right now Holly's hurrying me to get dressed. She's taking me to the Sydney Opera House to hear Puccini tonight. I forget which one they're doing, but you know how much I love Puccini. When I get back, if you're still not doing nothing, I got a great job for you at Gino's Gym. I told Guest you're not a bad guy and I want you to manage the original place since me and Guest are opening another Gino's Gym on the Island. With Kathy managing their new place in White Plains, we need people we can count on. What do you say, champ?

I ripped up the letter and the snapshot.

"Your mama's on the phone," said Marla, seeing that Pop's news hadn't done much for my sagging spirits.

"What are you doing today?" Regina asked me.

"Looking at apartments. We're about to sign our record deal, so I'll have enough money to move out of Marla's."

"Today's my big show. We're introducing the clothing line. You forget, Vinnie?"

"I guess I did. Sorry."

"It's not too late to come down. We don't start for another hour. You'll love it, honey. You'll be proud of your mother."

I didn't love it. I wasn't proud. But I was amazed.

In a small ballroom in a hotel near Macy's in Herald Square, Regina was wearing a silver lamé cape over a pink pants suit. Her eyelashes and eyeshadow and rouge and lipstick and fingernails and teased streaked hair were a little too much. She looked like Batman's mother.

"It's show business," she said, kissing me on the cheek and squeezing my hand. "I love it."

Jack Weinstein was wearing a baby blue tux with a ruffled shirt and going around introducing Mom to the press like he was her lapdog. "This woman is a genius," he was saying. "She's the brains behind Femmes on Fire. I'm just the bookkeeper."

In the show, Marvelous Medusa, Tiger Lady, Barbie and Brenda/Sasha, along with several other ladies, modeled the goods. If the chartreuse-colored leotards and leopard-spotted tights showed any more tits and ass, they'd have to call the vice squad.

I slipped out before the gals noticed I was there. I knew they'd be all over me, especially Brenda, and the last thing I wanted was to deal with a bunch of oversexed wrestlers.

I felt undersexed. I felt no sex. Maybe—I heard myself saying to Mueller—maybe it was 'cause there was just too much sex around me. My old man talking about it, my old lady selling it, and now me avoiding it. It wasn't 'cause I didn't love it. I always loved it. I always did it. But now I wasn't doing it. Now it wasn't working and I wasn't sure why except deep inside I still felt rotten, Doc, after all the shrinking and thinking, even with the big deal and the good money, I felt rotten.

Drew looked like he was rotting. I swear, that was my first reaction when I walked in the room. I never seen anyone look that bad. My heart started beating fast and there was this lump in my throat and I felt scared, real scared.

"Kathy told you?" he asked, barely able to pick up his head from the bed.

"She just said you were sick."

Drew's cheeks were hollow. Thin to start with, he looked like he'd lost forty pounds. He couldn't have weighed more than ninety. He had these awful reddish-brown blotches all over him and was coughing this horrible hacking cough. He was always so healthy and handsome and decked out in sophisticated suits from Paul Stuart that it was hard to believe this was the same guy.

"I've been sick for a while," he said. "I didn't say anything, I didn't want to be melodramatic and elicit pity, but now there's nothing I can do."

"You're going to get better, aren't you?"

"I'm afraid not."

"People are getting over it, I know they are. I just read something that said they got a cure and with these new drugs..."

"It's rough, Vince, and it's not going away. Complications have set in more quickly than the doctors anticipated. Would you mind sitting close to me?"

I pulled up a chair next to his bed. On the nightstand he had a pile of tapes and a portable recorder.

"Wanna listen to something?" I asked, not knowing what to say. I was feeling so afraid and confused I could hardly sit still. Sure, I knew he was gay, but he was always so clean-cut and together, he was the last cat in the world I figured to get AIDS. I figured wrong.

"Let's talk before we listen to music," he said. "What I have to say isn't going to be easy. In all the time I've known you, Vince, we've never discussed my personal life. I never judged you and you never judged me. I always appreciated that. Appreciation is the key to our relationship. Your talent never ceased to astonish me. And I always felt as though you appreciated my feeling for jazz. I never wanted anything to get in the way of all the wonderful things we shared. Now I feel like I want to touch you, Vince, I want to take your hand, but I won't do it, I don't want to do it if it makes you uncomfortable, I don't want to..."

I didn't want to, but I did. I reached over and took Drew's hand. His hand was shaking and his voice was shaking and I know you can't get AIDS by touching someone's hand and I wasn't worried about catching the shit, except his hand was clammy and I felt creepy, but I held his hand anyway, I looked at him when he said, "I love you, Vince. I can't go away, I can't die without telling you. I love you like a brother and I love you like a lover and I've never loved any of my lovers, not one of them, the way I love you. I know it's hard for you to hear it, I know it's hard for you to think about men loving men, and I wish I could save you the embarrassment, Vince, but I must say this. I felt it when I saw you for the first time, when I heard you play and when I heard you speak. I felt it every second we've been together. 'Unrequited love's a bore,' Billie Holiday once sang, 'and I've got it pretty bad.' I've had it bad, Vince. When you left for Europe, when you left for Canada, I always wanted to tell you. I didn't want to disturb the respect we had for one another, I didn't want to ruin our friendship, but I promise you, Vince, I was dying inside. Kathy knows. Kathy's always known. You see, she and I have shared this love, we're both so much in love with you."

"Kathy's long gone, Drew. She's off in another world."

"That's what she says, but I know her. I know her heart. Her heart still hungers for you."

I was still holding his hand, and there were tears in his eyes, tears in my eyes.

"I don't know what to say, Drew."

"Just sitting there is enough for me. Just touching me, just letting me know you understand."

For a long time I sat there without saying another word and let the light outside the window turn from dusk to dark. There was no sound until Drew nodded to his tapes. On top was Lester Young playing "Polka Dots and Moonbeams." I slipped in the cassette and we listened as this man—the most tender and heart-breaking of all saxophonists—took us deep into the night.

I wanted to break Mueller's face. The fucker didn't understand; the asshole didn't have a clue.

"It ain't no latent homosexuality on my part!" I screamed at him as I stomped around his office. I was so mad I couldn't even sit down. Now Klaus was wearing a black turtleneck—like Gino used to wear—and black jeans. What the hell was going on with this guy?

"Maybe *you're* the latent homo," I said.

"An interesting projection."

"Bullshit! Look, I know myself. If guys turned me on, I'd tell you. They don't. If I was a faggot, it would have come out over in Europe with the Baroness and all her freakery."

"How do you account for this extreme reaction?"

"A friend—a guy I really care about—tells me he's dying.

This beautiful good-looking guy looks like a skeleton..."

"Then you *were* aware of his physical beauty—"

"Would you shut the fuck up and let me talk! Just 'cause I notice that a guy's handsome doesn't mean I want to butt-fuck him. Me and Drew, we been pals for a long, long time. Don't you see? It was like he was my teacher. He got me into jazz. He told me who the main cats were. He loaned me his records and tapes, told me what to listen for, made me believe I could do it. He showed me my roots, laid the foundation, convinced me I was an artist. I loved him for that. But it was never love like kissing-love or fucking-love. It was music love, heart love, friendship love, that kind of thing."

"Yet you always knew about his homosexuality."

"He never hid it, but he never pushed it. Drew never flaunted it. He wasn't one of these fairies whose feet never touch the ground. He was normal, a regular guy, a college graduate, a writer who everyone respects."

"Do you believe that most homosexuals are flamboyantly feminine?"

"Look, Doc, I was raised in Little Italy and I lived in the Village and I seen my share of every kind of gay guy there is to see."

"You sound as if you've been preoccupied with them."

"Did I say that? Did I say that I chase them or dream about them or beat off to *Honcho* magazine?"

"Isn't *Honcho* a gay pornographic magazine?"

"It ain't *Better Homes and Gardens*."

"How would you know about it?"

"I see it on the stands."

"And stop and look?"

"Goddamnit, Mueller, get off my case! I'm trying to tell you about Drew and you're trying to nail me for being a fag."

"I'm trying to get you to listen to yourself."

"Well, listen to me 'cause I'm telling you that this friend of mine is dying, and he's telling me that he loves me, and I don't know how to handle it."

"Handle what? The fact that you may love him as well?"

"I do love him, I told him I did, I sat there and held his hand, but I ain't 'in love' with him. I almost wish I was so I could make him feel better. But I can't. I can't lie to the guy, especially when he's being so honest with me."

"But are you being honest with yourself?"

"Yes, goddamnit! Can't you see that?"

"I see another issue here, Vince. Purity. Just as you witnessed the demise of your father's purity—the sanctity of his gym being tainted by what you consider Wilbur Guest's compromising commercialism—so too Drew represented the purity of jazz, a music immune from corruption. The fact that his immune system has broken down has shattered you, has—"

"The guy's dying, Doc, and you're sitting there thinking up fancy theories about purity. Do you hear what I'm saying? And do you understand that he ain't just dying, he's dying this awful fuckin' death with his body rotting away, day by day, and I don't know what to do about it... I swear I don't..."

"Our time's up for today, Vince, and I do need to mention the matter of your unpaid bill."

"I can't deal with that."

"We're approaching two thousand dollars."

"We're supposed to sign our record deal in a week. I'll pay you then."

"I'm counting on it."

I felt like saying, "Count me out, Doc." For the four hundredth time, I felt like quitting.

See, lots of times with Mueller I felt like I got shit off my chest. I felt like he was helping me see things I missed. But recently—and especially today—the shrink didn't help at all. He was accusing me of being queer, and that was completely and totally dumb. I wasn't. I know that some people think deep down everyone is AC/DC, but I don't. Some guys like dicks and some guys don't.

"Your problems with your own penis," Klaus had said at the start of the session, "are perhaps related to this recent development with Drew."

"Those problems started before I knew anything about Drew."

"But you always knew about Drew's homosexuality."

"I ain't talking about that. I'm talking about AIDS."

Mueller was twisting the shit around. Mueller was tripping me up. It also didn't help that I was tripping out over this record deal. Maybe that was good, though, 'cause it gave me something to focus on. At Nick the Greek's coffee shop, over a double-cheese tuna melt, I tried to think about the record deal, except I really couldn't think about anything, not with Drew dying, and not with Kathy calling.

"You wouldn't agree to see me in Dr. Mueller's office?" she asked.

"I've had too much on my mind."

"I know your parents' breakup hasn't been easy for anyone, especially me."

"I ain't even thinking about that. That was always bullshit. You got hooked into it, Kathy, not me."

"I'd rather not discuss these things on the phone, Vince."

"Then don't call me."

"You sound so bitter."

"I'm going through some changes."

"Drew told me you've been coming to see him almost every day. He says you sit there and listen to music with him for hours on end. I really respect you for that, Vince. That takes courage."

"He's the cat with courage."

"There are other things I'd like to discuss with you, but I'd rather do it in a therapy session."

"Have you ever thought that those therapists ain't what they're cracked up to be?"

"From the way you're sounding and acting, Vince, I'd have to say that Dr. Mueller has done you a world of good."

"Maybe, but after a while he becomes just another jones, another fuckin' addiction. Like being on the tit. I'm ready to quit."

"If you rather meet me at my therapist's office, I'd be more than happy to set something up."

"Why are you being so nice? Why do I have the feeling you're setting me up for a fall?"

"Will you meet me at Daphne's?"

"I'll think about it."

I couldn't think about nothing but Drew. It didn't seem right, it didn't seem fair. I knew the guy. I knew he wasn't one of these crazy faggots who went to bars where they put live chickens up their ass. I knew he wasn't no S&M maniac. I guess he knew his way around the gay world 'cause of how he warned me about the Baroness—I'll always be grateful to him for saving my ass—but I couldn't imagine him jumping into orgies and pigpens. From what I understand, though, you don't have to be a freak to get AIDS. It just takes a little bad blood.

All that time I spent with Drew in the hospital, I didn't ask any questions and he didn't volunteer any information. It was just about being there with him and listening to music.

"One of the greatest balladeers," said Drew, "was Sonny Stitt." It was snowing outside while we listened to "When Sunny Gets Blue," Stitt wringing the thing dry, making a monument out of an already beautiful melody, scaling up through snow clouds into sunshine and sad blue skies.

"Blue Skies," I told Drew, "is the name of a tape I bought you by this new singer named Cassandra Wilson. She's a cross between Betty Carter and Sarah Vaughan. You'll dig her."

He did. While the wind whipped up the snow and the day got darker, Cassandra gave us lots of joy. There was a VCR in his room and we watched *Round Midnight,* our favorite movie. Dexter Gordon tore us up—acting true-to-life tenor genius, moving towards death, soaring on soprano and making us weep.

During those days, we did lots of crying. At first, I felt funny about it. Once his parents walked in while we were listening to Hank Crawford playing "Misty." They got misty-eyed in a hurry, but it didn't matter, I wasn't embarrassed any more because our tears were real and releasing shit that couldn't be released any other way.

I didn't think I could do it. I didn't think I could spend so much time with Drew 'cause the decay was pretty disgusting—I gotta be honest about that—the way he looked and smelled and coughed. But after awhile I didn't see him that way. I couldn't tell this to Doc Mueller—he wouldn't have understood—but I didn't see Drew's body, I saw his soul. And his soul was beautiful, like a tenor solo, like a lush melody. His doctors said I could bring him a bird so I bought him a pair of gorgeous diamond firetails that sang in their cage while we quietly listened to their song.

The birds were singing the day Drew died.

Kathy had been there the night before, but I was there when

he closed his eyes. I felt it, I knew the very moment when the last bit of life drained out of him. He wasn't afraid; he was peaceful and relieved. Anything was better than what he'd been through. He deserved better. In my heart, I felt he'd be going to a better place. It happened on a Tuesday, the same day me and the Righteous Rippers were supposed to sign the deal with Sue Kawisha, the same day Gino got back from England.

WOUNDED HEALERS

IT WAS a title on the cover on this highbrow magazine I spotted on the newsstand on my way to the lawyer's office. It said, "Wounded Healers: The old joke that therapists are more disturbed than other people may be no joke."

I bought it and thought about Mueller and why I hadn't been back. He'd been calling about the money I owed him. For some reason, I couldn't call him, couldn't tell him about Drew. For some reason, I didn't trust the guy. If I told him that, he'd turn it back on me—he'd be asking me to look at my problems with trust—so all I could do was stay away. Plus, I didn't wanna keep reporting that my gas gauge was still on empty. Sure, hanging out with a guy dying of AIDS won't do wonders for anyone's sex life. Fact is, it got *me* paranoid about having AIDS. After all, I'd been doing my fair share of fucking around. I thought about Brenda and Claudia and this Rita Scavullo. None of them were nuns. They all had an open-legs policy and what did I know about Sue Kawisha's sex life? I thought about taking an AIDS test, and I did, and when I found out that I was clean I was relieved but still bugged about sex. Everything was bugging me. Mom was bugging me about how Pop was bugging her by sending her pictures of him and this Holly in an Australian bodybuilding magazine.

"He flaunts his floozie," she told me, "to make me feel bad. But I don't, Vinnie, I don't feel bad at all. I know your father. I nailed him a long time ago. Once I thought I could make a man of him, but I was wrong. I was wrong the first time and I was wrong the second time. And believe me, *caro mio,* this second time is the last time. Never again. The sex therapist, she agrees with me, Vinnie. She says your father's chronically impotent. *Chronically.* That means he'll never get better. The more famous he becomes, the worse he gets. He thinks he's fooling me, he thinks he's fooling the world, but with all his big muscles, that one muscle still won't get bigger. Jack Weinstein may have problems, Vinnie, I'm not saying he's a saint, but he's good promoter and when it comes to you-know-what, he knows how to satisfy a woman. For too long I've done without. For too long I've sacrificed and lived like a saint. No more. I can't sacrifice for Kathy, and I can't sacrifice for you, Vinnie, not anymore. I have to live for myself. I'm making a living, this much I know. With the shop and the wrestling and the clothing line, I'll make nearly $200,000 this year. For a woman like me that's a fortune, Vinnie. That's the reason this divorce is important. He doesn't deserve and he's not getting any of my money. Soon as my cash flow improves a little, I'm buying back the stock I sold to Wilbur Guest, which is something your father will never do. Guest owns Gino; he owns the copyright to Gino's book and every last dumbbell in Gino's Gym. No one owns Regina Viola, and no one ever will. I'm independent, Vinnie. I'm moving to Forest Hills. I'm buying a beautiful condo, but I don't want to sell the house in Seaford. I want to give it to you."

"Sell it, Ma," I said. "I don't want to live on the Island. Besides, Tyrone and I have this record deal. I'm getting a good advance."

"You know I'm not against anyone, Vinnie. The colored aren't bad people. Marla's managing the store and she's a doll, she's a gem, she's worth her weight in gold. I'm not one of these people who hate the colored, but shouldn't Tyrone be playing for you rather than vice versa?"

"It doesn't work that way, Mom. It's his band. He invited me in. I play at his pleasure."

"But that picture in the paper up in Canada—that's what did it. You looked gorgeous. *You're* the star."

"I don't feel like a star, Ma. Especially today. Drew died today."

"Who's Drew?"

"My friend, the jazz critic. The guy I went to high school with. The one who taught me about jazz."

"That nice-looking colored guy? He's too young to die. Was it a knife fight?"

"Ma, this guy was a writer. His father's a professor. Drew was never in a fight in his life."

"The colored are different than us, Vinnie. I keep trying to tell you that."

What was the use of trying to explain to Mom? Marla was right—sure, Gina loved me, but she didn't have the faintest idea of what I was about. Neither did Gino. They were my parents, but they were also space cadets.

"Look, Ma," I told her. "I'm late for this lawyer meeting. I'll talk to you soon."

My head was still dizzy from thinking about Drew. He'd be buried the day after tomorrow. I wanted to cancel the meeting today—I was in no shape for it—but the lawyers had been playing ping-pong with our contract for so long that enough was enough. Sue kept adding on these little stipulations, but she also kept adding on money. Other labels had heard about us, and she wanted to avoid a bidding war.

She kept calling me, saying shit like, "I'm interested in making a side deal with you on the poster."

"What poster?"

"The photo from the Vancouver paper, the one where you're on your knees, wearing a sweaty tank top and hoisting your sax in the air. It's quite dramatic. So dramatic, in fact, that I bought the rights from the newspaper chain."

"How can you do that? It's a picture of me."

"Photos are like anything else in this world. They can be bought. For the sake of goodwill, though, I'm willing to cut you in. I'm doing an initial run of fifty thousand."

"You're crazy."

"I'm calling it 'Sax Sex.' What do you think?"

"I don't want you doing it."

"I'm afraid I don't require your permission, Vince."

"I'll sue."

"You'll lose."

"Why can't we just make a record? Why do we have to sell posters?"

"Multi-media merchandising is the key."

"I got the key to the executive washroom," said T in the lawyer's lobby. "Why don't we go in there before Squeak shows up."

"What about Weasel?"

"That's who I wanna talk to you about."

The washroom was all mirrors and marble lined up with bottles of colognes and deodorants. T was wearing a Yankees jacket.

"Weasel was offered a job with Cameo," he told me.

"The funk group?"

"*The* funk group, yes. He felt bad, but the bread was too big to pass up. Bigger than what Kawisha is offering."

"When did this happen?"

"Couple of weeks ago."

"Why didn't you say something, T?"

"You've been with Drew, man. I respect that. I didn't wanna fuck with your head any worse than I had to. You were being a buddy. Meanwhile, though, me and Sue have been out scouting drummers."

"You and *Sue?*"

"The chick's got a nose for this sort of thing. We came up with someone, and it turns out to be a drummer you know."

"Who?"

"English chick named Jasmine. She's playing with this reggae band in Jamaica. Been in the country for only a month. She said she played on your jazz album. Plays her booty off too. And what a booty! She's gorgeous, man . . ."

I wanted to smash my head against the marble countertop. I wanted to cry. I wanted to bang out my brains and scream for help.

"I can't do it," I said, thinking of Jasie.

"What are you talking about, V? She's a sweet chick. She's got nothing but respect for you."

"She's a bitch and Sue's a bitch and I'm just not gonna do it."

"Were you fucking Jasmine?"

"She fucked me, man. Look, T, this whole deal is fucked. I just can't go through with it."

"That's what Sue said you'd say."

"'Cause that's what Sue wants. She wants me out. Don't you see? She's got plans of her own."

"I'm sticking with you, V. I'm going in there and telling the lawyer to tell Kawisha to get screwed."

"Don't. Let her dump me. Let her get chick singers and let her sign Jasmine. Jasmine's great, I promise you. Maybe she's a conniver, but she's a show drummer and she'll sell albums. Let the deal go through, T. Take the money. You deserve it, I swear. I couldn't do it now even if I wanted to, even without Jasie or Sue. My attitude would hold you back. You've worked too hard to blow it now."

"What's wrong, man? Is it Drew?"

"Drew's dead."

"Oh shit . . . I'm sorry. It happened so fast."

"He had it for a while, but didn't say anything. I just caught up with him at the end. Right now I don't know what I'm doing, except I can't get my head into the band and I don't want to hurt you, T."

"Say the word, bro, and this deal is down that toilet, with no regrets."

"I'll kick your ass if you don't sign with that bitch. Take the money, man. Cut an album. Maybe I'll catch up with you later—I don't know what I'll do—but your songs are gonna go over better with singers than a sax anyway. I know your grooves are gonna catch fire."

"Without you, V, I wouldn't even be looking at this money. Whatever you do, I'm giving you a taste."

"That's good of you, T, but I need some time off. I gotta get away."

"Your old man just got back. Mom says he's been calling you at the house."

"I'm going back to pack and tell Marla goodbye. I love your mama, and I love you, Tyrone, but I gotta be alone. I gotta think."

* * *

I wasn't thinking. I just grabbed my sax and went to the funeral. A few famous jazz musicians were there, and a bunch of writers from the *Village Voice* and some other magazines. Professors from NYU, friends of his parents, maybe a hundred people. The preacher said something that I didn't hear. I rode out in the limo with his folks and didn't say nothing. Maybe some of them thought I was a lover. I didn't give a shit.

Kathy was at the service and she was at the cemetery. She was wearing a black dress and tears were running all down her freckles. She came over and took my hand. She said she'd call me. She said we needed to talk.

When they put him in the ground, I took out my sax and played. No one had asked me to, but I knew it was the right thing. It was freezing cold with a nasty wind cutting my face. The grave was on top a little hill and I stood next to my friend, dead at only twenty-seven, and I played the blues. I played the blues for Drew just the way he liked 'em—salty and straight-ahead.

The next night I moved out of Harlem into a furnished apartment uptown on Amsterdam Avenue big enough for my birds. I didn't wanna go back downtown. I didn't wanna be near Pop. Before I left, Marla gave me a check from Tyrone for $25,000. He had signed with Kawisha. "This is your finder's fee," the note said.

"I found your number through Marla," Pop said. He called a week after I moved in. "When you coming down to see me? If you need money, I got it. I'm getting rich. My book's a big hit. Wilbur wants to see you. He wants to hire you. I think that's big of him, don't you? And Holly's here. She's dying to meet you."

"I'm not feeling good," I said. "I'll call you when I feel better."

"You'll feel better," said Kathy, "if you stay in therapy. You've made so much progress, you can't stop now. Especially with what you went through with Drew. You need to sort it out. You need to go back to Mueller."

I needed to pay Mueller. I didn't know why, but I couldn't get myself to do it. I couldn't get myself to do anything.

"Will you at least meet me at Daphne's office?"

"I don't know."

"I do, Vince. If you can't do it for yourself, at least do it for me."

"This Christmas."

It'd been a year.

Last Christmas and this Christmas, and all the shit in between. A year since I'd seen Kathy in Daphne's office.

"This Christmas" was one of my favorite songs sung by one of my favorite singers, Donny Hathaway, who killed himself. No one knows why; he just jumped out a window.

It was ten in the morning and my birds were sitting on the window ledge and singing along with Donny. Donny had so much soul. Like Drew. Except Drew never knew much about pop soul singers. Drew had been hooked on Holiday, Fitzgerald and Vaughan—the Holy Trinity, he called them. Drew was a jazz purist. Isn't that what Mueller called him?

Mueller didn't understand, so why would Daphne Edwards? Why should I meet Kathy over there at noon? What was the purpose?

I didn't have a purpose. I was drifting, lifting my weights but wondering what the hell this whole thing was about. What kind of world was it that would waste a good guy like Drew?

Thank God for my birds and my barbells. They got me through the morning. They didn't talk back. They let me lose myself... curling iron, feeding canaries, anything to get my mind off me.

At the shrink's, I'd have to talk about me. I'd have to listen to Kathy. What was the point?

"The point is to express our feelings about each other," said Kathy, "in a way that's constructive."

The office was lavender—I remembered that and I remember the small sketch of Billie Holiday hanging next to Daphne's Harvard degree. It was sure nicer looking at Billie Holiday than the picture of cranky ol' Sigmund Freud in Mueller's office. And naturally it was nicer looking at Daphne, in her chic wide-shouldered suit, than creepy Klaus. Daphne looked like a movie star.

"Why don't you look at me?" Kathy asked.

"Okay, I'll look."

She looked beautiful. She was wearing a fuzzy gray sweater and a full black wool skirt. Her red hair was cut in bangs and framed her face in a new chin-length style. At the same time, she looked both hip and lost. Her green eyes seemed wounded. I wondered why.

"I don't know why I'm here," I said.

After too many seconds of silence, Daphne asked, "Do you want to tell Vince the reason you arranged this session?"

"No, not really," Kathy answered honestly.

I laughed. So did Kathy. It was great to see her smile.

"Okay," she finally said, "I'll try, but I guess he still intimidates me a little."

"Address Vince, Kathy, not me," Daphne instructed.

Kathy looked at me and said, "We've both made progress, Vince. I know I'm a different person than I was a year ago, and so are you. The way you comforted Drew made me so proud of you. That showed so much character."

In spite of myself, my heart started beating fast and I started thinking, *So this is why she wants me here—she wants me back, but she's so nervous to say it that she needs her therapist to help her through the conversation.*

"You see, Vin," she said, "I've always thought you were a very special and wonderful human being."

Man, it felt good to hear that. For the first time in so long, I was feeling warm all over. I was remembering how much I'd loved living with Kathy—the way she fixed up our place on Jane Street, the way she made everything comfy and warm, all those good times we shared.

"I hardly know where to begin, Vince," she said. "So much has happened to me. And to you. I'm finally realizing what and who is important to me. And I'm also able to acknowledge that importance without sacrificing my own identity. You are important to me, Vince. Very important."

I wanted to say so many things—that I'd been lonely, and lost, and confused, and hurt, and hungry for love, maybe even hungry for Kathy's love—but I kept my mouth shut. I let Kathy do the talking. I was waiting for her to say, *Come back, Vinnie, let's try it again, baby, only this time we'll get it right.*

"It's only right you know the truth about how I feel," she said, swinging her head slightly to one side, her eyes still fixed on me, half-longing, half-fearful.

"The truth, Vince, is that I've successfully separated from your mother and father. That hasn't been easy because, as you know, for too long Gina and Gino served as my surrogate parents.

With Daphne's help, though, I've seen how I was futilely trying to create a family structure. That structure proved false. That structure collapsed and I'm afraid in the process I caused you further pain. I apologize, Vince."

"That's okay, long as you see it now."

"I see it and I see other things quite clearly. I've fought for and won a measure of happiness, Vince. I'm happy in my work."

Suddenly something snapped in me. "You like managing that goon's club out in White Plains?"

"That goon is not such a bad guy."

"He's jive."

"He's my fiancé."

"You're marrying that asshole! What happened to all those nice things you were saying about me?"

"I meant them."

"How could you mean them if you're marrying this creep?"

"Why do you have to call the man I love a creep?"

"'Cause you don't love him, you can't love him, you're too goddamn good for him."

"Will you just be good enough to hear me out?" She started crying, but I couldn't hold back my anger.

"Why should I be good," I asked, "when I feel like a fuckin' fool? I been fooled again by coming here so you can fuck me up with your rotten news."

"How can you say it's rotten?" she asked. *"How can you call having a baby rotten?"*

I felt like Kathy had just kicked me in the balls. I knew it'd been over a year since I'd slept with her, so the kid couldn't be mine. "You mean, you and the goon are having a baby?"

"In September," she said, her red eyes now on Daphne, who motioned to her to look back at me. She couldn't. All she could do was look at the ceiling, tears streaming down her face now, and say, "I want this baby . . . I really do."

What I wanted was to punch out God. I know that sounds stupid and horrible—that's not how my mother raised me—but I swear that's how I felt. God was fucking me around. God was torturing me. God was taking the things I loved and turning them against me. The expression on Kathy's face told me that she was as miserable as me—she was still bawling when I left the office—and I couldn't comfort her and she couldn't comfort me 'cause the thought of her having a kid with my father's boss was more than I could stand. I love babies, but not this baby, not a baby made by Kathy and Wilbur Guest. If it wasn't God's fault, then it was these shrinks' fault. These shrinks thought they were God; these fuckin' shrinks were making me crazy.

"Quite the contrary," said my shrink. "I see this as a healthy development. It's a way for us to finally focus on what we've referred to before as your Jesus complex."

"How am I supposed to take you seriously," I asked Mueller, "when you're wearing a New York Athletic Club sweatshirt? You used to wear three-piece suits. Now you're dressing like a jock, Doc. What the fuck does it mean?"

"Obviously it means a great deal to you, Vince."

"You cheat, goddamnit, you and that Daphne both! You sit there like gods, like priests, like princes and princesses. You hide. All this time and I still don't know who you are, and to tell you the truth, Doc, I don't even care anymore 'cause this is it. I came by to let you know I've had it."

"Just as you've let me know so many times before."

"I've suffered enough of your shit."

"Just as Jesus suffered."

"Jesus! What do you have to get blasphemous for?"

"You just got through cursing God, Vince. You just told me how you were angry at God for abandoning you. At the hour of his greatest need, wasn't it Jesus who cried, 'Father, Father, why hast Thou forsaken me?' And aren't you, in fact, the sanctified son, both blessed and abandoned by your own father? Until you found he had feet of clay, wasn't Gino your god? Didn't you, in fact, view both your parents with abnormal righteousness and reverence? For the nearly two years I've been seeing you, Vince, we've witnessed the dissolution of that family, a family which, even when your parents lived together, was essentially dysfunctional. I understand your rage, Vince, and I understand your shame. Your entrance into adulthood has been not only belated, but excrutiatingly painful. Twice you've been forced to face Father's highly neurotic narcissism—first, at age sixteen, when you quit high school, and now, over a decade later, his godlike purity, symbolized by his gym, has been polluted before your very eyes. Your relationship with your mother has been just as bewildering. Her own purity—especially after leaving Father—was something you considered permanent. Time and again you've commented how she's sacrificed her love life in order to raise you. Regina—doesn't that mean 'queen' in Italian?—was your Mother Mary, and you her perfect son. To discover her sexual involvement with a man other than Father, with, in fact, the father of your former lover Brenda, had to be devastating. Just as devastating as the death of your friend Drew—Drew, who like Father also fathered you in purity, the purity of jazz, only to disappoint you by dying from a disease which seems to symbolize impurity itself. Your other brother Tyrone took you

251

into his family, Vince, but that relationship has been nearly ruptured by his entanglement with two women—the Japanese manager and English drummer—both of whom have deeply disappointed you.

"Family disappointments, family dissolutions, dysfunctional families—and now another family, another situation in which you find yourself odd man out—Kathy's marriage to and pregnancy by Wilbur Guest, Gino's surrogate son, the very man who replaced you as family savior. I must be honest with you, Vince. Given the complexity of your relationships, it's a wonder you're walking around. What I suspect and strongly hope, however, is that you've gained in here some sense of your own worth, your own emerging independence from these failed familial involvements."

"You're paying me a compliment?"

"I'm giving you the reason I haven't cut off our own relationship, even though your current bill stands at two thousand, eight hundred dollars."

"Because I haven't gone nuts?"

"Because I find you—and your sense of emotional survival—both phenomenal and fascinating."

"I was going to tell you about this fascinating article I read, Doc. I even brought it with me. It wasn't easy, but I read the whole thing. It made me mad, it made me think something was wrong with you, not me. But after hearing you today, I feel bad about being mad at you. I see that you've really been listening to me."

"What is it?"

I showed him the "Wounded Healers" thing from the highbrow magazine.

"I'm familiar with the piece," Mueller said. "And I can certainly see why, given everything we've just discussed, you'd rather find fault with me than further face these issues. This article must have represented some sort of relief for you."

"Don't you think I need relief from all the stuff you've just said, Doc? Plus, you didn't even mention nothing about my dick going soft on me."

"Everything I mentioned is a contributing factor to your sexual dysfunction. Yes, Vince, you do need release."

"When it's coming?" I wanted to know.

"When you're ready."

"I'm ready now."

"Are you ready to face your father?"

"Haven't I done that before?"

"You've backed off before. You've toyed with intimacy, but your pattern has been to escape, to run away not only from Gino, but your feelings about him. There's something to say for confrontation—not the confused confrontation of a teenager, but the mature confrontation of an adult and centered son. Along those same lines, Vince, I must confront you with this: without payment, I will not continue to see you. I must insist that on your next visit you bring a check for the amount in full or this therapy will cease. Given how we're just beginning to break through with insights into your personal dynamics, I would consider the interruption of our time together another tragic dissolution of a relationship which, emotionally at least, you can little afford to lose."

Mueller was right, never mind that he was too wordy.

I didn't want to lose him. For all his bullshit, he was probably the one person in the world who listened to me, who really understood me. I wasn't a dope; I knew he saw me as a case study and I figured one day I'd wind up in some book he was writing, but what he said made sense. The guy had my number; he cared about me. He'd hung in there with me. For all the times I'd been pissed

253

at him, I could see that at least I could count on him. He could put together the pieces of my puzzle and there were times, like today, that he even made me feel better—like I wasn't going nuts, like I wasn't falling apart, like I could look the old man in the face and finally tell it like it is.

I couldn't look him in the face.

Gino was facing Wilbur Guest, and when he turned to face me I looked away. I saw him only out of the corner of my eyes, and I'll tell you—he looked grotesque. The black dye on his hair was wearing off and flecks of gray were showing through. The way his skin was pulled tight around his eyes and ears, it looked like he'd had a face lift. I never thought I'd see Gino wearing a gold Gucci workout suit, but that's what I was seeing.

"I see you finally made it," he said.

"Vince!" Guest greeted me with a big handshake. "How wonderful to see you!"

I hated Wilbur; I hated his nice-guy routine. It was sickening and insincere, especially coming from someone I'd had a fistfight with, someone as slimy as this overblown blonde beach boy.

"I came by to see the old man," I told Guest, not wanting to acknowledge his existence or the fact I knew he was fathering my girlfriend's baby . . . my ex-girlfriend, I should say.

"I'm glad you came," said Wilbur, still smiling his toothpaste smile. "You're always welcome."

You don't gotta tell me I'm welcome in my own father's gym, I wanted to tell him but didn't. Why should I say shit to him?

He and the old man were standing by the juice bar. The place was packed. Female and male members were all over the pale peach carpet, doing sit-ups, working the fancy machines, even lifting free weights. Remembering what the joint used to look like,

the turquoise and orange color scheme made me sick. I also remembered the last time I was here, at my parents' wedding, when
I actually did get sick. I was glad I hadn't eaten anything today or I
might have puked all over again. Something about seeing Guest
and Gino together turned my stomach.

I finally turned to Pop and said, "Can I talk to you alone?"

"Of course," Wilbur answered for the old man. "Feel free to
use my office."

"*Your* office?" I asked, wondering why he needed an office in
Gino's Gym.

"The company office," he answered.

The office belonged to Wilbur, there could be no doubt. All
his college degrees were on the wall. "I thought his office was over
on Eighth Street," I told Gino when we were alone.

"He likes it here," said Pop. "He likes being around me. Why
should I mind?"

"You don't mind anything he does, do you?"

"You're pissed because of me and your mother, ain't you?"

"I'm pissed because I don't have a father." There, I said it; I
told him.

"What are you talking about?"

"We never talk."

"Look, I been back for two whole months, champ. You don't
call, you don't come by to see me, so how are we supposed to talk?
I should be pissed at you. I'm a big star now and my own son, my
own flesh and blood don't give two shits about me."

"Did I say that?"

"That's how you're acting. Do you realize my book's selling in
six different countries. Arnold Schwarzenegger, he's got a book
too, but his ain't selling near as big as mine. I'm getting letters
from all over the world. They all want my advice. Everyone wants
to know how Gino does it, how he stays in shape. I been working

255

out again, champ," he told me, taking off his top. "The pecs are pumped, baby," he said, slapping his chest and striking a pose. "Take a good look. Holly calls me the Rock. You just missed Holly. She was here all morning answering my mail. Did I tell you she's only twenty-five? That's younger than you."

"That's what I mean," I said. "That's how you fuck me up. You tell me you're fucking some chick younger than me. That's using me. Don't you see? That's fuckin' *abusing* me."

"What are you talking about? I never used you to get me broads. If anything, you got some of my leftovers."

"Listen to what you're saying, Pop. Your sex life and my sex life shouldn't be mixed up like this."

"You're mixed up, that's the problem with you, champ."

"Not no more, not since I started seeing things straight."

"What—you got a shrink or something?"

"And what if I do? My shrink happens to be good."

"Those fuckin' eggheads will eat up your money and leave you more mixed up than when you started. Didn't I go with your mother? Didn't I try it?"

"You couldn't take the heat. You're like those guys you used to laugh at who couldn't take the pain at your old gym when it was still a real gym. You called them wimps. You made fun of them 'cause they ran. Well, you ran."

"And you think you're hot shit 'cause some know-it-all shrink is feeding you a line you're buying. Well, I ain't buying."

"It's too late. You've already been bought. You sold out," I said to the old man.

"I get a pretty penny for what I sold."

"How much is your soul worth?"

"What the fuck are you saying?"

"I'm saying that I used to respect you. I'm saying that you used to be tough. I'm saying that, yeah, maybe you were always a little crazy, but at least you had the balls to run your gym the way you wanted it run. No one could tell you nothing. You were the boss. Well, not no more. Not since Wilbur turned this place into a fancy-schmancy 'health spa.'"

"Look, Vinnie, a long time ago I told you what would happen if you let Kathy get away from you. I told you she was a gem. I warned you to pay better attention to her. So what do you do? You run off to Europe and you run off with your nigger friends and now you've lost Kathy to Guest and it's your own fault, not mine."

"I ain't talking about Kathy, and I ain't talking about my *black* friends who happen to be musical geniuses, I'm talking about you."

"You're taking it out on me, that's what you're doing. You're sore at Guest about getting Kathy, so you're dumping on me."

"You walked out of my life, and when you came back you had another son."

"What kind of memory do you have? You don't remember me coming by your place on Jane Street to ask you—shit, I practically begged you—to come work with me?"

"I tried it, but no one can work with you, no one can put up with your ego."

"Wilbur does a pretty decent job."

"Wilbur found the only way to control you. He fuckin' bought you."

"Why the hell do you keep saying that? Why does it bother you so much to see me with money? Look, you wanna have an honest conversation? Is that what you want?"

"Yeah, that's what I want."

"Okay, I'll tell it like it is: you're jealous. Ever since you were a little squirt you've been jealous. And from what I can see, you ain't changed one bit. You're jealous that I got a fat bankroll while

you're still on your ass. You've been struggling with your goddamn music for so long it's a joke, except no one's laughing. No
wonder you're jealous of a kid like Wilbur who's got the smarts to
make a million bucks—"

"The only smart thing he did was to get born to a rich father."

"These health clubs are his idea. He put together my book,
he's turned me into a celebrity. You talk about geniuses, well, that's
what he is, a business genius. This guy is the future—he's a man of
the nineties—and you're history. If you weren't such a hothead,
champ, you'd play your cards right and get Wilbur to deal you in."

"Goddamnit, you still don't see what I'm saying."

"I'm saying you're also jealous that I got a broad younger
than you."

"From that picture you sent, she looks at least forty. That
bitch looks like she's really been around the block."

"That picture don't show her good. She's got a body like Rita
Hayworth."

"Rita Hayworth died of Alzheimer's disease. And your dick
died a long time ago, didn't it?"

"That's your mother talking. She's been poisoning you against
me. She and some two-bit shrink."

"Blame it on everyone else."

"I don't have to put up with this shit. I'm selling member-
ships, I'm selling books, I'm getting fan letters and all I got from
and your mother is grief. Fuck it—that's how I feel. Fuck the both
of you!"

"Before I leave, I want you to hear what I came to say: you
used me."

"You already said it."

"I'm saying it again. You needed someone to make you feel
big, and that someone was me. To make yourself feel big, you

made me feel small. When you didn't like the way your body was looking, when you were too lazy to do killer workouts, you lived through me, you lifted through me, you pushed me to be what you wanted—not what I wanted."

"And look what you've become—a bum. When you were a kid, I trained you, I made you into a champ. Now you're nothing."

"Maybe I'm nothing, but I'm my own man, which is a hell of lot more than I can say for you."

There was a knock on the door. Wilbur opened it halfway, flashing his perfect pearl-white smile. "Sorry to interrupt," he said, "but you'd best get back out on the floor, Gino."

"He'll be right with you, boss," I said. "Him and me are through."

All through the night, I kept waking up, remembering only pieces of my dreams. Gino was with Jasmine—that was one dream. She was playing drums and he was singing opera. He said they were getting married. They were taking a shower together, washing each other with soap. Drew was in another dream. He was a reckless race-car driver, driving this Ferrari around the track at a zillion miles an hour. Regina was in the stands wearing curlers in her hair. Jack Weinstein was selling T-shirts and souvenirs. Under the stands, Brenda had been stabbed by a crazy man. I ran to help her, but Drew lost control of his Ferrari; his car was speeding right at me. Just before it hit me, I woke up, shaking.

Seven in the morning. My birds were unusually quiet. I felt nervous, like something was gonna happen. It did. The phone rang, startling me even more. It was Kathy.

"I feel terrible," she said.

"I don't feel so great myself."

259

"I didn't really say what I wanted to say the other day."

"You said enough," I said.

"I want to say that I didn't want to hurt you."

"Is Wilbur there? Is he in bed next to you listening to you tell me this stuff?"

"He's already gone to work."

"Did he tell you I saw him yesterday?"

"He said you had words with your father."

"What else did he say?"

"That he'd like to help you."

"Why the fuck does everyone think I'm a charity case? Why does everyone think I need help?"

"Are you working?"

"I'm working on myself—okay? Weren't you the one who told me to do that two years ago? Well, I listened to you. I'm looking after my mental health. Yesterday I was able to go over and tell Gino how I honestly felt about him."

"I'm proud of you."

"That's what you said in Daphne's office—before you decked me with the left hook."

"I'm sorry...I'm—"

"Look, Kathy, you're a sweet kid and all that, but if you think we can be friends, we can't. I know you feel bad about making me feel bad, but there ain't shit you can do about that. Just get married and have your baby and leave me alone."

"I...I..."

"You what?" I barked. "If you got something to say, say it."

"I'm teaching an exercise class for pregnant women. I'm late. I better go, Vince. I'm...I'm sorry...I'm really sorry..."

"You and me both."

* * *

260

At first I thought I was dreaming. But how could I be dreaming at two in the afternoon at Nick the Greek's coffee shop. I just happened to be in my shrink's neighborhood 'cause I'd been called to a studio on Lexington Avenue to play a commercial. It was for a new liquid detergent. My tenor was supposed to represent dirt so the producer kept telling me to play dirty. Altogether I played for less than five minutes and picked up five hundred bucks and didn't feel too dirty about the whole thing. It was a way to make a living. Word from Tyrone was that they were recording, they'd found a couple of chick singers, Jasmine was dynamite—"she's kinda shy, but really a nice lady and she always says nice things about you, V," said T—so why didn't I come to check out the tracks? Thanks but no thanks, I said. I told T I was trying to settle down and didn't want too much excitement right now. But right now at Nick the Greek's my head was about to explode. I couldn't believe my ears.

There was a high partition between booths and the people sitting behind me couldn't see me, but I sure as hell could hear them. I actually pinched myself to make sure I was awake. That's how crazy it seemed. I wanted to be wrong; I wanted not to know these voices, but I couldn't deny it, I couldn't fool myself, I couldn't stop myself from listening to every word they said.

"I feel betrayed," said Daphne Edwards.

"I was careful to explain this about myself before we were ever married," Klaus Mueller was saying. "You knew exactly who I was."

"That's not how you explained it at all. You weren't speaking personally, Klaus. You were simply generalizing how all of us, at least in your view, are essentially bisexual. I sharply disagreed then, and I disagree now."

"This is no longer an academic matter, Daphne. Our marriage has been seriously dysfunctional for some time."

"*You've* been dysfunctional, *you've* been uninterested, *you've* been withdrawn. I saw that your preoccupation with improving your physique had deeply homosexual overtones."

"Yet you said nothing."

"Whatever I said you didn't hear. You weren't listening to me, Klaus. You weren't even looking at me. We weren't married six months before I sensed that you were having second thoughts—and affairs. It was last November when I felt you emotionally moving away from me."

"And still you remained silent."

"I did no such thing. I spoke up. I urged you to seek help. I practically begged you to go back into therapy."

"And I explained that I had completed my own therapy."

"And I wondered about the competence of your therapist."

"I'm afraid that your hostility borders on homophobia."

"What self-respecting woman willingly loses her husband to another man? That's enough to make anyone furious—and rightfully so."

"You see it as a matter of right and wrong. Your Baptist upbringing has a way of tripping you up when you least expect it."

"Your years as captain of the Dartmouth debate team make conversations like this futile. You turn into a smug little college boy."

Hearing their voices was making me crazy. Hearing them trying to out-shrink each other out was too much to take. I wanted to jump up and scream. I wanted to jump over the partition and kick Klaus in the teeth. I was so fuckin' mad I wanted to wreck the coffee shop, but I also didn't want to miss another word. So I just sat there, listening, spellbound.

"You needn't be so defensive, Daphne. I'm not saying that I'm leaving you."

"And I'm not saying that I want you to stay. The fact is, I don't."

"You're overreacting."

"Am I? Well, let me overreact some more. I don't want you coming back to our apartment. I don't want you sleeping with me. I don't want you touching me. God only knows that you've risked my health as well as—"

"I can assure you that—"

"You can't assure me of anything, Klaus. But I can assure *you* of one thing. This divorce is going to be neither easy nor cheap for you. Do I make myself clear?"

With that, she got up from the table and left without passing my booth.

I counted ten before I got up, turned, took two steps and stood right there in front of Mueller. My fists were clenched so tight I could feel my knuckles cracking. I was ready to crack his head, ready to knee him, strangle him, pulverize him until every bone in his fuckin' body was broken to bits. But the funny part is that I couldn't move. I was crying too hard.

My dick was hard and I was happy. Daphne was moaning low and telling me I was the best she ever had. She was sitting on me, taking it from the front, riding me fast and making it last. Now she was flat on her back on the counter at Nick the Greek's coffee shop. "I love you," she kept saying as she kept me up so strong and long I thought my shlong would snap in half. Man, it was great to be fucking again, especially fucking a chick this gorgeous and hot, fucking her until she screamed "I'm coming again" and screamed it again and again until I woke up with cum all over my stomach.

Here I was, age twenty-seven, still having wet dreams.

At first I felt ashamed, like I did when I was a kid, but then I realized I was glad. Hell, my cock was still bone-hard. The thing was working again. But then, with my birds singing their morning

263

song, I started remembering what I'd forgotten during the night. Klaus and Daphne were *married*. Klaus was *queer*. All that therapy, all that "progress" he talked about, all those hours on the couch ...I'd been had.

"I don't believe you," said Kathy when I called her.

"You don't have to. Ask Daphne."

"It's just hostility on your part. You're angry and you want to hurt me."

"Call Daphne. Ask her."

"I will."

Ten minutes later, Kathy called back. Her voice was shaking.

"I can't believe it," she said.

"So she told you the truth."

"She said she was going to tell me anyway. She said that when I started therapy they weren't married. And they weren't married when she recommended Mueller for you."

"Yeah, but they were already fucking."

"Why do you have to be so crude about it?"

"Because we've been fucked, don't you see? In my gut, I knew it all the time. I knew they were in cahoots."

"But they're splitting up. She said so."

"They're *messed up*, that's what they are. Just like the article said. They're crazier than their patients."

"Maybe Mueller, but I still think that Daphne—"

"She married him, didn't she? What does that say about her? This is the woman who's been giving you such great advice about your love life while her own love life is a joke."

"Their problems don't disqualify them as professionals."

"*Professionals!* While Drew's dying, this guy, this fuckin' shrink is sitting there telling me I got the hots for Drew—which I know goddamn well I don't—while it's Mueller who's got the hots for me. I'm the reason he started working out, I'm the guy he's imitating and competing with, I become his fuckin' obsession while he's analyzing my ass like he's the sanest motherfucker in the world. Now ain't that a bitch! Man, I'm just glad I owe him all that dough 'cause he'll have to sue me, he'll have to go to Washington fuckin' D.C. and get the Supreme Court to make me pay, 'cause, believe me, I ain't coughing up a goddamn penny. Something told me not to pay him, and I'm glad as hell I didn't. I knew something was wrong with that bastard, and I was right."

"All your therapy couldn't have been wrong, Vince. I can tell by how you've changed. You're calmer, you're stronger."

"I'm so strong I'm thinking about going over there and busting up him and his office."

"You could have attacked him yesterday, but you didn't. You could have attacked your father, but you didn't. Don't you see, Vince, you've gone beyond that."

"Listen, Kathy, to me you ain't no different than Daphne and Klaus. You're just as full of shit as them. If you wanna go on seeing that lady..."

"She admitted she was wrong not to reveal her relationship with Mueller, but they didn't want to interrupt our treatment."

"They didn't wanna lose money. It ain't about nothing but money."

"It's about more than that, Vince. After three years with Daphne, I know myself better—I know I do."

"Keep convincing yourself, baby. If you wanna buy your own bullshit, you don't have to convince me."

"It's not bullshit! I'm having a baby. Don't you see? *I want this baby.*"

BABY LOVE

A COUPLE of weeks later it's the beginning of March and I'm in midtown walking down 48th Street, past the flower stalls and fruit stands on my way into the Sam Ash music store to buy some reeds when I see it in the window. It's me. It's the cheesecake picture of me from the Canadian newspaper—me in my tank top, me on my knees—only now it's a poster and, just like Sue said, it's called "Sax Sex."

I turned around and walked away. I couldn't even walk into the store. I could sue Sue Kawisha, but that would fuck up Tyrone. And besides, only the lawyers would make out. Same was true for Klaus Mueller. In my mind, I'd written him a thousand letters, calling him a pig and a fraud and a fuckin' hypocrite. In my dreams, I'd reported him to the governing board of shrinks, I'd beaten him to a pulp; I'd ripped off his head and smashed his skull. I'd taken his designer paper towels and stuffed them down his throat. Finally, though, I figured the best thing to do was nothing. I'd given the guy enough of my energy. I just wanted to forget him. But that wasn't easy. He wrote me this letter that said, "Our last encounter was uncomfortable for us both. I strongly suggest that you call for an appointment so you might have the opportunity to express your feelings directly to me. That's the least we owe one another."

I don't owe you shit, motherfucker—that's the letter I wrote back. I didn't send it, though, thinking the best way to hurt him was to ignore him. See, anything I wrote or said he'd just analyze and turn back on me. But if he never heard from me again, he'd see that I didn't need him no more. I'd cut him out like a cancer, and that'd be that.

I also had to cut out of New York. Femmes on Fire were all over the place, even in Madison Square Garden. Brenda/Sasha was still chasing me, but I couldn't deal with her; I just didn't wanna be around Regina or any of her wrestlers.

"It's nothing personal, Mom," I told her one night when we had dinner down near the apartment where I was raised, at the Grotta Azzurra in Little Italy on Broome Street where they put fresh fruit at the bottom of the wine pitchers. "But every time I look up I see you on TV or Pop in the muscle magazines."

"You got your own poster. People are talking about you, Vinnie. They're seeing it everywhere. Marla said that Tyrone's manager gave you part of the profits."

"She ain't a total sleaze. She sent me a big check the other day."

"With that poster, you call your own shots," said Mom, wearing this new sky-high platinum wig. "You could model—"

"I tried that once, Mom. I couldn't do it."

"You could help me. I know you could. You could play your saxophone before the fights, you could play the national anthem or 'America the Beautiful.' I'd give you your own spot in between matches."

"I know you're trying to help, Mom. You've asked me before,

and I appreciate it, but I'm going away for a while."

"It's the divorce, isn't it? I wish it didn't have to be so messy between me and Gino, Vinnie, but there's money involved and he's mad. He says I've poisoned your mind and he thinks he's entitled to—"

"That's between you and him. I don't wanna hear about it, Mom."

"I can understand. And with Kathy..."

"I got nothing to say about Kathy."

"If you need money—"

"I *don't!* Look, Mom, you're nice to offer, but you offer all the time and all that does is make me feel like I can't make it on my own."

"Can you?"

I couldn't believe she even asked the question.

I needed some quiet, some time alone. I needed to get out of town.

I went to the country.

I admit it; I wanted to be noticed. I've always wanted to be noticed. I felt that whenever I saw that poster of me. Part of me felt happy. My body was hard; my muscles were big; my tenor looked sexy. I couldn't argue that's one of the reasons, even as a kid, I picked up the horn and started lifting. I got excited by the sound of the sax; I loved feeling the pump of blood rushing through my arms and legs.

Another part of me, though, didn't want to see that picture in Times Square poster shops where the junkies and whores were looking to score. The poster turned me into merchandise, and cheap merchandise at that. I was better than that. Drew always said so. I was no fake; I could play for real. And here in this little country house on the side of a hill that Drew's parents said I was free to use for as long as I liked, I liked the way my sax was sounding again. See, I was in the middle of upstate New York, in the middle of nowhere, playing for the birds and the bees and the start of springtime, with the new grass growing and the buds blossoming and the smell of wildflowers all up in my nose. I'd brought up a set of barbells and that kept me happy in the mornings, and in the afternoons I'd take long walks, and sometimes I'd take my sax and sit by this little lake and watch the sun reflect on the water and just play to the wind and the clouds floating by and the sunset turning my world purple and pink and lavender and blue. My heart was happy, at least until night.

At night I stayed inside. At night I looked through the books Drew's parents kept on the shelves. I read a little about the Civil War. I never knew it was so bloody. I read this skinny little Bible where Thomas Jefferson took all the bullshit out of the big Bible and reduced it down to nothing but the words of Jesus. I liked that. I liked listening to lots of music—when Sarah Vaughan started singing in the late forties, sounding so silky and smooth, doing shit no one else dared do; when Sonny Rollins played with Clifford Brown and Max Roach; when John Coltrane played and Johnny Hartman sang; when Ray Charles and Betty Carter did a duet on "Baby, It's Cold Outside." And it was. It was chilly and lonely at night. I hadn't ever been alone for this long, but it was good for me. I was going back to nature, back to my musical roots. I kept thinking of Kathy, but Kathy, like Klaus, was history. You're supposed to learn from history, that's what these books said, and I was learning to be alone. It hurt, but it helped. I spent lots of time listening to the crickets, and sometimes I'd just sit and stare at the moon, thinking that, no matter how big we wanna be, we'll always be small. It was strange, though, 'cause little by little— don't ask me why—I was also feeling connected to something big.

I had every reason to go crazy, but I didn't. I had my binoculars and my bird-watching book and, at daybreak, after being up all night, sometimes I'd spot some pals I'd never seen before. They all had their own songs and every song was gorgeous. On my flute or soprano, I'd play back those melodies and, believe me, we had beautiful conversations. I kept busy. I grew a beard. A week passed, then two, then three. Then this telegram came.

"I want to come see you," it said, signed, "Kathy."

Kathy came and looked awful. When I picked her up at the Greyhound station, her eyes were watery and her skin pasty and pale. I had told her not to come. I had called her and said there was nothing to talk about.

"Yes, there is," she had said. "I need to ask you something. I need your advice."

"Then ask it."

"Not on the phone. It's too personal. I need to talk to you in person."

"Personally," I had said, "I don't want to be disturbed right now."

"Do I have to beg you? Is that what you want?"

"I want to be left alone. Can't you understand that?"

The sound of her sigh changed my mind. I don't know why, but it did. "Okay," I said, "you can come up here if you really want to."

"You want to tell me what this is about?" I asked her as we drove up in the rent-a-car to Drew's folks' house in the woods.

"Not right now," she said. "Now I'd just like to breathe in the fresh air."

It had rained that morning so that the woods were wet and

270

smelled like heaven. Kathy smelled a little like heaven herself. She had this Kathy-smell all her own, a sweet-skin smell, with just a little light perfume, a woman's smell, a smell that made me realize how long it'd been since I'd slept with a woman.

"Does the goon know you're here?" I asked when we reached the house.

"I had to lie. I said I was visiting a girlfriend in Connecticut."

"That's not good. It ain't like you to lie."

"None of it is good."

"What are you talking about?" I wanted to know.

She sat in a rocking chair with this pretty embroidered padding. In her blue denim skirt and flowery blouse, she looked like she belonged there. I could tell her breasts had swollen up some, but the skirt was hiding her stomach so I couldn't see how big she was.

"I like your beard," she said, changing subjects.

"Thanks."

"Thanks for letting me come. Thanks for listening to me."

"I haven't heard anything yet. You just said things aren't going good for you. What'd you mean?"

She sighed a sigh just like the sigh on the phone. "I don't want to marry him."

My heart started racing. "You tell him that?"

"I told him that I don't want to have his baby."

"And what'd he say?"

"Get an abortion."

"Is that what you want?"

"I want to think about it. I came to talk to you about it."

"*Me!* You've been fucking me over with your shrinks and your horseshit boyfriend—I kept saying you didn't love him—and now I'm out here meditating and getting my head together and just when I'm practically chilled out 'cause I could be bouncing off a wall at Bellevue—you know that, don't you?—just when I'm feeling halfway calm, you show up talkin' 'bout divorcing this asshole before you marry him and killing the kid."

"Is that how you feel about abortion?"

"Look, Kathy, I don't feel nothing about abortion, I don't feel nothing about any of this 'cause this here is your problem. Get it? *Your* goddamn problem, not mine. Your problem and Wilbur's problem. Why didn't you ask my mother what to do? Why didn't you ask Gino? And how 'bout Daphne? She's your guru, ain't she? I thought everything was going so great for you, I thought—"

".I thought we were friends."

"Friends! We were a hell of a lot more than friends. We were lovers and lovers are different than friends, lovers love each other and sleep together, lovers go deeper than friends, you were the one who always said so, Kathy, you were the one who—"

"I'm sorry," she said, starting to cry softly. "It's that nothing quite turned out the way I had imagined."

"What did you imagine?"

"My own independence. My own health spa."

"I thought you got it. Didn't he give you that new one out in White Plains?"

"I manage, but he controls. He tries not to—he means well —but he's a control freak, down to the last detail."

"Couldn't you see that from the start?"

"I saw he was different from you. I saw he was interested in giving women a chance. With you, Vinnie...well, I always felt overwhelmed by your energy and your talent."

"Why didn't you tell me that? That might have made me feel good."

"I told you, but you weren't listening. You had this image of me as a prim and proper schoolteacher. Anything more was a threat."

"So the goon comes along and sweeps you off your feet."

"I suppose in my mind I made him into something he wasn't. After all, he did give me responsibility and allowed me to prove myself."

"And what'd you prove?"

"I got stronger, just as I promised myself I would."

"So why are you making me crazy, Kathy? What are you doing here?"

"I've come to say what I couldn't say in Daphne's office, not the first time and not the second time. In a weird way, Vinnie, I'm strong enough to say it now."

"Say what?"

"I want you back."

"Great! With the goon's baby, you want me back."

"I'm considering an abortion."

"And that's supposed to be *my* choice? Is that it? I'm supposed to tell you whether to have an abortion or not?"

"I didn't say that. I only said I was considering the option."

"Look, I know what you wanna do, Kathy. You wanna dump this shit on *my* head. Well, that's fuckin' nuts. This whole thing is nuts. But I'm *not* going nuts. I tell you, I'm not. I've been working my ass off to stay straight, and just when I make it, just when I'm feeling halfway mellow—in spite of my crazy parents, in spite of my crazy shrink, in spite of my own crazy ways—you come around 'cause *you're* going nuts and start saying things to make me nuts all over again. Well, I'll tell you what I'm going to do, Kathy, I'm not going to go nuts, I'm going to make you a cup a tea instead and if you're hungry I'll make you a grilled cheese sandwich or

273

something and then I'm packing you up and driving you back to town to catch the six o'clock bus back to the city. And that's that."

It rained that night. It thundered like the gods were angry. The sky boomed, crashed and crackled with lightning. A big bolt ripped through an oak tree just outside the house and Kathy grabbed me. We were both naked. We had made love twice, and twice it had been beautiful beyond words. At first I couldn't do it. I thought I'd hurt the baby. I kept imagining the blonde beach boy screaming at my father, or Brenda throwing Barbie Doll down in the ring. I kept seeing the Baroness or Drew dying or Jasmine behind her drum set. Too many people, too many memories, too many images crowded my mind.

"Let me just massage you," Kathy offered. "Let me just kiss away the pain."

It'd been so long since I'd been touched tenderly. It'd been so long since a single kiss had felt sincere. I'm not saying it wasn't sexy—it was—but it was more. It was quiet, it was sweet, it was deep. All the old images started to fade. I was with Kathy, alone and together, just me and my baby.

"I want you to have the baby," I told her afterwards, thinking of how Kathy had been an orphan and how badly she wanted a child of her own.

"I want it, too. I always did. But it bothers me—it tortures me—that it's not yours."

"And what do you think it does to me?"

"Does it do enough to destroy our relationship?"

"Our old relationship is dead, ain't it? We're gonna have to see if we can start something new."

* * *

274

I kept seeing this baby version of Wilbur Guest. The kid was blonde and blue-eyed and wore this tiny little Village Health Club sweatshirt with the abstract artsy logo. He looked nothing like me and every time me and Kathy took the kid for a stroll in the carriage, people stopped to stare, asking, while looking us straight in the eye, "Who's the father?"

"I don't think I can live with it, Kathy," I said when I drove her to the bus two days after she arrived. "I'm trying, but it's still driving me nuts. You're asking for a lot."

"I'm not asking for anything. I'm canceling the wedding and leaving him. Afterwards, whatever happens happens."

"What happened here was beautiful," I told her. "What happened here is something . . . something else."

We had walked into the woods where I pointed out my bird pals. I brought along my alto and played some new songs I'd written. I'd really never had the patience to write my own songs before, and now the alto gave me the right voice. Melodies were coming to me from out of the sky. Maybe that's cause I'd been listening to Bird, the greatest of all alto players. Bird didn't intimidate me like he used to. Kathy showed me these great stretching exercises in the middle of a field of daisies. With the breeze at our backs, we rode bikes around the lake. Color came back to Kathy's cheeks and I could see, no matter how depressed she'd gotten, that she was still strong. We hiked up a hill and sat still, just watching the clouds roll by, neither of us saying a word. It was enough to hold her hand. It was enough to breathe.

Fact is, we hadn't done much talking. I guess we both felt we'd talked enough to our shrinks. We didn't mention them, we didn't mention Gino or Gina, and we sure as shit didn't mention Wilbur. Maybe we were just pretending none of that ever happened, pretending we were alone in the world and starting out fresh—no complications, no fuck-ups.

We also knew, though, that it probably couldn't last for long. I waved to Kathy as the bus drove off down the bumpy country road.

I liked my beard. It grew in thick and black and I kept it neat and trim. It made me feel a little like a different person, not that hunk on the "Sax Sex" poster, which was selling like hotcakes. The country had done my head good. My apartment on Amsterdam Avenue was dim, but my spirits were a little brighter until I thought about Kathy. I didn't know what to do about Kathy. I needed more time to think.

"You need to come out and see us tonight," said T. "Don't want no excuses, bro. Wanna see your raunchy ass right there up front. Wanna see you taste our latest dish."

The debut Righteous Rippers album was due out, and the group was performing at their own press party at some hip hotel in Soho. When I got there, the far-out characters were out in force.

It was one of those turned-out turned-on New York crowds —the artsy-fartsy funk fanatics, the sleek and slippery music moguls, the press pimps and whores, the glitter groupies, the egghead critics cruising for free booze. They were scooping up caviar and guzzling down champagne, looking important like they knew everyone and I didn't know no one until Marla came up and gave me a hug.

"How's my baby?" she asked. "With them whiskers, you look like a mountain man. Does your mama know about this beard? You looked a lot younger when your face was clean. Wish you'd shave it off, sugar."

"Can't afford a razor, Marla."

"Wish you were up there playing, Vinnie. Tyrone says it's not the same without you."

"Tyrone deserves all the glory. This has been his baby from the start."

"We want to get started," Sue Kawisha announced from the stage at the end of the small ballroom. Looking at her long legs under her black-and-pink pin-striped business suit, I remembered how I'd gotten into so much trouble. Hearing the tone of her voice, I also remembered how she could be one of the world's bossiest bitches. "Quiet, everyone. We'd like to get started. We'd like to thank you for coming out. We're terribly excited about sharing this moment with you, so without further ado, I give you the Righteous Rippers, featuring the fabulous Tyrone Newborn and Jasmine Jetstar!"

Jasmine Jetstar?

Standing sideways so people could view her curvy contours, Jasie was jumping; she was playing standing up. She was wearing this white outfit with one leg covered in white skin-tight Spandex and the other leg bare and black all the way up her butt. With one cheek covered and the other cheek nude, her booty was the focus of everyone's attention and, believe me, no booty ever looked finer. It was hard—it was impossible—to look at anything else. Maybe that's what got me in trouble with Jasmine to begin with. Maybe, like with Sue's legs, I got sidetracked by the sexy sideshow. Anyway, Jasie jammed on the congas and beat the shit out of the bongos, she surfed over the snares and hit the highhat with all the flare of a seasoned star.

"She's the next Sheila E.," said some press flack standing next to me, referring to the Latin percussionist Prince had groomed into a hit-making headliner. "Her outfit even looks like Sheila's."

The Righteous Rippers had realigned themselves around Jasmine. It was Tyrone's same great grooves, Tyrone's same slick dance moves, Tyrone's same pumping thumping bass, but instead of featuring my sax, it was Jasmine out front, doing some fancy highsticking and even some soul-licking singing. I didn't know she could sing. Didn't know that she loved the spotlight as much as she did. I remembered her being shy. I remember how she had shied away from me once we arrived in London.

"I'm very grateful for all you did for me," she told me after the show, after the photographers had popped her picture and she'd posed with Tyrone and Squeak and the sexy backup singers. "I just wish you would reconsider and join the group."

I did reconsider—for a second. I thought of those times when I loved to see that spotlight shining on me. But then I saw that Jasie and T were holding hands. He was wearing a sweatshirt with the red, green and black African liberation logo—a fist high in the air pointing to "Positively Black!" I felt the vibes, and I knew—just by the way Jasie and T were looking at each other— they had to be bumping. Their music was fresh and funky, and fucking was definitely part of it. Right now—no matter how much I loved and respected T and his talent—I didn't want any part of it. I'd had enough complications.

"You're part of this scene," said Sue, sliding up to me while the band was being interviewed by a cub reporter from *Rolling Stone*. "There could still be a profitable exchange between us," she added, brushing her long left leg against my thigh.

I was glad my dick did a little dance—I was glad to feel it back in action—but I was also glad I had the sense to look the other way.

"You better take care of T," I told her.

* * *

"People are starting to talk," said Pop.

"About what?" I wanted to know.

"About Wilbur and Kathy. They say they're on the outs."

"So why are you calling me?"

"I thought you'd know why."

"Why don't you ask Wilbur?"

"It ain't none of my business."

"If it's none of your business, Pop, it sure as hell ain't none of mine."

"I thought I smelled a skunk, champ. I thought maybe you were in the middle of their mess. I thought you were so pissed at me you'd found a way to fuck up my deal with Wilbur. All I can tell you is that he's crazy about Kathy, so, if you know what's good for you, you'll leave her alone."

"I like this," I told the old man. "I like this a lot. It's like Kathy's your property. Like she's your angel. She finds you a backer and now you gotta keep your backer happy. If not, you're scared he'll throw you out on your ass, is that it?"

"That ain't it. That ain't it at all. I told you what's wrong. *You're* what's wrong. The green-eyed monster is what's wrong. You're jealous—jealous of Wilbur, jealous of me, jealous of anyone doing good 'cause you ain't doing worth a shit."

I hung up in his ear.

But all night long I screamed at him in my sleep. In my dream, he was Conan the Destroyer or Conan the Barbarian, I don't know which, but he was Arnold Schwarzenegger with a red wig that I ripped off and found these horrible snakes underneath and each snake turned into a Gino, I was fighting a hundred Ginos wrapping themselves around my neck and choking me, hissing and pissing poison on my face until Regina came with a sword and started chopping off their heads with Pop screaming, "She's killing me, the bitch is killing me!" "Fuck you!" I screamed back. "Don't call my mother a bitch!" Kathy came driving up in the back of a cab, crying, "I'm having a baby! I'm having my baby in the taxi!" and I ran to help, except it was Wilbur or Schwarzenegger who was driving, and then the driver turned into a guy with a black hood and no face, the driver was Death, and Death started laughing and Kathy tried to get out of the cab but the door wouldn't open and I smashed out the front window, trying to get to Death, trying to stop him, but my hands were bleeding and the blood got all over Kathy and the baby was born in the blood, not a baby at all, just a skeleton, nothing but the bones of an infant, no face, no flesh, it was so fuckin' awful I woke up shivering. I had to call her.

"You all right?" I had to know.

"I haven't been feeling great," Kathy confessed.

"You didn't have an abortion, did you?"

"Does it matter to you?"

"I...I..." I didn't know what the hell to say. I just blurted out the truth. "I had this dream."

"Did the baby die?" she asked.

"How'd you know?"

"I had the same dream."

"Did you tell Daphne?"

"I'm not seeing her anymore. I didn't tell anyone."

"Have you told Wilbur?"

"I'm telling him tonight that I'm moving out tomorrow."

"Where are you going?"

"I'm not sure, but if you're worried that I'm going to bother you, I'm not."

"I'm not worried...I mean, I am worried. I just want you to be all right."

*　*　*

"I want you to leave Kathy alone."

Wilbur Guest had caught me just as I was leaving the apartment building on Amsterdam. It was one of those wet May mornings, humid and drizzling, and I was on my way to the little gym around the corner where I'd been working out.

"First of all," I told the goon, "get your fuckin' hands off my jacket. And secondly," I said, "get the fuck out of my sight."

While he considered his next move, I heard the soul song "I Am a Spy in the House of Love" blasting out of someone's radio.

"I came to warn you," he said.

"Yeah? You and what army?"

"I know you've ruined your own life, but you're about to ruin everyone else's life."

"Who's everyone?"

"Your father and mother, for starters."

"My mother bought you out."

"She *wants* to buy me out. She hasn't done it yet. I not only own a substantial interest in her wrestling promotion, but her clothing line as well. If I wanted to, I could make it impossible for her to stay in business. I could tie her up in court for years. My lawyers could drain her dry. As far as Gino goes, he's child's play. He's nothing more than an employee. In spite of his braggadocio, his book has done only moderately well. I have half a mind to can him."

"You got half a mind and no heart. That's why Kathy can't stand you no more."

"Kathy doesn't know what she wants."

"She knows she don't want you."

"You're influencing her and undermining us. I'm telling you, Vince, stay far away from her. I want her to see a counselor with me. I'm insisting and she's refusing. I know you're the reason why."

"She's wised up. She's too smart, she's too fuckin' good for the likes of you."

"You're a loser."

"You've lost her. Now you're desperate."

He grabbed me by the collar and threw me against the building, yelling, "That's my baby she's having. *Mine.*"

I kneed him in the nuts. It wasn't a fancy move, it wouldn't be legal in the ring, but here on the street it did the job just fine. When he came back at me and I kneed him again. I also think I might have broken his jaw with a right hook. As a kid, I was known for throwing a hard right hook. Anyway, he went down and stayed down. A cop came by and asked what was wrong. Guest tried to say something but his mouth wouldn't work. Mine did. I said, "Nothing's wrong with me, but this guy needs help."

He did what he said he would. He fired Pop and even changed the name from "Gino's Gym" to "Guest's Gym." He sued Mom, and he also sued Kathy for trying to steal from him. And he did it all in one week, the same week that Gino and Gina were arguing in court over money.

I kept dreaming the baby was dying. Sometimes in the dream the baby would be Wilbur—with Wilbur's hair and eyes and skinny legs—and sometimes the baby would be me. The baby would fall from a crib or drown in a lake. The blades of a helicopter would chop off the baby's head or a rodent would rip at the baby's throat. I'd wake up in a pool of sweat, frightened to death, and reach over to see whether Kathy was all right. I'd put my ear to her stomach and listen for the baby's heartbeat. We were back at Drew's parents' place in the country. They were off in Europe and we were waiting for spring to become summer and the baby to be born.

It isn't my baby, I kept thinking as I kept falling deeper in love with Kathy.

Kathy was knitting baby things and I was reading baby books about how the kid grows in the womb and we didn't have a phone and we didn't care about the lawsuits we left behind—they were all jive anyway—we just cared about getting to know each other again and Kathy cared about my music so much she made me play for her night and day, she encouraged me with my songwriting, and, driving upstate, we found a broken-down gym in Saratoga Springs for sale and we thought of buying it and fixing it up and running it together.

"Is that crazy?" I asked Kathy.

"Very crazy," she answered.

So we put down a down payment 'cause money was pouring in from my poster and two songs I'd written with Tyrone were on his album and his album was selling like crazy and Kathy had some savings and it looked like things might turn out okay until I got the telegram from Mom saying Dad was in the hospital.

When me and Kathy got to the city, though, Gino wouldn't see us. They said it was a heart attack and he'd be okay, but he'd have to slow down. All his life he'd made fun of guys who had heart attacks. All his life he said he had a heart strong as a bull. I felt like bawling. If it happened to him, it might happen to me. I worried about my own health; I started listening to my own heart.

Regina was there. A red-and-gold Femmes on Fire baseball cap covered her hair which she hadn't had time to set. "He's blaming you," she told me. "He's blaming me. He's got no gym, he's got nothing to do so he figured he'd have a heart attack. That's how I figure it. He wants us to feel bad. Me, I'm going to California with Jack Weinstein. We have bookings out there, we have matches lined up between L.A. and San Diego, we have stores who want to sell our leotards. Kathy, your friend Wilbur, he's a fool if he thinks he can threaten me with his lawyers. He's a nuisance and nothing more. You shouldn't be afraid of him, Vinnie."

"I'm not, Mama," I said, trying to figure out whether Pop's heart attack was real or fake. I didn't know who to believe.

"I'll come back when the baby's born," Regina promised.

"I want to see Pop."

"Don't," she said. "You'll only make him feel worse."

There was a small community hospital where Kathy and I took birthing lessons. I liked the lessons. I liked bathing the baby doll and putting diapers on it and doing stretches with Kathy and helping her with her breathing. She led the class with exercises to strengthen what she called the "pelvic floor." Sometimes, driving back to the house on the side of the hill, I'd get angry all over again that the kid wasn't mine. I remembered that for a long time Kathy had been fucking the goon, but I also remembered that I hadn't exactly been a saint and sometimes I'd feel the kid kicking and Kathy, with her breasts so full and her cheeks so rosy, got more beautiful every day.

We got threats and letters from Guest, but in late August, a week before Ginger was born, we saw an article in the Sunday *Times* that said he'd sold his health spas to some conglomerate and was moving to Sydney where him and his old man were building the biggest resort in Australia. Just to show you the kind of goon he was, he never even called to ask about the baby. Just to show what kind of gal Kathy was, she talked me into letting Gino take over our Saratoga Springs gym. The old man was delighted, and I never did figure out whether he'd had a heart attack or not. Or for that matter, who was telling the truth about his sexual powers. The last time he called he said he and Brenda were making an exercise tape together, an iron-pumping video. He said Brenda was like Jane Fonda with balls.

Kathy wanted us back in the city. There was this guy with a record label who'd heard the tape I'd made in Rome and thought I needed a record of my own. I told him I'd changed since then. I told him I'd been writing. I played him my new songs, "Blues for Drew" and "Tyrone's Tornado." It was jazz, but it was also balls-out funk, and there was even this one miracle melody called "Ginger," which the guy said he wanted to record with strings 'cause it was prettier than anything Kenny G ever played.

Ginger was prettier than anything I'd ever seen. She was bald, and that was good, 'cause I didn't want her to be no blonde. She was a little chubby, but she came out in a hurry—I was there for the whole thing, never closed my eyes once—and naturally Kathy delivered like a champ. Natural childbirth and all that. Kathy was setting up her own series of exercise classes all over the city, and I was helping her during the day and recording at night.

Look for my record. It'll be out any day now. It's called *Family Album* and you'll see this picture of me and Kathy and the kid on the cover, plus our birds are flying free all over our loft on Lower Broadway and if you look closely in the background you can even see an old photo of Mom when she was a young woman and Pop when he was Mr. Olympia of 1948 and even though I'm wearing a shirt you can bet that if I took it off you'd see I'm still plenty pumped, except I don't gotta prove nothing to nobody no more, but I wouldn't mind making a bundle off the record, so don't forget, pick up a copy—*Vince Viola's Family Album* is the whole title—and when you listen to it, even if you don't like all the numbers, least I hope you'll say, "Damn, this guy's blowing from his soul!"